Praise for
What Makes You Think You're Awake?

What Makes You Think You're Awake? is a wonderful debut; a
collection of frank, funny, and heartbreaking stories that delve
into the mire of human loneliness.

> —Carmen Maria Machado, *In the Dream House*
> and *Her Body and Other Parties*

What Makes You Think You're Awake? invites us into an uncanny, atmospheric world, where violence lurks under the surface of daily life and portals abound, beckoning characters into
the midnight logic of the surreal. Maegan Poland's surprising,
incisive, and powerfully imaginative stories make for an unfor-
gettable debut.

> —Laura van den Berg, *I Hold a Wolf by the Ears*

This is my favorite kind of collection, beautifully written and
full of surprises. Maegan Poland is a terrific new talent. Her
stories make strange normal and normal strange.

> —Tom Franklin, *Crooked Letter, Crooked Letter*

D1358174

Maegan Poland's strange and extraordinary short stories exist in a world like ours but not quite: a shed can literally stop time, a nest burns down to barbed wire, solar flares knock out the power, and a pandemic doesn't quite put a damper on infidelity. All is not well in this world where Poland's characters, straight and queer, struggle with trauma and loneliness while searching for love and connection. *What Makes You Think You're Awake?* is a prescient and eerie collection that perfectly captures the surreal quality of our times.

—May-lee Chai, *Useful Phrases for Immigrants*, winner of the American Book Award

Reading one of Maegan Poland's stories feels like walking through a familiar place at dusk with a bright flashlight in one hand and a big, beautiful magnifying glass in the other. Everything you see is so clear, so fine. So much closer than before. And so hard to look up from. But later, when you do, you are surrounded by darkness, even—especially—after you finish reading.

—Maile Chapman, *Your Presence Is Requested at Suvanto*

WHAT MAKES
YOU THINK
YOU'RE
AWAKE?

WHAT MAKES YOU THINK YOU'RE AWAKE

?

MAEGAN POLAND

BLAIR

Printed in Canada
Cover design by Laura Williams
Interior design by April Leidig

BLAIR

Blair is an imprint of Carolina Wren Press.

*The mission of Blair/Carolina Wren Press is to seek out, nurture,
and promote literary work by new and underrepresented writers.*

We gratefully acknowledge the ongoing support of general operations by the
Durham Arts Council's United Arts Fund and the North Carolina Arts Council.

These stories are works of fiction. As in all fiction, the literary perceptions
and insights are based on experience; however, all names, characters, places, and
incidents are either products of the author's imagination or are used fictitiously.
No reference to any real person is intended or should be inferred.

Library of Congress Cataloging-in-Publication Data:
Names: Poland, Maegan, 1981- author.
Title: What makes you think you're awake? / Maegan Poland.
Description: Durham : Blair, [2021]
Identifiers: LCCN 2020049883 (print) | LCCN 2020049884 (ebook) |
ISBN 9781949467505 (paperback) | ISBN 9781949467512 (ebook)
Subjects: LCGFT: Short stories.
Classification: LCC PS3616.O5567 W48 (print) | LCC PS3616.O5567 (ebook) |
DDC 813/.6--dc23
LC record available at https://lccn.loc.gov/2020049883
LC ebook record available at https://lccn.loc.gov/2020049884

For Michael

CONTENTS

THE SHED

At first, Amy didn't even notice the worn shack that sat in the backyard on the edge of a deep ravine. It was easy to overlook. Groves of waist-high grass and thick vines of wisteria had nearly swallowed the tiny box of a building. When she discovered the shed and its secret, she pored over her inspection report and the sales contract, but there was no mention of it. Nonetheless, the shed was on her land. She decided it belonged to her, that it was a gift for her alone.

Before she witnessed the anomaly, before she knew what the shed could do, Amy resolved to make use of the unexpected space. Inside, a rusted bed frame was pressed against the wall, and a pile of old twine and rope sat near the baseboard, frayed and faded. She found a bottle of ink stashed in the corner, surrounded by old tools without handles—saws, hammers, screwdrivers—as though the handles had been made of wood and termites had feasted upon them long ago. Yet the weathered floorboards remained intact, worn smooth in areas as if by heavy traffic, marking paths between the bed, the door, and the only window. The glass was so old that you could see it for what it was: a fluid that had gathered thick like molasses at the base of each panel.

She scrubbed the floor and walls and coated the wood in thick oil, allowing it to dry for days with the shed's door propped wide, letting the humid spring air swirl through the room at intervals when the wind was blowing from the south, from the gulf two hundred miles away. The window, warped by the years, would not open. She untwisted the ropes she found on the floor and made oakum to fill the gaps in the walls. Wary of the frequent storms that blew through town, she caulked all the crevices she found, sealing the shed tight.

She was charmed by the simplicity of the space and found herself spending more time renovating her shed than decorating her house—a midcentury ranch with a gravel drive set a mile away from the street. Before she left the city, she had suffered from unpredictable panic attacks. She felt jittery inside, like too much energy was coursing through her, waiting to short-circuit her brain or zap her into oblivion. Her decision had been methodical. She needed somewhere with a slower pace where she could have a more flexible schedule. One of her work friends, someone who knew what she'd been through, called in a favor for her with her alma mater, a small community college five hours away, deep in the hills of Alabama, and landed her a job with a flexible schedule. Most days, she could work from home, prepping materials and engaging with students online, but twice a week she had to log hours at the writing center on campus, forty-five minutes away. It wasn't much, but money stretched a little further in the country, and she no longer felt she had other options.

She bought a desk at a used furniture store down the highway, not far from the town center, and paid the man who ran the place to haul the heavy, walnut piece to her house on his truck. He had to drive into her backyard, where she guided him to the front of the shed, then helped him unload the desk and narrowly squeeze it through the entrance. For a moment, before they'd positioned the desk below the window, she realized she was trapped inside the shed with this man, and even though he'd done nothing to indicate malicious intent, she became suddenly aware of how remote her property was and how removed the shed was from the drive.

He used his flannel sleeve to wipe the sweat off his brow and surveyed the room, barren except for the metal bed frame and the desk he'd just deposited.

"This a mother-in-law suite?" he asked.

Amy grimaced at the antiquated designation. "No, it's just for me."

"Why're you wasting time on this little hut then?" he said.

"I like the smallness of it," she said. "The house is nice, but it can feel empty sometimes."

She immediately regretted saying the last part, because now there was an implication: the emptiness needed to be filled.

"If you ever need a hand with anything, let me know." He gave her a business card with a phone number, his name, and the embossed title of his store.

"Thanks, Joe."

She pocketed the card and watched as he backed his truck out of her yard, leaving twin tire tracks in the grass. She used her hands to rake the blades upright and hoped they'd survive.

It was her first time owning a yard, or a shed, after years of renting a city apartment, and she reveled in the quiet space that belonged to her. Toward the end, before the move, even the helicopters would wake her. Often, she'd emerge from sleep soaked in her own stale sweat, even though the helicopters had nothing to do with her trauma. If a car backfired, if a drunk person hollered out in the street, or if a neighbor's door slammed, she would feel her chest tighten. Eventually she discovered that it helped to sit in her closet with her hands grasping the top of her head, fingers interlocked, counting as she breathed as slowly as she could. Perhaps the shed was an extension of this need, but, she reasoned, this was more mindful. She was making this space her own.

She hauled a chair from the house across the lawn, set it in front of the desk, and sat down. The window faced the ravine. The kudzu and oak leaves shook in the wind, sending shadows dappling across the dark gulch below. The breeze chilled her, so she crossed the room to shut the door. When she returned, she laid her head on the smooth desktop and set to the task of daydreaming.

It was only then that she noticed the stillness. The leaves no longer rattled. The shadows were perfectly still. The ravine appeared as if in a photograph. At first, the uncanny resemblance to nature, distilled into artificial permanence, filled her with a sense of dread manifested as nausea and a scratch of electricity running up her spine. She ran out the door to the back of the shed and observed the trees lining the edge of the ravine, now rustling in the wind. When she went back inside and peered at the window, the light was still shifting, oscillating in brightness as clouds drifted by.

It was when she shut the door that the world stopped. Once the knob clicked tightly into the frame, it was as though she had pushed pause on the outside world and the scene beyond the window. She sat and watched for what felt like an hour, eyes straining to find any detail of change: a shifting leaf, a lower angle of sunlight, a flitting insect. Nothing.

When she accepted the nothingness, she felt an ache in her muscles melting away. Her shoulders dropped and her back unseized. She inhaled deeply, suddenly realizing that she had been taking only shallow breaths for who knew how long. When she left the shed, she felt the breeze, and the small shuffling movements of the foliage resumed.

She had to know the nature of the anomaly. She bought plants that were already half-dead, with spotted leaves and yellowed stems. She put them in the shed and made a point of keeping the door closed as much as possible. Several days passed, and the plants persisted, still sickly but never dying. When she wore a watch in the shed, the hands stopped moving as soon as the door was closed. Numerous times, she would sit in the shed and count the seconds—saying *One Mississippi, Two Mississippi*, and on and on—and she would mark off the minutes on a notepad. After she'd done this for more than an hour on three separate occasions, she decided that the anomaly was real, because each time she left the shed and entered the house, she would see that no time had been lost. The world had stood still.

The last day she'd done the counting exercise, she'd chosen the final minutes before sunset. She counted for two hours, but when she emerged, the sun was still hovering just above the horizon, its nimbus streaking the sky.

She dragged the unread books from her nightstand to the shed and read two in one sitting. She discovered that hunger did not affect her. Although she remained as tired as she had been upon entering the shed, her fatigue neither waxed nor waned. It seemed that all biological processes froze in their current state. Entropy did not exist here.

———

Amy went back to Joe's furniture store and bought a used bookshelf. This time, she had him park in the front of the house, and together they hauled the shelving unit across the lawn and into the shed. Amy made a point of propping the door open, letting the breeze carry away the magical cessation of time. Joe observed the new mattress on the rusty frame, the braided rug spanning the length of the room, and the photographs lining the desk. In particular, he lingered over the picture of an older woman wearing a sun hat, beaming in a garden.

"My mother," Amy said. "She's not around anymore."

"Sorry to hear that," Joe said.

Amy shrugged, not to negate the information, but to make Joe feel more comfortable. "It's been a while."

He nodded, then gestured at the room. "You live here now?"

"No, but I like to spend a lot of time here, reading and drawing mostly."

"You're an artist," he said, like things were coming together.

"Not exactly. But I do draw."

She had always wanted to be a serious artist, but the careful blending and stages of drying required of oil paints had overwhelmed her, so she stuck to graphite and—once she had predrawn so that she could safely trace her own lines—ink. These days, she mostly doodled on old furniture catalogs, drawing dogs and children and large families onto glossy pages of empty, staged living rooms and kitchens. She'd never had a large family—she was an only child—but she liked the look of it on the page.

Joe took off his baseball cap and squeezed the bill in his hands, doubling the brim over on itself, and with a white-knuckled grip, he asked, "Can I take you for a bite to eat sometime?"

Amy felt cornered, but not threatened, or, at least, no more threatened than she felt on a consistent basis. He looked so earnest and vulnerable in the moment that she couldn't think of a way to say no that wouldn't leave her feeling guilty for hurting his feelings, and yet, she couldn't wrap her mind around an actual date: the prerequisite sexualizing of him, the implicit goal of peeling off shirts and taking the other to bed.

She was still pondering how to turn him down when he added, "There's a real casual barbeque spot down the street. The place used to be a gas station. I thought we could grab lunch there, when you're not too busy."

Lunch was more manageable, Amy decided. She nodded and smiled. He could be a friend, she thought, as she watched him stroll back to his truck, whistling the whole way.

Joe texted her the next day and set a time, that Friday, for the lunch.

"I'll meet you there!" Amy texted back, pleased with the casual distance that was unfolding.

For Amy, she still had eons before Friday anyway. It was only Monday, and she spent the days pondering the possible uses of the shed. She could learn anything, she thought. She could read all the books in the world as long as she could bring them with her to the shed. She decided she would learn a new language, possibly French, but she soon realized that the shed would only allow her to learn how to read it, and only with careful self-study. When she carried her laptop into the shed, hoping to play the audio of a French lesson, the battery immediately drained. The same was true for lamps. It was therefore useless to visit the shed at night unless she wanted to light a dozen candles or sit in darkness, which sometimes she did.

In the timeline of her experience, the days before Friday amounted to months. She read dozens of books. She spent more time thinking from the perspective of the characters in the novels she read than she did contemplating her own life. Could that be enough, to slip into the minds of others in perpetuity? She came to be like some sort of other, like dancing versions of a danceless self. Ceaselessly, she flipped the pages, the dried and pressed sheets of wood pulp pulling the moisture from her fingertips, but she only noticed when the skin cracked, leaving faint streaks of red in the margins.

She had cultivated an almost endless present. She went to work, yes, but the work was a cyclical routine interspersed with sleeping and cooking, the days blurring together, the slippage of time deepening each session she spent reading in her secret sanctuary. She set alarms on her phone to remind her of any real-world obligations, but she had to leave it in the house so that whatever magical vortex that stopped time didn't also suck away the life of its battery. When Friday arrived, she woke to the chime of a notification informing her that the lunch was today.

She immersed herself in her morning tasks of work emails

and marking feedback for students online. When the lunch hour neared, she retreated to the shed, shut the door, and spent an unknowable amount of time steadying herself for unscripted conversation with a stranger. She wouldn't mind having an acquaintance, maybe even a friend. She played through the possible scripts like planning moves in quantum chess. By the time she'd envisioned all the outcomes, she felt like she'd already lived the lunch, so she returned to her house and decided to crawl onto the sofa, pull the blanket over her shoulders, and sleep. As the cocoon of fatigue swathed her brain, she tried to send a cancellation text, or an apology, but she couldn't think of any words that would suffice, so she let the phone slide between the cushions of her couch and succumbed to drifting dreams.

———

Amy woke to insistent knocking. When she opened the door, Joe was standing on her stoop looking mournful and pissed at the same time.

"I'm sorry," she said. "I fell asleep."

"It's one in the afternoon," he said, incredulous.

"I'm sorry," she repeated, quieter this time, unsure of what she could say that would neutralize his disappointment and need.

"I was worried that something had happened to you, so I just thought I'd drop in to check," he said. "My aunt Rose nearly died from accidentally leaving the gas knob on her stove slightly askew. You just never know . . ."

"Thank you for making sure I'm not dead."

"Listen," he said. "I still need to grab a bite. I left when you didn't show. Do you want to come along?"

She couldn't really see how to say no at this point, so she acquiesced. He held open the passenger door and offered his hand to give her a boost, but she grabbed the handle that rested just above the window and hoisted herself up.

They drove down Main Street, a speck of road with a few surviving historical buildings from when there used to be a train stop here, but most of the tiny city center consisted of rundown franchises: a Popeyes and a McDonald's going toe-to-toe, a Super Dollar, and a BP gas station with a mini-mart that could tide you over until you could make the longer drive to Walmart, two towns over. There was a smoke-spewing stand surrounded by picnic tables called Whole Hog BBQ, which had stopped serving whole hog barbeque several years ago but no one wanted to invest in changing the sign since money was tight. No one wanted to invest in a town that was barely hanging on.

Joe drove past the barbeque joint, explaining that he was embarrassed to go back since he'd just left not even an hour ago. Instead, they went to Mike's Grocery, which didn't even sell groceries, just booze, basic grub, and jukebox tunes, but Joe insisted that the burgers were worth it. The front porch had long since lost any paint or varnish, and two orange traffic cones cordoned off a splintered gap in the planks. Joe held the door open for Amy so that she had to enter first, eyes struggling in the dark interior to make sense of the layers of tarp and strings of lights woven into the ceiling beams. Joe ordered at the bar, then led her to a card table, its surface shellacked with a collage of stags cut from hunting magazines.

An old man sat hunched at the bar, sipping at his beer and gazing into the mirror behind the shelves of cheap liquor and potato chip bags. Every so often, he'd peer over his shoulder at Amy, stare long enough that she couldn't help locking eyes with him, and then turn back to the mirror, satisfied.

"Hey, Billy," Joe gave a perfunctory wave, then added quietly to Amy, "Poor bastard. His wife died a few years ago and now he just sits here all day, most days, watching whatever game or court show is on the TV, or just sitting like a bump on a log."

"You ever live anywhere else, Joe?"

"I lived in New Orleans for a couple years with a few of my buddies, but it wasn't a good mix for me, all that fast living. Plus, I inherited a spot of land here." He took a sip of his Coke. "What about you? What brought you here?"

"The quiet."

He raised an eyebrow. "People don't just up and move to bumblefuck Alabama. Maybe Tuscaloosa or Mobile or something, but this," he twirled his finger, pointing at the room at large, "this ain't that. You running from something?"

"Yeah, I killed someone," she said, and he immediately laughed, sensing it wasn't true.

"What's so funny?" she asked.

Joe lost his smile. "I'm trying to have a real talk with you."

"I don't want to get into the details," she said, "but someone really messed me up, and I don't mean broke my heart or played a few mind games, although that could be bad too, I guess. I mean, someone made it so that I couldn't live anywhere I lived before. I needed zero reminders."

"That sounds serious."

"It is, but," she said, forcing brightness, "moving on."

Joe nodded, then leaned back in his chair, splaying his fingers out in surrender. "Just trying to get to know you."

"I like pizza, drawing, and books. I probably don't vary my routine as much as I should. I don't like crowds or loud music or multilane highways. And your friend Billy may be a sad bastard, but I don't like how he keeps leering this way, like he might just whip his dick out any moment and we're the ones who are supposed to avert our eyes."

Joe looked over at Billy, who was still midstare, oblivious. "Sorry about that," he said, turning back to Amy.

"These better be damn good burgers."

Joe laughed, so Amy smiled. She wanted to grimace, to show him that the Billy thing wasn't leaving her in a laughing mood, but he'd apologized, and it wasn't his fault, even if he wasn't doing anything to fix the situation. The burgers came and they ate in awkward silence for a while. Amy wasn't much of a cook, and she was scared of underpreparing meat at home, so this was the first burger she'd had in months. She was on her last bite when she realized Joe was watching her with a smirk.

"What?" she said, deflated, lowering the last morsel of meat.

"Just enjoying how much you liked that burger."

She pushed her plate back a few inches and wiped her mouth, her hunger draining away from her. This was one of the trajectories she had envisioned, the smarmy endearments, the oblivious persistence. Out of the many possibilities, only a slim fraction played out as congenial, mutual curiosity between two people passing time together. She focused on slow breathing, inhaling through her nose, but then she was overwhelmed by the sour smell of days-old beer and sweat.

"I'm suddenly not feeling well," she said. "Would you mind taking me home?"

She thought about walking—the town was too small for cabs or ride shares—but it was nearly a hundred degrees outside, she was miles away, and there were no sidewalks. She wouldn't feel safer walking along the shoulder of the country highway, she thought, still uncertain.

Joe nodded.

Amy pulled her wallet out, and Joe waved his hand at her, insisting she put it away. "I know Dan, the bartender. He always gives me a deal."

What sort of deal would that be? she wondered. Surely everyone here knew the bartender but her.

"I'd like to pay for my part," she said.

Joe ignored her and walked up to the bar, flagging down Dan, a man with a dark beard and a heavy metal tee shirt. Whatever Joe said, Dan laughed and slapped him on the shoulder, then shook his head. Amy imagined the possibilities, but she couldn't land on one that felt kind to her.

In the parking lot, Joe insisted on holding her door open, and now she resented his proximity. She wanted it to all be over. She wanted to be home, hidden between the walls of her own space.

He drove past the two fast-food restaurants onto the highway, a grandiose term defined by the technicality of where the road led rather than the local upkeep or traffic density. The road was elevated, descending into gullies on either side with deep, dark forest stretching beyond, seemingly forever.

"Do you want to see the lake?" He slowed the truck, already veering toward the shoulder, preparing to turn down an old road with remnants of pavement from years ago.

"I told you I was feeling bad."

"We'll just loop by it. Doesn't add much to the driving time." She forced a smile, shifting into placating mode.

"You'll see," he added. "Makes living here not so bad."

She had her cell phone by her thigh, wedged between her and the door. She peeked at the screen, saw the low bars indicating bad reception.

To his credit, there was a lake, and the road led directly to it. One minute they were in a tunnel of black-green leaves and then the sky opened up, an amber gray reflected in the still waters below.

Joe rolled down the windows and leaned his arm out the side. The air smelled too pungent, like organic matter, maybe leaves, had accumulated too many layers and were concentrating the gasses of their own decay.

"Do you want to get out? There's a bit of a beach, even if it's mostly mud."

She shook her head. There was nowhere to go, really, except into the forest, or into the water. She had a faint memory of being in a lake as a little girl, her mother holding her hand, dragging her in as she wailed. She had hated the way the warm mud sucked on her toes. She could feel the slime swallowing her feet.

"You feel that bad, huh?" He squinted at the sky, looking re-morseful. "I thought maybe it was a mood thing."

"How considerate of you."

Amy noticed a large heron wading near the shore, its neck collapsing into itself, then extending, over and over, piercing the surface with its sharp beak. Finally, the black-striped head retracted with a tiny fish flailing, trapped in its mandibles.

"You misunderstand me." Joe's stare was intense, unflinch-ing. "I'm speaking to something I go through myself. I get real low and need to change scenery, but sometimes I don't remem-ber to do it for myself, but once I'm there, I remember how it always feels better, even if for just a second. Now, if you feel real sick, especially if that burger did it, I'm going to feel sorry for-ever. I just thought I could cheer you up, is all."

His response confused her. She couldn't figure out which script they were on.

"Thank you," she said, trying to force soothing tones into her voice. "I think I just really need to get some rest."

"You're shaking." He reached for her hand and, without any conscious decision to do so, she threw her weight against the door. In a blur, she found herself half leaning out of the truck, her seatbelt still on, cutting into her waist.

Joe leapt out of the vehicle and ran to the passenger side. When he looked up at her, she could see his eyebrows were raised. He's at least performing concern, she thought. He might mean it.

"You okay?" he said.

She ran her hand over her mouth. "I got really nauseated all of a sudden. I didn't want to puke in your truck."

He nodded. "I'll get you home."

The relief cascaded through her. By the time they were back on the main road, she felt the aftermath of her adrenaline sending her into a state of forced calm, and she struggled to stay awake. Joe was rambling on about all the things she could draw by the lake, listing all the local flora and fauna. White oaks and hickory. Tupelo gums and cypress trees in the swampy areas. The mockingbird, the muskrat, but, he reassured her, no alligators in this lake.

When they got to her house, he dropped her off. He let her go.

She went to the shed and curled up on the rug she had placed in the center of the room so that she could stare out at the still evening sky. She lay there in the forced sleeplessness of the timeless space, and she realized no one could open this door, the one that stood behind her, and surprise her while she rested in this closed room. Outside, nothing was moving at all.

She thought about what it would mean, to stay forever. Would she have stopped the world? Would she have, in effect, ended it? If a storm came and destroyed the shed, time would never stop again, but if time were already stopped, the storm would never come.

———

She read the books on her shelves. She read them all. On the outside, it would take her an hour to read forty pages. Here, in the shed, she read thousands of pages before she even considered leaving, but she did eventually decide to leave. She felt outside of herself, like she'd lost a sense of embodiment, and she found herself missing something as simple as sleep, a bio-logical process that would let her thoughts wind down instead of spiraling forever. She returned to her house, to her bed, and folded into herself and her dreams.

———

One day, not long after the day of the lake and a hundred books, when the sky was taking on a worrisome green cast and the clouds were stewing low, Amy returned from work to dis-cover a young woman fawning over flowers in the middle of her yard.

Amy rolled down her window and pulled her car along-side the large hibiscus bush the woman was inspecting. She wore overalls with a gray tee shirt underneath. Her short curly hair was mostly tucked under a baseball cap. Despite the ob-vious sound of crunching gravel and a rumbling car engine, the woman made a point of turning slowly and smiling, un-ashamed by her trespassing.

"Can I help you?" Amy said.

The woman held out a recently plucked hibiscus blossom, large enough to hide her palm. "Have you smelled these?" she asked.

"You know this is where I live, right?" Amy asked.

The woman walked up to the car and extended her free hand. "I'm Fran."

They shook hands through the window.

"I used to know the lady who lived here, when I was little," Fran added. "That was years and years ago. No one's lived here in a decade. Not sure why her family was sitting on it, but here you are now. Didn't even know you'd moved in." She held up her saucer-sized blossom in a gesture approximating half apology and half shrug.

"The woman who lived here," Amy said, "did she ever talk about the shed in the back?"

"Not that I can recall," Fran said. "Why?"

"Just curious. It was full of junk when I moved in, but it's probably all worthless."

"Miss Arleen was pretty reclusive, but she'd have garage sales from time to time, and I'd buy her old romance novels. She was pretty kinky, turns out, but she never mentioned the shed to me."

Amy laughed, suddenly charmed and surprised to find herself desiring the company. "Looks like it's about to pour. Would you like to come in for tea?"

"That'd be nice," Fran said.

Fran carried her plucked blossom with her into the house, and Amy brewed some herbal tea with dried berries in sachets. They sat at her kitchen table, sipping the sweet tea from their mugs. The rain came, and Amy cracked the window so they could hear the drops pelting the leaves. Fran breathed deeply and said, "That is one of the few things that never gets old."

Amy smiled. "I forgot how good it smells when you're not near pavement."

Amy told Fran she had been ready to leave Memphis, but she shared a few things she still missed, like the concerts by the river, the live music, and, preposterously, the McDonald's with the drive-through going the wrong direction so that everyone had to reach across the passenger side to grab their food.

"Couldn't they just drive the other way around?"

Amy suddenly realized that she couldn't picture the layout of the parking lot well enough to determine the cause of the poor design. "I guess I don't have any idea why they made it like that."

Fran laughed hard enough to send Amy laughing with her.

When the moment passed, Fran asked why she'd left Memphis, and Amy told her about her need for quiet.

"I hate my job," Fran said, revealing that she worked in the office of a car factory an hour away, but she currently lived with her parents down the road to save money. She wanted to start a nursery someday, to grow plants for people's gardens.

"Is there a market for that sort of thing around here?" Amy hadn't seen many nice lawns since the move.

"I'll find a place where it makes sense." Fran said it in faith. "My parents think I should stick with Toyota forever, save up retirement, keep up the insurance and all that jazz. They don't see anything wrong with the endless filing of paper. I'm their black sheep," Fran added, pulling on her hair. "Wasn't always so. I was a debutante down in Vicksburg. My grandma made me. They still do that shit, you know."

"No way."

Fran gave her a stern look and asked, "Which part you placing doubt on?"

"Both," Amy said weakly, unable to lie when put so directly on the spot.

"I was pretty!" Fran said. "And now I'm handsome. I am at peace." She took a swig of her tea. "Girl, you better have some more tea to serve after a comment like that."

"I didn't mean you couldn't be a debutante, aesthetically. I just meant, you seem too free in spirit to do that sort of thing."

"Free in spirit. That silliness. I'm deliberating all the time on each aspect of all the minutiae of my existence," she said. "Are you free in spirit?"

"No," Amy said.

"That's what I thought. And who is, really? No one, that's who."

They made the tea a ritual. She would come on the weekend and leave after an hour or two, sharing nothing more than words. The first couple of times, Fran simply wandered by and Amy spotted her, acting as though it were incidental, but in truth she had hoped Fran would return. She would peek out the window from time to time. After a few weeks of this, Amy found herself spending fewer sessions in the shed, wanting time to pass faster.

Even as Amy was hopeful for Fran's visits, even as she would usher her through the front door and say, "Please, come on in," she was thinking of how to avoid Joe, who had taken to texting her and asking if she needed any help around the house. Sometimes she would ignore these messages. Sometimes she would send a quick reply, like, "Thanks so much but I'm good for now!" And she would add a smile emoji, to appeal to his kindness, hoping it would buy her goodwill if he pressed the issue and forced her to outright reject him.

One day Joe showed up unannounced. He knocked on her front door, and she ran to open it, imagining Fran on the stoop.

He held his cap in his hands and smiled. "I'm so sorry to bother you with this, but I have some bad news."

Amy couldn't fathom what such news could possibly be. Joe didn't know anyone that she cared about. Her mother was already dead, she never really knew her father, and the only person she cared about in her new hometown was Fran. He'd never seen them together, so it couldn't be about Fran.

"What is it?" she asked.

"I have a termite issue at my store," he said. "I'm thinking the shelf I sold you may have tracked them into your shed."

He went on to describe the horror of termites.

"You haven't noticed them swarming, have you?"

She shook her head. She hadn't noticed anything, but now she wondered if termites could proliferate in the timeless space. Would they lose all desire to reproduce, to feed? Did they exist like living fossils in the nooks and crannies of her wooden furniture?

"I'll just give it a look to make sure," he said.

"That's okay," she said.

"Really, it's no trouble." He was already stepping off the porch and onto the grass, heading to the back of her property. Anxious that he might discover the shed's secret, she followed him, insisting again that she didn't need the inspection, but he waved off her polite protestations.

She quickened her stride to outlap him. She considered insisting that he couldn't enter the shed, but in the flurry of the moment, she thought that would appear strange to him, and she wanted everything associated with the shed to seem casual and disinterested. She unlocked the padlock and propped the door wide open with a large stone she had kept there for that purpose.

As soon as he crossed the threshold, she realized that her desk was strewn with portraits she had drawn of Fran. They were drawn from memory. She didn't want Fran to know, not yet anyway, that she fixated on capturing her likeness on paper, her profile especially, when her eyes were cast downward, examining her tea, fingernails, or stolen flowers. The most prominent drawing on the desk was a large charcoal piece with Fran's bone structure roughly rubbed into the grain of the thick, beige paper. In this portrait, Fran's head was bowed, but her eyes were focused sideways, peeking at whoever was holding her in this two-dimensional form.

She tried to put her back to the desk, obstructing Joe's view as he squatted in front of the shelf, running his fingers along the edge of each plank of wood. He plucked a couple of books from the shelf, pulling them away by hooking his finger on the spine, a gesture that bothered Amy, but she would never say so, at least not now while trying to avoid deeper revelations.

"May I?" he said, already clutching a few books and pantomiming his intention to remove them all.

"Sure," she said, not moving to help. Not daring to leave the desk as he pulled dozens of books and piled them on the floor.

He peered behind and beneath the shelves. He lifted the bottom edge and examined its underbelly. After he'd touched all the surfaces, he wiped his hands on the thighs of his jeans and sighed.

"You're lucky," he said. "I think this piece is clean."

"Glad to hear it."

He leaned against the shelves, peering down at her. She felt suddenly small and girlish.

"I never did get to take you to that barbeque."

"I've been real busy these days."

"A girl's gotta eat."

Amy could see that there was no gentle way out of this. She gripped the edge of the desk behind her, steeling herself. "I don't want to go out with you, Joe. I'm sorry. But I'm not looking to start anything."

"Like, now, or ever?"

Amy couldn't help but laugh a little, a nervous, involuntary response. The question was so off-putting. He'd cornered her into lying or hurting him.

At her brief chuckle, he shook his head and narrowed his eyes. "You're just being cruel now."

"I'm not in a healthy place for anything serious. That wouldn't be fair to either of us." She shifted her weight away from him, preparing to pivot past him.

He surprised her by smiling. "Who said anything about serious? I was just looking to spend some time with you, is all. I'd just like to converse on things, have a friend, maybe go fishing. No need to make it this big dramatic affair."

"I have to put in hours at the writing center on the weekdays." Amy knew the barbeque spot was only open for lunch.

"What about Saturday?"

Amy had made plans with Fran that day, but she didn't want to tell Joe that. She didn't want him to know more about her personal life than he did already. "I can't," she said. "Not this week," she added, hoping that would be enough.

For a moment, he stared with no discernible reaction. Then he gave a quick nod. "Okay. Then I'll shoot you a message next week to find a time." He tapped his fingers on the bookshelf. "Could you recommend a book for me? Let me borrow it? I'll give it back at lunch next week."

"*To the Lighthouse*," she said. She just wanted him gone, and she could see the title on top of the stack nearest him. There'd be no need to search for it, no need to linger.

He plucked the book off the pile and tipped the bill of his cap at her. "See you soon."

With the book sandwiched under his armpit, he left her alone in the shed. She waited until she heard the truck's engine fade, then she shut the door so that she could rest her mind and ease her breathing in the stillness.

————

She told Fran about Joe and his last visit. They were making bruschetta and dicing tomatoes Fran had walked over from her parents' garden.

"That doesn't sound right," Fran said. "Besides, it's nearly July. I don't think termites swarm this time of year."

"You think he's lying to me."

Fran shrugged. "I've only talked to Joe in passing. He's ten years older, so it's not like we overlapped any at school. But I hear things. When he's sober, he seems to lay low. But he has his drunk spells, and then people will talk about some trouble he's stirred up. Nothing serious that I know of, but this pushiness you're describing? Sounds shady. I don't like it."

"I don't know what I'm supposed to do. He hasn't technically done anything." Amy put down the knife and slid the chopped tomatoes and onions into a bowl.

"Want me to stay over?" Fran asked without even looking at Amy. She poured some olive oil into the bowl and raked her fingers through the vegetables.

"You going to be my bodyguard?"

Fran looked up and smiled. "I can try."

The offer felt earnest and unassuming. Amy felt, for the first time in years, that someone was offering to shoulder her burden. "Okay," she said, scooping salsa onto crostini.

They had their dinner on the front porch. It was Fran's idea. She wanted to watch the sun set. They spread a blanket for their dishes. Amy gathered citronella candles and lit them along the edge of the porch and on each step leading to her front walkway. They shared wine.

Despite the candles, Amy could feel the bugs biting her, already leaving welts on her arms and legs, but she didn't want the night to end.

"I want to show you something."

"Now?"

Amy nodded.

"What time is it?"

"It's eight thirty," Fran said. "Why?"

"Leave your phone here."

Amy motioned for her to stand up. She picked up two candles, handed one to Fran to carry, and then led her around the house and across the overgrown yard to the shed.

"Are you going to paint me or something?" Fran said with a cocky smile.

Amy unlocked the door and led her inside.

"What did you want to show me?"

Amy shut the door behind them. "It's hard to explain, especially since it's dark out. It's hard to tell by just looking outside."

"Tell what?" Fran said, her smile fading.

She put their candles on the window ledge, above the desk. In the flickering glow, Fran could see an unfinished portrait. When she recognized it for what it was, a portrait of herself, she lowered a candle to look closer. She touched the lips, which were so artfully drawn they appeared to be glistening.

"Be careful with touching it," Amy said. "I haven't set the charcoal yet."

Fran put the candle down and pulled Amy into her arms. She hugged her so that Amy's face was cradled against her shoulder and she breathed deeply of the nape of her neck.

When Amy finally lifted her head, she found Fran still looking down on her.

Amy kissed her. She rose on her toes and pressed into Fran so that she stumbled back against the desk, and they both laughed. Then Fran grew serious again.

"What did you mean about looking outside?"

"It's not important," Amy said. "I'll explain in the morning."

She kissed her again, guiding Fran to the bed, pulling her down with her. Fran peeled away both of their shirts and traced her fingers in a spiral around Amy's breast, lightly closing in on the nipple, then kissing it. She ran her lips along the ridge of her ribcage, grazing the top of Amy's jeans before pausing and cocking her head to the side.

"Something's not right," Fran said. She climbed off of Amy and lay beside her.

"What do you mean?"

Fran held up her finger to shush her. After a long silence, she asked, "Do you hear that?"

"What?"

"Nothing."

"I'm surprised you'd let that stop you."

"No, it's weirdly quiet, and not just that." Fran gestured between their bodies. "This doesn't feel right either."

Amy felt panic rising. "I thought you wanted this."

"It's not like that. I *do*. But don't you feel it? Like I can barely feel my heart beating," Fran said. "Is there a leak, carbon monoxide, some sort of gas?"

"There's no gas hooked up to the shed," Amy said. "Hold on."

Amy scooped their shirts off the floor and handed Fran hers. As soon as Fran was dressed, Amy opened the door. A profound wind swept through the shed, and Fran placed her hand to her neck, like she was feeling her own pulse.

"Are you alright?" Amy asked.

Fran nodded, but her eyes still showed too much white. Her gaze roamed around the room, zigzagging, unable to land focus.

"There's one last thing I need to show you."

Amy led Fran back to the porch and handed her the phone.

"What time does it say?"

"Eight thirty-five," Fran said, "but we were in there for at least twenty minutes. Maybe longer. Weren't we?"

"I know how this sounds. It's why I had to show you first," Amy said. "The shed, it stops time."

"That's not possible."

Amy explained what she knew about the shed. Her experiments. The effect on her hunger. The long hours she had dedicated to reading and art, living outside of time. She explained how it made her feel safe because no one could harm her if the outside world was still.

She told her about the time someone had drugged her. She'd been at a bar, celebrating a friend's promotion, but the friend left before she did, and she wanted to have one last drink. She was always careful, only ordering drinks from the bar, never taking drinks from strangers. But the bartender was the one who did it. It didn't take long for her memory to fail. She had flashes of stumbling in front of a crowd of people, of him scooping her up. Quick bursts of memory of him on top of her. Then nothing. She woke up in a cheap motel. Her first conscious thought was the raw pain between her legs. In the following days, she would find bruises and scrapes from the way he had handled her—like a doll, an object, something to drag over carpet. She later learned he'd paid the motel in cash, that he wasn't even a bartender. He was just some guy who'd hopped behind the bar. She would never be able to identify him in a lineup, so she just had to live with it. There was nothing to be done.

Fran held her until she fell asleep that night. In the morning, Fran was already awake, sitting cross-legged at the foot of the bed, watching her.

"I don't think you should use the shed anymore."

"The shed gives me peace. Maybe you just need to see it in the daylight—"

Fran shook her head. "What if there are side effects?"

"I need it."

"It felt like sinking," Fran said.

"You were only in there that one time," Amy said, "You don't know what you're talking about."

Fran reached over and squeezed her hand. "I just want you safe, is all."

Amy laughed at this, at the absurdity of casting the shed as the primary threat out of all she had just shared.

Fran pulled away, rose from the bed, but lingered at the door to say, "Does it really not scare you?"

Amy shook her head, but she wasn't sure if she meant it.

After Fran left, Amy returned to the shed, wondering if she could feel what Fran felt—some sense of inherent wrongness—but the void of any outdoor noise soothed her. She experimented by working on her portrait of Fran with the door open and then closed, in alternating intervals. The right side of her face was etched within the flow of time. The left side was the product of the anomaly, constructed entirely with the door closed and with time frozen. Was there a difference, she wondered? Or had Fran's insinuation burrowed into her subconscious, weighing her hand more heavily on the left side's lines, making the charcoal thick and jagged on the page? She had meant to reflect admiration, maybe even love, but what else guided her hand when she was in the timeless space?

———

Some days she would do anything to make the weekend come sooner, to be with Fran. But Amy worried that the shed—and therefore she herself as the defender of its virtue—had scared Fran away. Sometimes this would trigger an adolescent desire to obsess over each possible outcome, and then she'd return to the shed and imagine what may or may not be, and when she'd leave the shed, an anxious thought would recur: at least now she could look forward to Saturday, but if Saturday led to an end of some kind, if Fran no longer wanted her, then what use would the future hours be now that she'd grown attached to the idea of Fran in her life? She had known Fran for less than three months, but she had thought about Fran for much longer. She had carved out the hours where none existed.

Saturday came without any word from Fran, but she received texts from Joe on each day leading up to the weekend. At first, they presumed their plans were made. "When should I pick you up?" he wrote, as though she had already consented to the date and inked it in her calendar. When she failed to respond, he wrote a series of increasingly erratic messages: *what a flake—I'd still like to see you though—At least let me return ur book—what changed?* When her cell chimed, she read the name of the sender with disappointment, then with mounting apprehension. The last message lit up her phone at two in the morning, and she finally responded with: *Never text me again*.

So when she walked out to the shed that morning and found the door torn from its hinges with a chunk of a plank missing where the lock once was, she immediately thought of Joe. Inside, the bookshelf had been toppled over. Her art was scattered on the ground, some papers torn to pieces. In the middle of the rug, Fran's likeness was split in half.

She saw a shadow fill the rectangle of light cast on the floor by the empty door frame. She knew it was him. Who else would it be?

"You've ruined it," she said, her voice thick with grief.

"I'll help you fix it," he said. "I'll fix everything."

She finally turned to look at him. His eyes were red with spent tears; his shoulders, hunched. His hands cradled his elbows.

"I don't know if you can."

He lurched into the room, then swayed, and she realized he was deeply inebriated. She backed away from him until her body was against the desk. To her surprise, he collapsed to his knees and began picking up papers, placing them in a pile. He tidied them into something resembling a stack and then offered her damaged art back to her.

She took the pages and placed them behind her, on the desk, while keeping her sight trained on him.

"I'm sorry," he said, his voice full of remorse until he continued, "but you weren't honest with me."

"Please, you need rest," she said, trying to keep her voice steady. "We can talk about this later."

"You won't talk to me." He grabbed the fabric of her pants, pulling slightly to steady himself.

She felt her chest tightening, like she couldn't get enough air. If only she could shut the door and have the stillness, but then he'd be in here with her, in the timeless place forever. He had tainted it. He had stolen her one thing.

"I will," she told him. "But not when you're like this."

He peered up at her, his chin grazing her waist, his pupils dilating as his vision took in the window light then readjusted to render her visible.

The drawers of the desk were askew, some left gaping open. She hid her hand behind her back as she explored the crevice, feeling the various writing utensils she'd come to know so well during her countless sessions here. She knew the rough metal grid of the X-acto. She slipped it out, palming it, nicking herself in the process.

"Now," he said, then repeated it. "Now!" He stood quickly, shoving off her to get his footing.

She lunged, sliding the knife into his neck, the long arc of her swing creating an equal and opposite arc of blood spraying in a stream, spiraling as he stumbled and staggered, then pooling over his fingers as he pressed on his own neck. He fell to his knees, and she watched the blood gather on the rug. It misted the window, refracting rosy-hued light. The blood kept flowing, even after his startled eyes lost focus. She thought she saw them flatten.

She was still holding the knife, staring down at him, when Fran found her. She had no sense of time. Fran screamed, then knelt to check his pulse. She looked up at Amy, her hands covered in his blood.

"Did he hurt you?" she asked.

Amy nodded.

"We need to call for help."

"No, you can't." Amy grabbed Joe by his feet and tugged on him, pulling his body over the loose drawings and torn pages.

Fran was sobbing. "Stop this. Please."

But Amy had already crossed the threshold. Joe was lying in the grass, his blood marking a wide path back to the shed. She ran to the door and propped it up, then struggled to jam the damaged hinges into place. Maybe that would be enough. Maybe that would work. Or maybe if she added a piece of wood and nailed the door shut from the inside. Then he would be frozen on the outside, maybe not dead yet, and she would be in the timeless place. She and Fran. She could make her understand.

"Help me put it back," Amy said. "I just need time to think."

MILKING

She and Kyle were caviar farmers. It always made for a good introduction at parties. *What does it take to farm caviar?* someone would always ask. *Now,* Diane would say, *a total commitment.* At first, she thought farming meant being in control of the fish, the pH levels, the water temperatures, and the schedule of the harvest, but you had to be ready when the fish were ready. You had to care for them with the all-consuming devotion of a parent, which was funny, funny in the way that something is the opposite of funny, because that was the thing they really wanted and the thing she could not provide.

That's why they were having this dinner, she and Kyle, with this vegan woman, trying to impress her, to show how deserving they were. Diane had hoped the night would feel warm and bonding. She had lit candles and wall sconces, their oiled wicks flickering against the oak paneling of their dining room. She had set the table with embroidered serviettes and brass plate chargers, an added touch that she normally skipped out of lazy, daily convenience. Those niceties were for holidays and anniversaries.

Their plan had been to wow Cindy with the best food northern Mississippi had to offer. Diane had bought local grass-fed beef and set it on the counter to adjust to room temperature. The steaks were still sitting there when Cindy arrived and revealed that she was a vegan. The young woman had wrinkled her nose at the sight of raw meat and then apologized. "I should have warned you," she had said. "I thought I said something at the gallery, but obviously this is my fault." Diane was inclined to agree. She had played their interaction at the art exhibit on a memory loop, seeking the telltale of veganism, but there was no indication that she could have deciphered, and it had been so long since she'd lived in California or spent time with anyone outside of her culinary community that the question of dietary preferences had entirely escaped her.

Now Diane could feel Cindy watching her as she seared the bloody meat in the cast iron. She could feel the woman's scrutiny, like the sensation of flies crawling beneath the crepe fabric of her dress. All they could feed Cindy now was a plate of roasted root vegetables. Cindy insisted brightly that the carrots, beets, and potatoes would be "more than enough."

Diane tapped Kyle on the shoulder and murmured for him to take over. She leaned against the kitchen island that doubled as a bar, where she had left Cindy to sip on a crisp albariño in front of a spread of appetizers. Diane scooped up a dollop of caviar and deposited the marbled gray eggs directly on her tongue. She closed her eyes and let them sit there, firm spheres waiting to burst, until they did burst, her tongue pressing them against the roof of her mouth, releasing fresh oils with a hint of ocean, a primordial hors d'oeuvre. She opened her eyes to find Cindy smiling at her.

"That good?" Cindy said.

"Are you sure you can't try the fish eggs? Don't some vegans eat eggs?" Diane said, stroking the stem of the stone-white spoon that sat beside the caviar jar, her caviar—she'd harvested

it herself. You couldn't use a silver spoon on caviar. A lot of people made that assumption: that the symbolically fancy spoon
would pair with the fancy delicacy of fish roe, but they were
wrong. The metal interfered with the sharp salinity of the eggs,
which needed to be presented on a neutral canvas, like ivory.
Ivory, Diane suddenly realized with a plummeting twist of her
gut, was an animal product—the worst kind of animal product. Shit, was this real ivory? It had been a gift from a client.
Even fake ivory, Diane knew, could come from the bones of
less-endangered species. She pulled her hand back and hoped
Cindy wouldn't notice the flat whiteness of the utensil.

Cindy shook her head. Her hair was loose and unbrushed;
her face, unmade. She was so beautiful she could afford to forget herself, to let the usual tasks of grooming slip away from
routine. Only the young could be like that, Diane thought. Her
daily routine was now a fight against entropy, lotions to correct
various signs of time and sun damage. Now she had persistent
rough spots emerging on her stomach. The night before, as she
undressed, she had discovered a couple of scaly blemishes near
her navel. She had tugged at the skin, and although she could
slide her fingernail beneath the edge of the gray scabby tissue,
she couldn't pull off the growth. She had called Kyle into the
bathroom and held her shirt up for him to inspect the spots.

"That's a nice look," he had said, flirting in the way he always did these days, like it was for her benefit, to make her feel
wanted, when they both knew their sex life had turned maud-
lin and perfunctory.

"What if they're cancerous?" she had scolded.

Several years ago, her mother had a melanoma, a black scab

blooming like cauliflower above her knee. She recovered, but a huge chunk of her thigh was indented now. Diane couldn't understand how her mother still went to Orange Beach with her friends each summer, slathering on sunscreen, yes, but nonetheless lying for hours in a chaise, her freckled skin freckling more and more. The same mother had always warned her this might happen, that if she waited too long to try, the child might never be. Like the choice was easy, like the relationship had always been a sure thing, like the business had not been new and struggling.

Kyle had suggested the scabrous growths might be a delayed reaction to her injection sites, but that was nearly a year ago. Nonetheless, it seemed fitting, albeit unscientific, that signs of her trauma would rise to the surface, leaving tally marks.

"I don't eat any kind of eggs," Cindy said, shrugging. "Nothing with a face, and nothing from anything with a face." She laughed. "But don't worry. The vegetables look lovely."

Diane could see Kyle falter as he ladled the autumnal medley of veggies into a bowl for Cindy. They had been meant as a side, a small portion for each, but in order to offer a substantial meal to Cindy, Diane had to convince Kyle to sacrifice each of their own servings.

"Do fish count as having faces?" Kyle asked.

"Yes," the women said, in unison, and Diane was grateful for this moment of agreement despite their dietary conflict.

Diane ushered them into the dining room. She had hung floor-to-ceiling cream curtains, which she liked to keep closed in the evenings, when the windows became mirrors against the deep darkness of their rural acreage. She'd grown up in Birmingham, in the suburbs, and she could never shake the feeling that someone could pass by and notice you, without you even knowing. She had done it herself, as an adolescent girl. When dinner was over, when her father was in his office and her mother would draw a long bath, she would go for walks around the neighborhood and see the other families, the ones who had left their curtains undrawn, watching their televisions and finishing their late dinners. There was one house down the street where the parents would sit with the children, doing homework, the pendant light shining brightly on the tops of their heads.

Now she had a row of simple pendant lights, rustic exposed lightbulbs running the length of their farmhouse table. She set the plates on one end, so that she could face Cindy, leaving Kyle between them, at the head.

Once seated, they all stared expectantly at each other.

"You can dig in," Kyle said. "We're not religious."

"Or pray if you'd like," Diane added. "That's okay too."

"Thank you for this meal," Cindy said, then stared down at her plate for a moment so that Diane could not tell if she was praying or simply waiting.

"We're happy that you came," Diane said, hearing the intensity in her voice and reminding herself to tone it down.

Cindy was a maker of nests, or nest art, or, as she worded it for the gallery flyer, she recuperated nests as mixed-media projects: the nest as found object with strategic enhancements. She would take actual nests—abandoned, usually found after they'd been dislodged from some branch or gutter—and weave cut-out words and trinkets into the twigs and grass. The manmade matter that the birds themselves wove into the natural fibers was often shocking—strips of plastic grocery bags, cigarette butts, holiday wrapping paper that had somehow not disintegrated. One nest contained a piece of barbed wire. That was the first thing Diane asked Cindy: was the barbed wire her own addition? But no, the barbed wire was chosen by the bird.

This rhyming of the nests and the caviar, it was not coincidence. In a speech at her exhibit, Cindy explained that she was drawn to the representation of the Anthropocene, it was true, but she couldn't avoid the effect of her surrogacy upon her subject matter.

"Yes," Cindy had said with a self-deprecating laugh, "I was a surrogate, and I collect nests. I will leave it to you to connect the dots, my friends."

Standing in that small-town gallery, a plastic cup of cheap wine in hand, Diane, who historically had scorned the idea of fate, felt that things were finally clicking. When Diane had the miscarriages, when miscarriage pluralized into two, then five lost pregnancies, she secretly began to wonder if the fish had cursed her. She didn't believe it in the front of her mind; she just acknowledged that a hidden part of her worried, the same way she still couldn't bring herself to walk beneath a ladder.

But whether it was a curse or not, the effect was indisputable: she couldn't carry a baby to term. One doctor told her that she and Kyle shared similar genetics, and they therefore bestowed their embryo with genes so similar to her own that her body was failing to produce the right antibodies for pregnancy. She imagined a shared ancestor. She questioned her subconscious and the nature of her attraction. She even began to notice similarities in their phenotype. Did they share the same divide between their brows? The same pronounced pinching of the nasolabial fold?

Relatively speaking, it came as a relief when a new doctor told Diane that she had a "hostile uterus"—his clinical diagnosis, those words. He told her she could go through another round of IVF and blood thinners for a slim chance of success, or she could consider surrogacy. Kyle wanted to keep trying IVF, but Diane had begun to resent her body, to think of it like a house filled with carbon monoxide, a silent killer, and no opening of windows could vacate the noxious fumes.

Then she'd met Cindy, a curator of fertility symbols and a former surrogate. It was as though fate had advertised the art walk, pinned the flyer for her exhibit on the bulletin board of the local bookstore where Diane had sought solace in the testimonies of formerly barren women. At the gallery, Diane had asked Cindy more than a dozen questions about the nest art. Each time Cindy finished answering, her eyes drifted to a spiky modern light fixture or the table of cheese cubes and magnums of wine. Diane had felt panicked that she had not secured enough of a connection with this woman. *Not yet*, she had thought, scrounging for one more question, then another, and another, no matter how inane. Finally, when she could no longer deny Cindy's cornered exasperation, she revealed that she was going to buy one of her pieces.

"Which one?" Cindy had asked, suddenly revived.

"The one I first asked you about," Diane said, no longer recalling the title of that particular nest.

Cindy had offered to pack the nest that night, to hand it to

Diane in a baker's box, but Diane had insisted that the nest remain on display until the end of the evening. Even as she had said it, she flushed at the realization that the exhibit was nearly over. A couple of stragglers sipped their drinks near the snacks, no longer paying attention to the art. But she wanted an excuse to see Cindy again.

"I really am happy to give it to you now," Cindy had said, already reaching for the nest, careful to avoid the thorns of the interwoven barbed wire.

"I noticed that you put the wall-mounted ones on driftwood," Diane had said, pleased with her improvised request. "Would it be possible to do the same thing with this one? I would pay you extra, of course."

Cindy had looked down at the nest in her hands. "All in all."

"Excuse me?"

"The title of this one: All in all." She held it up like an offering, and Diane could see the carefully clipped newsprint half buried by metallic fibers.

"I love it the way it is," Diane had said, suddenly concerned that she'd offended Cindy. "I just know I want to hang it on a wall."

Cindy nodded. "I understand. It's fine. I'll get it ready for you."

A week after the exhibit, when Cindy had emailed her, Diane insisted that she come over for dinner, to compensate her for her trouble. "That's really not necessary," Cindy had responded, forcing Diane to reveal something adjacent to complete honesty. That was when she called her and told her that she wanted to "pick her brain about surrogacy."

Now, in the foyer, there was a piece of driftwood with a nest, pinned by a nail, like a wreath, to the branch. Now, in the dining room, there was a vegan eating carrots as Diane struggled to swallow her achingly rare meat. She mulled over how to make surrogacy sound like a light topic, a casual exchange of chit-chat, when such a topic could never be anything other than the sequel to a tragedy.

"What is that picture, with the dark circular things?" Cindy pointed with her fork to the wall behind Kyle where Diane had hung a gallery of photos in gold frames.

"It's a picture of our fish tanks, from above." Kyle had taken the photo from the roof, through a skylight they later removed in order to better regulate the temperature and lighting schedule of the tanks below.

"They live in those circles?"

Kyle shot Diane a look, as if to say, *I got this*. She saw it through Cindy's eyes. He reclined in his cane-backed chair, indulging in that masculine tradition of luxuriating in physical space to broadcast complete assuredness, and said, "Our operation actually saves the lives of fish, might even save an entire species from extinction. So, if you're worried about the ethics, we're on the same page. That's why we do what we do."

"Don't you shank them in the ovaries?" Cindy said, adding in a subdued tone, "I saw a video once."

Diane cringed. They weren't set for life. The business could still fail. She might have to start over, yet again, building up from nothing, but they were part of a world where fine dining was an extension of their expertise, and she liked to believe there was artfulness, an elevation of experience, that they offered. But what must they look like? Her little black dress and statement necklace. Her husband's crisp blazer. Kyle never dressed up except for dinners with prospective clients and investors. He dressed up tonight because she asked him to. "We need her," she had said to him, his face in her hands, his stubble grazing the calluses she'd developed from years of caring for the fish, years of chemicals, the many harvests.

"That's not really accurate," Kyle said. "We can show you the procedure. The hatchery is just down the street, down our driveway, really."

The procedure. That morning, Kyle had cradled the flailing sturgeon against his chest as he carried her from the tank to the milking trough, the metal cradle designed to hug the supine body as they took all the eggs from her swollen belly. He had held the head in place as one of the hatchery employees prepared the collection bin. Even after all these years, Diane couldn't shake the impression that the sturgeon, at this angle, had human faces with upturned noses and surprised mouths, which is why she spoke to them sometimes when it was time to slide the catheter into the oviduct inlet, a term that made her think of the ocean, and therefore of all the eggs roiling around in this internal sea of a fish belly. During the procedure, she would slide her hand down the pearl white underside, over and over, guiding the inky beads out of the sturgeon in gushing rivulets.

Most nights, Diane would dream of them, a drifting slideshow of the sturgeon in their tanks, prehistoric, older than dinosaurs, with bony scutes scarring their sides. If you sliced open the ridges, rings would mark the age of their bones, just like the trunk of a tree. Recently, perhaps spurred by this fact, she would dream of the fish in cross sections, their heads detached with mouths still gulping as eggs fell thick from their partitioned bellies, spilling to the concrete floor, into the Cloroxed muck, and down the drain. Unconscious, she would flail, displacing Kyle to the couch. Often, she woke to her arms stretched over her head, like she was reaching for the window.

It was Diane's idea to convert the hatchery from catfish to sturgeon, to farm sustainable caviar. She researched the method, the nonsurgical use of the metal tube paired with the deep massage. In little over a year, the fish would heal and grow more eggs for the next harvest. The reproductive irony was impossible to miss. There was a horrific symmetry to the proceedings: the stealing of their eggs for a nice family business, something to pass on to generations that might never come. Used to be, everyone just killed the fish. They killed so many that they nearly eradicated sturgeon from the Black Sea. You would cut out the ovary and slide it back and forth over mesh to separate the eggs. What was left looked like broken pieces of placenta. The entire life of the fish reduced to a tin of caviar and silken pink membranes, washed down the drain.

"What we do," Diane said, "it's the gentlest way possible."

Cindy was cutting her carrot into tiny pieces, dicing all of her vegetables, her jaw visibly clenching and unclenching.

"We've upset you," Diane said. She felt her hope being masticated in Cindy's mouth.

Cindy put her fork down with a big sigh. "Look, I'm used

to seeing things differently than most people. I try not to force my views on others. But no one needs to eat caviar to begin with, do they?"

"I'm sorry you feel that way. I really am," Diane said. "Obviously, I didn't bring you here to discuss caviar. But you know how worried you are about the fish being poked and prodded? I've lived it. I'm sure you think that's some sort of karmic retribution. I know I do, most days."

Even at the thought, she could feel the skin beneath her dress itching, the feeling of a thousand flies landing, their proboscises touching, tasting, looking for sweet rot. She scratched through the rough fabric, feeling it scrape against the barnacled scabs beneath. Tears sprang hot but she widened her eyes, willing the excess fluid to sink beneath her lids, to reabsorb, disappear.

Across the wide expanse of table linen, Cindy looked horrified, keeping her eyes downcast as she said, "I empathize. Really, I do."

"I want wine," Diane said. "Let's start over. Would you like some wine?"

There had been some champagne to accompany the caviar, but for ages, all she'd allowed herself was the taste, a hint to complement the roe they were pushing on buyers. She pulled a dusty bottle from the wine rack, a Bordeaux heavy with sediment.

When Diane hovered the bottle over her glass, Cindy nodded.

They steered the dinner to ostensibly safer topics. Cindy asked how Diane and Kyle had met. They met at a wedding,

Diane said, sanitizing the truth: they actually met on Bourbon Street when she was a bridesmaid at a bachelorette party. She had ordered a complicated martini at a dive bar that only served daiquiris and beer, and Kyle, a total stranger, had laughed uproariously at her. She told him to fuck off, expecting to never see him again, but soon ran into him at a different, fancier bar, and so he had the exact martini she had tried to order at the first place sent to her table. "I know what I like," she had told him, and he asked for her number.

Back then Kyle was a catfish farmer, living exactly the life his father had lived, exactly the life his father had laid out for him, and although the perpetual sameness sometimes disappointed him, Diane felt stirred by his determination to carry the family legacy. There was security in his commitment that she had always lacked, the daughter of a mercurial mother and a father of various business trips with nondescript objectives. She was still in her twenties then, and her career had already changed three times. When they met she was working at a vineyard, a sommelier gig that exceeded her credentials, but she knew she'd never be a master sommelier with a steady career. She lacked the nose for it. Her body had disappointed her, even then.

They had married. They had planned on children. All those years ago, they had taken his business and tried something new. She knew what the restaurants were buying in Napa. They still wanted caviar, they just didn't want the optics of obliterating a natural population. They kept the catfish running long enough to fund the gradual transfer to sturgeon. It took years for the sturgeon to mature enough to produce the eggs. It was a ten-year plan. Ten years to see the return on their investment and to finally start a family. All things led back to this in any conversation they had.

"May I see a picture of your niece?" Diane asked.

Cindy smiled indulgently as she pulled out her cell phone, tapped and scrolled through her screen, then slid it across the table.

Diane held it up so Kyle could see. A baby with tiny pink pustules across her cheeks and a deep brow crease glared up at them. "Oh," Kyle breathed, and Diane pressed her knee against his under the table.

"She's sweet," Diane said.

Cindy burst into a quick cackle. "Neva had a mean case of baby acne. I didn't even know that was a thing, but that's how she came out, red and angry at the world. I thought my sister would blame me. Like my diet gave her acne or something." She sighed. "She's beautiful now though."

Diane swiped to the next few pictures, a slideshow that aged Neva into a toddler with spiky black hair and gaping smiles.

"My sister has a story like yours," Cindy said. "She's my big sister. They'd tried everything."

"Did she ask you?"

"No, she'd never. I offered."

Diane swiped to a picture of Cindy, moonfaced and pregnant in a long floral dress. A woman with some kind of chemical formula tattooed across her clavicle embraced Cindy from behind, an arm curved over her stomach. In the photo, Cindy stared up, neck twisting to adore her.

Diane held up the screen. "Is this your sister?"

Cindy flushed and reached for the phone. "No. Sorry. That's my ex."

She put the phone back in her purse and took a large sip of her wine. They all took sips of their wine. Diane felt she'd seen something she wasn't supposed to. A glimmer of Cindy's what-might-have-been.

"Where's your restroom?" Cindy asked, folding her napkin and placing it on the table.

"Just past the kitchen, to the right," Kyle said.

Diane watched as she walked away, ducking into the dark foyer, then leaned into Kyle and asked, "What do you think?"

"We just met her."

"I know, but keep an open mind."

"Do you want to be married to this person? Because we will be linked to her, for life," he said. "Do you want that?"

"Maybe that's not a bad thing."

"I don't like her. She's arrogant."

Diane felt mildly stunned, the same sensation she'd had as a kid roughhousing with her brother when he'd accidentally bopped her on the nose. It was akin to embarrassment, a form of rejection.

"Arrogant?"

"If we do this," he said, "we need someone we can trust."

"You keep saying these words, and I don't know what you're attaching them to." But she wondered. She knew Kyle grew up in a small-town Baptist family. His mother still said things at Christmas dinners that alarmed her. That was their usual holiday couple's fight: sharing harsh whispers in his childhood bedroom, a room that had thankfully shed its camo bedspread years ago. "You need to speak up to her," she would say, and Kyle would reassure her that they were on the same team but his mother was stuck in her ways. What good would it do, he had asked, to only share bitter words with a woman who would never change, who had aged rapidly in recent years? Last year, Diane noticed that his mother could no longer walk with a straight back. She leaned on the counters as she worked the kitchen, shooing away anyone who tried to help her. Diane felt trapped by these visits. They sullied her admiration for Kyle, a man she thought agreed with her about the poisonous aspects of what some people called tradition, but whose priorities became contradictory when faced with family. But she felt it too, the futility of trying to change a woman who cried easily at any gesture of familial generosity and who also assigned articles before categories of people, spouting offhand remarks about "the gays" or "the Mexicans," failing to connect these terms to townspeople she did business with every week.

"I'm just saying, she's clearly a flighty artist type," he said. "We need someone who will be healthy and reliable."

"You thought I looked healthy and reliable, but joke's on us both," she said, then added, "Don't take away our options." Even as she said it, she felt a jittery rage coursing through her, a desire to swipe her arm across the figurative tabletop of options and see which pieces Kyle would glue back together.

"You're the one who said no to IVF," he said.

"Shush, she's coming back."

She could see Cindy checking her cell phone. Whatever she read, it made her smile. Another picture of her niece, perhaps, but no, it was probably too late in the evening for that. Maybe, she worried, it was a new girlfriend. How could you convince a woman to carry your child when she was trying to start a life of her own?

"Would you like dessert?" she asked, as Cindy situated herself. "We have lavender sorbet. You can eat that, right?"

"That's really nice of you, but please don't trouble yourself," Cindy said.

Diane worried that Kyle seemed relieved. She squeezed his knee under the table and glanced pointedly at him, prompting him to say, "Really, it's no trouble."

Diane forced a smile, like she was having a sudden inspiration rather than following a script she had mapped out days before, and added brightly, "And we have sherry, a really wonderful sherry that you absolutely should try."

"That sounds nice," Cindy said, "but I can't stay out much later. I have to open the bakery in the morning."

"You mean The Basket? I didn't know you worked there." Diane would go each Friday morning, the one morning she allowed herself to arrive late to the hatchery, and buy a cinnamon roll and a latte served in a large ceramic bowl. It was one of her purest mundane pleasures, and now she pictured herself sitting at the counter, talking to Cindy as she arranged the baked goods in the display; Cindy smiling as she wiped the flour down the front of her apron and, with any luck, that apron stretching across an expanding belly until one day Diane would insist that Cindy stop working. *Please*, she would say, *I'll cover your expenses. Just stay home and relax*. Maybe she would bring cinnamon rolls to Cindy's apartment. Or whatever baked good that Cindy could eat. Maybe Cindy, great with child, would crave the yolky, soft dough.

"I just started," Cindy said. "My resumé is pretty random at this point."

"You're still young," Diane said.

"Not that young," Cindy said. "Old enough that I can't write things off as simply having fun or *discovering myself.*" She said the last two words like she was mocking someone real, someone who had judged her harshly.

"You have time." Diane reached across the table and touched her hand. *You have time I may want to take from you*, Diane thought, feeling suddenly disingenuous. But couldn't it be a ripe year for them both? *I will make it count for her, as well as me*, she thought. *If this happens, please*, she wished. *Please, if this is allowed to happen.*

Cindy used her free hand to pat Diane's before pulling away. The evening was slipping. She wanted something to happen that hadn't yet. She knew it was too much to expect any resolution about surrogacy, but she wanted a token of progress, a sense that tomorrow would be incrementally different than the thousand days preceding it.

"Let's hang up your art," she said, rising from the table.

Cindy retrieved the chimera of driftwood and nest and asked from the shadows of the foyer, "Where do you want it?"

"I was thinking our guest room," Diane said.

She left Kyle clearing the plates, which he happily did to avoid further conversation, and led Cindy to the guest room on the other side of the house. Although their house was large, it was all one story, a sprawling midcentury ranch. The house had been on the property neighboring the hatchery that Kyle had inherited from his father, who had commuted each day before sunrise from his tiny hometown an hour away. The same week that Kyle proposed to Diane, he took her to this very house and told her of his plans to buy it: how work would always be close, they would always be close, and the kids would be just down the hall. She had teased him when he had said they could grow old here, explaining excitedly that there weren't any stairs.

Diane flicked on the lights of the guest room, revealing walls the color of lemonade and a fainting couch tucked beneath the window in the corner so that someday (she had originally thought) she could breastfeed there and watch the breeze swaying the wisteria vines, which were prettier than the gingko leaves that had once sprung from the now-dead tree.

"We want to make this the nursery," Diane said. "We'd take out the bed, obviously, and put the crib in that corner."

"I like that it's yellow. It's a happy color," Cindy said, still holding the driftwood. "Where were you thinking this would go?"

"I was hoping you could help me decide."

"It needs to be out of reach, wherever it goes," Cindy said, tapping a thorn of rusted barbed wire tucked into the nest.

"Oh, of course." Diane sank into the plush duvet of the bed. "I'm an idiot."

"That's not what I meant," Cindy said, sitting on the foot of the bed, a few feet away, the driftwood in her lap.

"Sometimes I think maybe I'm just not supposed to be a mother." There was no stopping it then. She felt an audible sob welling up in her.

"Supposed to?" Cindy said. "No such thing."

"Sorry," Diane said, wiping at her eyes. "It must be the hormones." Even though she hadn't taken those in ages. It was an old reflex, to use that excuse.

Cindy reached across the bed, placing her hand on Diane's knee. "Sometimes I dream that Neva is my daughter. Sometimes I wake up and I can't remember the dream itself, but I know that's what it was. When I do remember, it's like a memory of a thing that never happened, so real that it takes a moment to process that this is my life, not the memories of my dreams. But I have these visceral memories of her calling me Mom, memories of when she's grown up already."

"I don't know that I could handle that," Diane said.

"Thank you."

"For what?"

"Not giving me a platitude."

"If you could go back in time, would you still do it?"

Cindy nodded. "I think so."

———

They decided instead to hang the nest in the living room, where they found Kyle, absorbed by his phone and sipping whiskey, an unstopped decanter beside him.

"I think it should be high above the mantle," Cindy said. "High enough that it exists by itself, no visual clutter nearby."

Diane saw Kyle smirk into his crystal highball glass.

"Will you get the ladder?" Diane asked him.

"It's at the hatchery."

"I really should go soon anyway," Cindy said.

"Sobriety checkpoints at Highway Seven and along Jackson," Kyle said.

Diane jumped in before Cindy could respond. "Why don't you come with us to see the hatchery? Let the wine fade a bit."

"She doesn't want to," Kyle said. "She probably thinks it's a prison fueled by fish tears."

"Kyle!"

Perhaps it was pity or a need to resist Kyle's assessment of her, but Cindy responded, "I'll go. Let's go."

They crammed into Kyle's truck with Cindy sandwiched between them in the front bench seat so that her thigh was unavoidably pressed against the length of Diane's. She could smell something astringent, like eucalyptus but milder, wafting from her skin. When the truck swerved on gravel, Diane held onto the door handle, trying not to slide further into Cindy's space.

The drive was short. They could have walked if it weren't for the ladder. From the hatchery's parking lot, the windows of the house were still visible, leaking the amber interior light. The fishery itself was a large warehouse with a corrugated steel roof and sheet metal siding.

Inside, the water filters hummed and percolated. The tanks smelled like tide pools gone stale in the sun. Cindy wrinkled her nose, raised a hand to her mouth.

"You get used to the smell," Diane said. It was only half-true. You grow desensitized, she thought, but if she focused on it, she could still detect a hint of ammonia, a brackish taste to the air.

They had two dozen tanks. Diane led Cindy to a tank of fish that were three feet long, dark shadows circling beneath the water.

"We've had these since we started," Diane said.

"Siberian Beluga hybrids," Kyle explained. "They mature faster. We needed fish that would produce in time to see a profit."

"Hybrids," Cindy murmured. "You made them?"

"Yes," Kyle said, "and they're better than either fish by itself. Tastes like Beluga without the difficulties of raising just Beluga." Kyle smiled, then added, "They're a little bit cannibalistic."

"Stop it, Kyle." Diane knew he was taking a victory lap, trying to drive home to Cindy how wrong she had been to judge him.

Cindy was staring into the water. "They look so strange."

"Would you like to touch one?" Diane asked.

Cindy smiled with a childish earnestness Diane had not yet witnessed.

Kyle looked surprised, then stern. "Are your hands clean? Free of any lotion?"

Cindy nodded.

"Maybe you should wash your hands just to be safe," Kyle said. "I can show you where. The sinks are by the ladder."

He gestured for her to follow, but Diane cut in, "You go ahead Kyle. She washed her hands before we left the house. It's fine." She wanted the moment to feel spontaneous, for Cindy to feel swept up.

Kyle shook his head, then left for the back room.

The fish, stirred by the lights, were circling in a school, a stream of shadows closing in on itself. Diane wouldn't normally risk the touching. There was always the outside chance the fish could get infected by some unanticipated pathogen. So much had gone into cultivating these fish, these hybrids that were the foundation of their business. But connection required risk, and maybe even sacrifice. She was making her offering now, guiding Cindy's hand into the water, reaching for the closest shadow, a slower fish, curious to its detriment.

Cindy's eyes grew wide and she gasped. "It's so smooth. I thought it would feel different."

As she watched the younger woman slide her hand along the fish, Diane felt her stomach pulling upward as if corseted to her spine and yanked by laces. She pressed her hand against her abdomen, bracing herself, conscious of the patches of abnormal skin beneath. It would be impossible, but she thought she could feel heat emanating from them. She missed the smoothness of her own skin.

"They don't have scales exactly," Diane explained, "but if you touch them on the ridges that line their back or sides, you'll feel these bony growths that some people think are scales."

Cindy reached in again, searching, and again Diane felt the tugging sensation, then a feverish dizziness.

Cindy flung her hand out of the water and looked at Diane. "How unusual."

"What did it feel like?" She wanted to know, had Cindy felt what she felt?

"Like armor."

Diane dipped her own hand in the water and slid her fingers along the jagged spine of a fish, but she felt nothing inside. She motioned for Cindy to touch the fish again.

"It's okay," Cindy said.

"Each one feels different," she said. "Try it." It was technically true, but no one would ever notice the minute differences of the touch. But for a moment her mind ran wild. She thought, *What if I'm linked to them all, cursed by them all? Or if it's just one, if I could figure out which one it was, I could keep it safe, treat it better than the rest. . . . Sturgeon could live a hundred years . . .*

But Cindy wouldn't help her. "Really, I'm fine," she said.

"Just touch the damn fish!" Diane said, pointing.

As soon as she said it, Cindy backed away from the tank, retreated from Diane with the wariness of someone stumbling upon a snake on the trail, noticing it inches away when at first it seemed there had been only leaves.

"I'm sorry," Diane said.

She fled past Cindy, out the front door, and felt the sudden relief of the winter chill. She leaned against the cold exterior and wiped at her eyes, not caring that her hands were filthy with tank water or that her fingers came away sooty with mascara.

Cindy emerged, letting the heavy door slam behind her. She dug around in her purse, and for a moment, Diane thought she was about to pull out a Kleenex. Instead, Cindy produced a cigarette. The way she lit it, the way she took a deep, desperate drag from it, made her look ten years older. The act, which ran counter to all of Diane's expectations of a vegan artist and former surrogate, startled her into the numb aftermath of her weeping.

"That was really fucking weird," Cindy said, looking Diane steadily in the eye.

The openness of her assessment felt somehow more congenial than critical.

"I fucking agree with you," Diane said. "I'm not usually like this. I really am sorry."

"Okay," Cindy said, still wary but soothed. Diane knew there was no coming back from this.

"I can't believe you smoke."

"I quit for the pregnancy," Cindy said. "I'd hoped it would stick, but, here I am." She leaned her head back, exposing her neck, and let out an exquisite exhalation that sent the smoke moonward.

"I'd hoped it would be you, that you'd be our surrogate," Diane said. "When I met you, it seemed right. I was going to ask. Not tonight, but someday, maybe after we knew each other better. I know that's weird to say now. It's too much."

"I figured you didn't just want to hear about Neva."

Diane felt awkward and ashamed.

"There's a really good agency in Jackson," Cindy said.

Diane knew this. She'd done her research. Everything was so contractual. The surrogate sometimes lived a few states away. It would be like the pregnancy never happened except in emailed photos and, if they were lucky, a couple of doctor's appointments. She realized now that she had dreamt up a future based on a forced friendship with a stranger who would want her to be there each step of the way, each living vicariously through the other.

"Why did you come?"

"I thought I could do this for money, but I can't. What I did, I did because I loved my sister, more than anything. But this?" Cindy gestured at the space between them with her cigarette, the tendrils of smoke like pernicious sage. "This would have been a transaction."

"What changed? Is it because of our work? Or what I just said? I don't usually snap like that."

Cindy shook her head. "Stop."

"Is it because of a girlfriend? But," Diane paused, "you'd be helping people." She regretted it immediately. She could see the way Cindy became closed to her. Her fingers tightened on her cigarette. Her eyes narrowed.

"You know, some people don't have the money to try all the things you're trying, right? Some people just have to accept the hand they're dealt. Your husband, would he understand if you just never had a child?"

"This is what I want," Diane said.

"Okay," Cindy said, "I believe you." She said it like a dig.

"You don't even know me."

"Exactly." Cindy stomped out her cigarette. "Thanks for dinner. I'm going to walk to the house. Good luck hanging my nest."

Diane watched her walk down the gravel drive toward the house in the distance, where she would climb into her rusted sedan and disappear.

———————

That night, Diane opened another bottle of wine. She had nearly finished the first glass when she felt Kyle nuzzle the nape of her neck and slide his hand across her waist, grazing the paunchy skin beneath her navel. He was always placing his hand there, and she was always telling him to stop. She pictured the gesture as a subconscious desire to cradle her womb, to coax their future child from her.

"Don't," she said, peeling the fabric of her shirt from his hands and lowering it back down. She felt the rough spots on her skin and raised her top again to look.

"Stop worrying," Kyle said. "Let's go to bed."

But she knew he didn't really want to sleep, and she couldn't stop thinking about the strange shiny growths on her skin.

"I'm not ready yet," she said.

She poured herself a bath, an excuse to be alone, and held her phone over the tub's rim so she could safely scroll through various images of lesions that matched her search terms. She couldn't say which image would settle her, stop her compulsion to load more pictures, but she needed to keep seeing possible answers.

She couldn't remember falling asleep. One minute she was searching the aftermath of various Mohs procedures, including an aesthetically disappointing T-flap procedure on someone's forehead, and the next she was taking a knife to her own skin, now rough to the touch. She scraped and scraped at her belly, leaving piles of silvery strips on the concrete floor of the hatchery, and the raw skin bled. She ran her hands over her

slick stomach, then up and down her sides until she could feel
the prominent ridges forming, bony plates rising to the surface.
Something roiled within.

She woke in tepid water, her phone on the tile floor with a
cracked screen. At first she felt relieved that it had all been a
dream, but the two blemishes remained. She toweled herself
off and observed the sodden tissue drying out, turning to pert,
fibrous scales. She scratched one, and when she failed to remove it with her fingers, she took tweezers and pulled it away,
revealing red, shiny dermis beneath. She felt a moment of satisfaction, like she was whole again after removing the alien piece,
but when she glanced up, Kyle was standing in the doorway
with a look of repulsion.

"Why did you do that?" he asked.

"It's just a scab," she said.

It was closer to dawn than dusk by the time she pulled the
ladder to the living room wall by the fireplace. She took three
steps before she realized there was no way to ascend higher
without asking Kyle to hold the base, but he had already gone
to sleep. When she had told him that Cindy had guessed her
intentions and left in a hurry, he shrugged. "It's not surprising,"
he had said. He knew not to say the other part, the part that
she knew he was still thinking: that they should try again, but
they should try it his way.

She descended the ladder and looked at the blank space
above the mantle. Before the sky lost its darkness, she decided
not to wait any longer. She placed the driftwood in the fire and
watched the nest go up in flames first, like the kindling it was.
By sunrise, the driftwood had burned to ash, leaving behind a
crown of barbed wire, molten and glowing in the hearth.

THE NEIGHBOR'S CAT

The cat is crying again, has been crying for days, always from the neighbor's patio below so that its wail carries through the bathroom window into the musty bedroom of their apartment. To be fair, the cat didn't wake Shelly. The screech of chair legs dragging and the collective singing of soccer songs from the bar next door woke her. Now the drunks are outside, chanting and whooping, waiting on the predawn bus that stops below their bedroom window. But the cat—human-sounding, mournful—keeps her awake.

Shelly slides out of bed, careful to leave Paul to his sleep. With his hair mussed and his face smashed into his pillow, she can see the thinning halo of early baldness. She doesn't think he's noticed the change yet, but she knows it will bother him when he does.

In the tiny bathroom, she climbs on top of the toilet and pushes open the French windows. She has to lean her head out to see the patio of the unit below, a square of brown tile enclosed on three sides by concrete walls stained charcoal by the smog. The fourth side overlooks a three-story drop to the back of the beer hall where, every dawn, someone hoses kitchen detritus down a large grate-covered hole, conjuring the scent of stale yeast and hops. Shelly notices her breath turning to mist. In the middle of the patio, surrounded by buckets, brooms, mops, and a tattered vinyl chair, the cat moans so that his fluffy white body expands then deflates impressively.

In the States, Shelly would knock on the door and demand that the owner let the cat in. Or she'd call an animal rescue, or take the cat herself. But she doesn't really speak Spanish, and she doesn't know the local laws.

The cat looks up with amber eyes and meows. Shelly turns away and latches the window shut. After the fresh air, the stench of the sewage drain in the middle of the tile floor is stifling. This bathroom always leaves her feeling dirty. When the shower is on, the water hits the toilet so that each time she washes herself, she has to remember to take the toilet paper off the roll and put it on a shelf across the room. There's no tub or shower door, just a plastic curtain dangling from flimsy fishhooks on a clothesline that does nothing to contain any splashing. The violet-tiled wall shows black streaks where dirt has collected from dried rivulets of water, which is mystifying since the pressure is too low to ever fully rinse the shampoo out of her hair.

She washes her hands in the hot water, cherishing a moment of warmth. In the bedroom, she finds Paul awake, swiping the screen of his smartphone.

"The bus stop?" she asks.

He nods.

"That poor cat," she says.

Paul reads the text on his phone.

"We should do something," she says. "It's supposed to dip down to freezing tonight."

"The cat has fur," he says. "We're in the same temperature without fur."

"But we at least have a roof and walls. Would you let Atticus stay out all night when it was freezing?" Atticus was the dog his roommate had back in Kansas City, where he used to work in college admissions before he decided on a graduate program in Argentina.

Paul lowers his phone. "What can I do? It's not my cat."

"Just talk to her. Maybe she doesn't realize how cold it's going to get."

"You can talk to her too, you know."

Paul had been less than helpful with the language barrier. Part of her wondered if it was tough love. Maybe he was pushing her to use what little Spanish she'd already learned. But sometimes, like now, she wondered if he was just taking advantage of her monolinguism to avoid any conflict that would inconvenience him.

"You know I can't understand anything if she talks back at me," she says. "Please?"

"I don't care enough about the cat to jeopardize our relationship with the landlady. You know how hard it was for me to find this place."

That was the other thing. He was always reminding her that he had to do everything now. He had to do the apartment hunting. When the oven stopped working, he had to arrange for its repair. He even had to help her find out where she could take language classes in town. She used to be independent. She used to call restaurants to make their reservations because it made him nervous to talk to strangers. At parties, she would mingle with Paul in tow, enabling his introductions. She liked being a source of comfort, assuaging his social anxieties. She was good at it, but now she depends on him for nearly everything, and he's not always gracious about it.

"I need to get my run in," Paul says, putting down his phone.

She watches as he pushes aside the covers and pulls his jogging gear over his goose-pimpled skin.

"Want to come with?"

One of the soles of her running shoes has a crack, and her foot hurts for days each time she wears them. To replace them here, with the import taxes, would be too expensive, and she doesn't yet know the local brands or sizing, or how to ask for what she wants in any specific manner. And she's tired. She can never sleep more than a few hours here.

"It's not even light out," she says.

The apartment borders one of the diagonals, large avenues with busy traffic and littered medians. Even at this hour, she can hear the storekeeper below as he unlocks the metal security grate that protects his windows and spools it back like a garage door. Paul takes the antique key out of the ashtray and unlocks their front door. There are so many locks in Argentina. Shelly can't even go outside without first unlocking their apartment door with a large lever key and then unlocking the door to the building with a different key with large toothy bits at the end.

"Did you leave me a set of keys?" she asks.

"It's in the bedroom."

He slides the door shut and locks her in.

———

The night hovers near freezing. Shelly lights the oven and leaves it open for heat. She conjugates Spanish verbs in the kitchen, writing the same word over and over in her notebook. Later, they cook pasta with too much butter and stuff themselves for warmth. They wear their coats at the dining table—a collapsible card table with faux leather glued on top. Paul downloads a detective show, and they prop his computer on top of a stack of his textbooks to make it feel more like a television. His books are all about human rights violations.

When the broad-shouldered cop creeps through the shadows of the suspect's house on the screen, they hear a woman wailing.

"Is that the show?" Shelly asks.

Paul puts it on pause and listens. The wailing intensifies.

"I think it's the cat," he says.

After dinner, when Shelly brushes her teeth, she leans out the window. The cat just stares and stares up at her.

———

The cat develops a worrisome hoarseness. Shelly invites a new friend from her language class over for tea. They are stumbling through their poor Spanish when Melissa gestures for silence.

"¿Qué es eso?"

A strange, rhythmic croaking comes from outside.

"El gato debajo grita." Shelly feels proud of her sentence, and then—noticing Melissa's concern—recalls that the words signify something real.

"It's the neighbor's cat," she explains. "There's nothing we can do." But she feels like she's lying. She remembers her cousin's cat, Elmor, and how his arthritis got so bad he had to have painkillers every day, special pills that came from the vet. One day her aunt substituted a human dose of acetaminophen, not realizing how incompatible it would be, and they found Elmor in the playroom, struggling to breathe. They were too late.

"He sounds weaker," she says to Paul when he returns from his classes at the university.

"Who?"

"The cat. I really think he might be dying."

They sit in the kitchen, sipping wine, listening. Indeed, the cat's yowling grows faint, yet more urgent.

"It's raspier," she says, "like it's sick."

"It probably just has a common cold or whatever it is that cats get." He pours himself more wine, dribbles some onto his hand, then delicately licks the drops from the web between his thumb and index finger.

"This is just like when I had dysentery in Chile and you kept insisting that I was overreacting."

"You still don't know that's what happened."

"Or when you insisted on taking the bus to Santiago even in the middle of winter. When I told you that was a bad idea, you laughed. You said people never have a problem on that route."

"That was an unusual weather pattern."

"Dariela said it was a fifty-fifty shot that we'd make that pass in July," she says. "You acted like I was being crazy for worrying about it."

"Please stop bringing that up."

"It's relevant," she says, "to the cat."

"Have you noticed that you tend to fixate on what's wrong?"

"There just happens to be a lot that's actually wrong, Paul."

"I don't know if that's true." He holds her hands in his and really looks at her. "I hope it isn't."

She remembers their time in Missouri as easy. She would return from class or teaching and find him already home from the office, brewing an afternoon batch of coffee with her mug waiting on the counter. They would share accounts of their days—commiserating over the tedium, celebrating any minor success. Their lives overlapped enough in scope and routine that Shelly believed in their inherent relevance to each other. They were, she had thought simply, compatible.

Paul squeezes her thigh, then kisses her. She thinks about refusing him, but she wants things to be better between them. He takes her to bed, and she forgets about the cat until after, when her thoughts are drifting toward sleep and a soft mewling rises up from the patio.

———

Shelly translates and transcribes a series of possible sentences that she will need: "The cat is too cold." "Can you take the cat inside?" "The cat could die if you don't take the cat inside." That last one is particularly troubling as she hasn't yet studied subjunctive or conditional moods. She then writes down various possibilities of how the landlady might respond, in hopes that she will therefore be able to prolong the conversation toward actual understanding.

After Paul leaves for class and before her next English tutoring session, Shelly resolves to confront the landlady. She can feel the slick sweat on her palms as she knocks on the pale wood. A man opens the door.

"¿Qué?" he says, abrupt and rude.

Shelly asks for Angela, and he widens the opening so that she can see the back of a woman in a satin robe, the fabric sliding down her arm and exposing her shoulder. She wipes at her unseen face and turns, red-eyed and smiling. The man's eyes, Shelly notices, are clear and dry. She thinks, if they're fighting, he's steering the ship. Angela tightens her robe and shuts the door behind her, leaving the man in her place. She kisses the air near Shelly's cheek.

"¿Cómo andás?"

"Bien. ¿Y vos?" Shelly hated the automatic nature of the greeting. She felt like it was false advertisement for a language proficiency she lacked.

"Bien . . ." Angela laughs and points self-consciously at her clothes, saying something Shelly can't follow. She imagines it's an apology for being undressed, so she smiles and gestures— not a problem.

Shelly launches into her script about the cat. Angela stops smiling. There's something guilty about the way she stares at her tightly clasped hands, but perhaps that's a projection. What she does know is that Angela keeps saying she can't— No puedo. But she says a lot more than that.

Finally, unsure of how to extricate herself from a conversation she cannot follow, Shelly forfeits, telling Angela the catch-all phrase: "Está bien." It's fine.

"Disculpe," she says, then climbs the narrow stairs back up to her unit.

————

She buys kibble and sardines. From her bathroom window, she tosses them down. The cat ignores the kibble, but he eats the little fish. It pleases her to watch him licking his whiskers.

————

Paul takes her to a bistro down the street. After some calamari, Paul notices an old-fashioned black butler statue by the bar—the kind of statue with exaggerated features, a cartoonish grin.

"We can never come back here," he says.

"We can leave and finish dinner somewhere else."

He shakes his head.

"I'd leave," she says. "You can explain, but I can't."

"We'll just not come back."

When the waiter returns, she stares at Paul, willing him to complain, but he merely orders a burger. She bungles her order, and Paul just watches patiently.

"Can you help me?"

"I don't know what you're trying to say," Paul says.

"I want it medium-well."

Paul completes her order, and they eat the meal in relative silence, remarking occasionally upon the food, the greasy ham smothering the beef patties and the watery beer. "The fries," Paul says, "are actually good."

On the walk home, she can see her breath in the air. She tells him about Angela, how she couldn't understand her.

"I think she was having a fight with a boyfriend," she says. "I wonder if he's why the cat has to stay outside."

"You shouldn't have done that," Paul says. "This isn't Antarctica. The cat is going to be fine. It may not have the best life, but it isn't going to die."

He wraps his arm around her shoulders and adds, "I don't want to hear about it anymore."

It was a command. She clenches her teeth so hard the rest of the walk home that she gets a headache. She begins to wish that the cat would die, just to prove Paul wrong. Just to get rid of that smug assuredness he's had since the move.

She has to ask Paul to help her buy Tylenol because the only pharmacy that's still open is the kind that makes you take a number and wait on a caja to open, where you then explain to a pharmacist what you need, even if it's just some cheap shampoo, because all the products are kept behind the counter. She asks for Tylenol, but all they have is generic acetaminophen in doses she doesn't recognize.

"What's it for?" Paul translates for the pharmacist.

"A bad headache," Shelly says. "Really bad."

After another round of translation, the pharmacist smiles sympathetically and pushes the box of pills her way.

The idea comes later, when she's gathering water in her hands from the bathroom sink to swallow the white tablet. After she recognizes the thought for what it is, a violent, spiteful wish, she feels her breath catch with guilt. It's just a thought, she tells herself. She doesn't mean it.

But later that week, on a particularly cold night, she can hear the harsh, scraping yowls of the cat, and she wonders if it might not be a mercy. She edges out of the covers, careful not to disturb Paul, which is easy since he's rammed his ears with wax plugs to drown out the bus stop, the bar, and the cat.

Through the window, she sees the cat lying on its side, its belly moving with quick breaths. She tells herself he must be hurting.

She uses the back of a spoon to press the tabs into a powder. After a few failures with skinny sardines, she finds the fatter fish and stuffs the powder into careful incisions.

The cat stands up for the treat, stiff-limbed, stretching. He licks it all up and keeps licking long after the last fish is gone.

Her regret is immediate. She thinks about warning Angela and giving the cat hydrogen peroxide to make it throw up, like they used to do with Atticus when he'd eat the unraveled thread of his stuffed toys. The dog would jerk his head rhythmically, then belch up a foaming ball of bright yarn. Then he'd sleep, at peace. She imagined how he'd felt—relieved, pleasantly empty, most likely.

But she doesn't know the laws here. And she doesn't know how to explain what she's done, not in any language.

She sits in the kitchen all the next day, staring at her Spanish workbook without seeing it. She cannot help but hear the absence, the added piece of silence, despite the traffic and the people on the street outside.

When Paul comes home, she tells him, "I think the cat is dead."

"The cat isn't dead." He drops his books on the table.

"Will you please check?" Something in her voice softens him.

She can hear Paul climb on top of the toilet and unlatch the window. He stays there awhile. She can imagine what he sees. The still whiteness. He's watching, alert now, waiting for a sign of life.

SPORES

They met at Spook Fest, a film festival with a limited cult following. Betsey was one of the finalists with a short comedy about serial killers, and Mannie was a guest speaker on account of his having directed *Mississippi Machete*, a 1960s horror slasher that still made top-ten lists. She was thirty in a thrift store dress, and he was a craggy-featured septuagenarian wearing a brown cardigan that slouched over his broad, sloping shoulders.

Mannie sat in a plastic chair on the stage next to the moderator, a young guy with thick glasses and a leather vest.

"Can you tell me more about your relationship with Peter Minowitz?" the moderator asked.

Mannie jabbed his finger at the young man's chest. "I won't talk about that. I told you as much."

Mannie stood, and the moderator waved for him to sit back down. "I'm sorry. I forgot—"

"Like hell."

"Please. Stay. We'll just open it up for questions from the audience."

Mannie held on to the arms of the chair, supporting himself as he deliberated, then finally slumped back into his seat. Silence descended. The two dozen audience members eyed each other, waiting for someone to speak.

Betsey hated public speaking. She hated crowds, and she

hated addressing more than one person at a time. But she had a tickle in the back of her throat—it'd been festering for days—and now her lungs felt like they were burning and drowning at the same time. She burst into deep, wet coughs that echoed through the auditorium. She coughed until her sides cramped.

"Do you need water?" Mannie asked, gesturing from the stage to his own water bottle.

She shook her head, but Mannie passed the bottle to someone in the front row, and then the bottle was crowd-surfing its way back to her. She never shared drinks, but with all eyes on her, she felt she had to take a sip. She uncapped it and tried not to think about the moist rim, tried not to think about the likelihood of that being Mannie's saliva.

"You okay?" Mannie said, his voice magnified by his clip-on microphone.

She nodded. Everyone kept staring, so she asked Mannie, "What do you think of the *Mississippi Machete* remake?"

"I was quite pleased," he said. "The pacing is much quicker now, and they did a good job of adapting the narrative to current trends." He offered a flat smile, his lips stretched taut across his yellow teeth.

After the panel, Betsey intercepted Mannie. "Thanks for the water."

"I couldn't let one of my fans die," he said. "There are too few of you."

"I just have crazy sinuses." She gestured at her face. "Anyway, I think the remake is bullshit."

He nodded. "Thank you."

"They took the guy in the wheelchair out, and I thought that was such a stupid revision," she said. "His dynamic with the other kids, the way they ostracized him, that was the heart of the movie, wasn't it?"

"What do you do, Miss . . . ?"

"Moser. Betsey Moser. I'm a screenwriter. Well, trying to be," she said, offering her hand. His skin was mushroom gray and crinkly.

"And what do you write?"

"Everything, anything. Horror." She dug a disk out of her canvas messenger bag and offered it to him. "It has one of my screenplays and my short film on it. They're screening the film tomorrow, but I'm sure you have better things to do."

She said the last bit to be polite. She knew all his recent movies went straight to DVD.

"Thank you. I look forward to watching it," he said.

He took the copy of her film and left the theater.

―――――

It was a month before she would see Mannie again. Turned out, she had a sinus infection. The doctors gave her antibiotics, and the antibiotics caused a chronic bacterial infection of *Clostridium difficile* that sent her into a fever and delivered stabbing cramps to her gut. She passed out in a grocery store, in the dairy section where she was stockpiling yogurt in desperate hopes of recovery. She awoke in the hospital. The doctors informed Betsey that the bacteria in her system could germinate into microscopic spores. When her roommate Sarah visited her, a distant smile splayed across her face, Betsey warned her—with many apologies—that their place would need to be doused in Lysol. The sheets, the bathroom, the towels, and the laundry. She regretted having to inform Sarah of the spores, a term that brought to mind sci-fi movies of the week. Sarah had fled her room with her hands over her nose and mouth.

Betsey and Sarah had been college roommates, and they had remained together despite Betsey's antisocial preferences and Sarah's controlling tendencies. Sarah demanded little in the way of companionship, which suited Betsey. They symmetrically split the fridge. They each had their own set of dishes, kept on separate shelves. They traded vacuuming and trash duties, which were completed on Friday and Monday of each week. They had a system, and Betsey appreciated the structure in her life.

After much morphine, that sweet heady syrup waltzing in her veins, and a couple days of antibiotics, Sarah drove Betsey to their rickety studio apartment. She deposited Betsey at the front door and told her that she had already moved out.

"You're supposed to give two weeks' notice," Betsey said as she pulled at her plastic hospital bracelet.

"Harold is going to marry me," Sarah said, maintaining a distance between them.

"When?"

"I'll pay through the end of the month," Sarah said, and then she climbed into her car and drove away.

————

Despite being stabilized, the illness still lingered in the following weeks. Betsey had been a sickly child, suffering month-long bouts of strep throat that alienated her from her classmates and left her paranoid of germs and touching hands and turning doorknobs, so her reluctant immune system did not surprise her. Betsey tried several rounds of antibiotics, probiotics, and prebiotics to cure her ailing gut, but nothing fixed her. Her bodily needs became so unreliable that she could not maintain her job as an administrative assistant. Technically, she was a full-time temp, but she had worked the same desk for nearly a year. She soon learned the crucial difference between a permanent employee of the production company and a temporary employee of the studio that housed the production company. Her boss sent her an email with only the subject line *Come into my office and shut the door.* He did not address her health as a reason. He relayed euphemisms and alluded to a new permanent hire from New York. She cleared out her desk and packed up her belongings. As she carried her things to the elevator, her plastic orchid drooped, its petals bobbing with each step like a white flag waving in the wake of her retreat.

She could barely meet her monthly rent. The threat of nausea or diarrhea would only allow her to enter the public realm when she had fasted for twenty-four hours. She remained at the studio as a part-time temp, drifting between different offices and departments. She could only manage working every third or fourth day, avoiding food in the surrounding hours. She looked for cheaper apartments, but with rent control, her lease was already a steal. She placed ads for roommates. Each person sensed the unsettling cleanness of the place—or perhaps witnessed the ubiquitous presence of disinfectant wipes, one dispenser for each surface—and left without taking an application.

Betsey took to reading message boards on the internet that revealed horrifying possibilities for her health. She learned that the spores could live on surfaces for months. They could float through the air. She could breathe them. Betsey read about a woman in her twenties who had been sick with the same bacteria for ten years. No antibiotic would kill it. She had to drop out of college and now lived with her parents. There was an online support group full of people like her, all desperate sufferers, all unemployed and half-starved and living like hermits.

In particular, she liked to read about Jane in Melbourne. Until recently, Jane had worked in advertising. She posted pictures of when she was an avid surfer, ripped abdominal muscles gleaming in the bright sun. Now she was largely debilitated by her illness, but she managed to work some as a technical writer. To Betsey, working from home sounded like a dream. Never facing public failure in an office. Never worrying about one's health interfering with one's earning potential. Wearing pajamas all day, every day.

She found a listing for Mannie in the phone book. *He's that unfamous*, she thought. Or perhaps it was a different Mannie. She called, but the answering machine picked up with Mannie's prerecorded raspy voice. "Sorry I'm not home right now. Please leave your name, your number, and please briefly describe why you are calling, and I will get back to you as soon as possible. Have a wonderful day. Goodbye." Then there was a long fumbling, pause. "Where's the button?" And then the answering machine beeped.

"Mannie, it's Betsey, from the short-film fest. Betsey Mos—"

The machine beeped again. Then an automated female voice said in monotone, "I'm sorry. The tape is full."

Betsey tried Mannie twice a day for four days, but the answering machine was always full. Then, to her great surprise, Mannie called her back. He apologized for taking so long to clear out his messages and invited her over for tea.

Betsey suffered a great deal of anxiety whenever something strayed from her routine, so she left her downtown apartment two hours early in order to punctually arrive in Sherman Oaks.

Mannie lived in a small midcentury ranch house on the edge of the dying Los Angeles River. The dark, rotting wood of the shingles matched the splintered siding. Within, Betsey imagined a potbellied oven full of molten Hansel and Gretel. It had that vibe.

The door had a brass plaque at eye level featuring a lion-and-crown motif. After Betsey rang the doorbell, the plaque opened to reveal Mannie's face peering through a grid.

He pulled the heavy door open and smiled. "Come on in."

The house was full of horror paraphernalia, some of which she could recognize from his movies. A clown marionette hung from the ceiling, a skeleton hand from *The Morgue Keeper* served as a paperweight, and a zombie dummy sat in a club chair wearing a smoking jacket and clutching a pipe with its spindly finger bones. A series of framed Edward Gorey illustrations covered the walls of the foyer, and an open coffin—with a sheet of glass placed on top—served as a coffee table. Within, upon the worn satin fabric, a mummy lay supine with arms crossed over his linen-swathed chest.

A bronze teakettle and a plate of crustless sandwiches appeared to float above the mummy's head. Mannie gestured for Betsey to sit on the wine-dark sofa.

"It's oolong." He held up the kettle.

"Is there caffeine in it?" she said. Her stomach could no longer handle any beverage that contained caffeine or alcohol.

"An infinitesimal amount."

He poured the pale amber fluid into her blue teacup, and after a polite sip, she rested her saucer above the mummy's kneecaps.

"I've always wondered," she said, "why was *Phantom* your last theatrical release?"

"Peter Minowitz fucked me," Mannie said.

This shocked Betsey, since Peter was the celebrated auteur of all the best children's films from the '80s.

"There are rules in the DGA that you can't simultaneously direct a project," Mannie said. "Minowitz wanted *Phantom* for himself. He wanted it bad, but he already was signed up for *Alien Visitor*, so I got it. But he was still the main creative producer on the project, so he kept interfering with my shot list and adjusting things here and there. One day, a journalist showed up while Peter was fiddling with my camera, and next thing I knew, all the press was telling the world that I was some sort of directorial beard, a joke, a stand-in. That Peter Minowitz was the real director." He stared deeply into his teacup. "My next project was a TV movie. And then they were all VHS releases."

Mannie pulled a manuscript from beside the couch and set it on the table. He poked the title page, and she saw that it was her own screenplay, "Ice Castle of Doom."

"But this," he said, "this makes me happy. I could do something with this."

"Thank you," she said.

"Amazing. Those little ice boars? And the way they tunnel into the ice hotel and eat the oil moguls? It's gold. And there's a real market for those cheap CGI monsters."

"I was thinking more Diego Torres. You know, like a haunting fable."

"No one will green-light that. Not after that last one," he said. "And really, you could cut the budget of this in half with a quick rewrite. I mean, does the Arctic research facility really need to blow up in the end?"

"I guess not."

"So what I'm suggesting is how about you and I do a rewrite on this thing and shop it around?"

"I hate to go to this place in the conversation, but I could really use some money," she said.

"I know a guy who could help on that front."

"I thought you wanted the script."

"I want to direct the script," he said. "I know a guy who might produce it. We should prep a pitch. We should pitch it to him together. I've worked with him a dozen times. He produced *The Mausoleum* with me. He's got a deal with Tru Image."

"Tru Image. Is that the place that made the Conan spin-off as a reboot?"

"That's the one!"

"Oh," she said.

He rubbed his index finger back and forth across his upper lip, polishing it to a high gleam. "We should work on this ASAP. Rob likes things focused. Straight to the point. An elevator pitch."

It wasn't exactly the big budget dream Betsey had nursed all these years, but she thought about her finicky stomach and her dwindling funds and nodded.

"I have big plans for us," he said.

She wanted to believe him.

———

On her way home, secretly thumbing the button of her pepper spray as she swayed with the motion of Los Angeles's underused subway train, she decided that Mannie was probably overselling their potential, but that even an immediate release to DVD or the internet would be better than just temping twice a week. Hell, some people made their entire living off cheap horror movies. It might even be fun. She could invite Mannie and Sarah over for a viewing party. She'd decorate with black lights, ghost cookies, and rubber bats strung from the ceiling. She pictured herself in a not-too-distant future, healthy and financially secure, the type of person who could chat up strangers at bars. When someone asked her what she did, she'd take a cool sip of her wine and say, "I write horror movies." Maybe someday she would call her mother and say, "Turn on channel 150." Thousands of miles away in Terre Haute her mother would watch the television and spot her daughter's name in the credits. Her mother might say in a begrudging tone, "I'll be damned. You did it," and Betsey would know that her mother would never lecture her again about growing up and turning to real work.

Twice a week, on her good days, Betsey would meet Mannie at his house, and they would spread dozens of index cards out on his coffin table, brainstorming and labeling scenes to alter or add to Betsey's script. He would always brew a pot of tea, and she would adore that an innocuous beverage was waiting for her, although she fretted over hurting his feelings since she always had to decline the croissants and sandwiches he served.

Throughout her four years of college, she had worked and interned, so she had never relied on the usual social activities of a young adult. Once a season she would tag along with Sarah to a party. Now, without Sarah and without the ability to drink at bars or eat in public, she lacked any social conduit. Having tea with Mannie was the one social activity she could manage. What began as a necessary step to fulfilling her dream of screenwriting became a structured routine, and from that structure, she eventually derived comfort.

Mannie had a creative system. They would spend an hour "rearranging the blueprint," as he liked to say. They would argue over and finesse the index cards on top of the tattered mummy. Then they would pick a card at random and spend the rest of their session revising the scene that card referred to. Once done, if the sun had not yet set, he would often insist on showing her a random artifact from his attic, or they would sip more tea on the Adirondack chairs in his skinny backyard that overlooked (through the grid of chain-link fence) the concrete banks of the Los Angeles River.

Sometimes Mannie would bring down a box of old films from when he was even younger than she was. He would carefully extend the film from its reel through the projector, and they would sit side by side in the flickering darkness as the past rolled out before them. Usually it was a roughly hewn short about a rubber-masked sea monster or a talc-covered ghost.

When they finished the last scene of the rewrite and the script was finally complete, Mannie drank most of a bottle of wine and then screened a personal film. It was nothing more than gritty eight-millimeter. The young woman within those tiny frames rolled her loose jeans up around her knees and laughed as she waded into the waves. Her hair was wild, unfixed. Her face, without makeup. The camera followed her lovingly, lingering on the sun-crowned edges of her as she ate chowder at a seaside shack. After the film ran out and the projector's light shone plainly against the wall, Mannie returned the reel to its case. He pressed the canister closed, then rubbed his hands along the edges, wiping away any traces of dust.

"I married that woman," Mannie said. "Then Peter Minowitz married her."

"Mirabelle," Betsey said. It was an antique tabloid headline. A beautiful starlet who bounced from director to director. Even A-list marriages couldn't save her lack of acting talent. Her last film, a box-office flop about a trophy wife and stepmother who was secretly an alien invader, was shot twenty years ago, and she wore facial prosthetics for half of it.

"Didn't Cesare Lazzara marry her too?"

Mannie nodded. "And Kyle Platt."

"Who's she married to now?"

"I don't know," he said.

"She sells arm weights on the Home Shopping Network now."

"She always had great arms," Mannie said. "Sometimes I think how different things might have been if I'd done better with *Phantom*. If I'd never let Peter make a fool of me."

When Betsey was in high school, she fell for a guy in drama class who took her virginity and then came out of the closet. She had spent the rest of high school cataloging every clue she should have noted as a testament to his actual desire. It became an obsession that followed her in a shoebox to her college dorm. When she revealed her stash of love letters, journal entries, and photos to Sarah, her roommate was at first sympathetic but then insisted that Betsey needed to move on with her life. One day Betsey returned from class to discover that the box was empty except for an airplane bottle of vodka, a disposable camera, and a note that said: *I stole your shit. Now take new pictures. Love, Sarah*. It was too bad, Betsey thought, that now she had a stash of photos with Sarah in them, and Sarah too had left her.

"Mannie," Betsey said, pulling the canister away from him. "That bitch belongs in the L.A. River."

"Excuse me?"

"A little snip snip," Betsey said. "A little fire."

"Stop joking around," he said.

"I'm dead serious." Betsey held up the film canister, well aware of the garish shadows the projector cast upon her. "This is bad juju. Bad celluloid. It's a one-way ticket to what-if land."

They pulled apart the film like party streamers. They wrapped themselves like mummies in the dangling strands of eight-millimeter and marched into the night to the concrete bank of the river, that trapped trickle of tainted water. She helped him strip away the memories, piece by piece, and set them ablaze. They threw each flashing ember over the chain-link fence that kept them from the narrow stream, and the flames disappeared even before they touched the ground.

———————

Betsey's infection took a bad turn. It was three weeks before they could meet again. In the meantime, Mannie scheduled a meeting with his producer friend Rob. It was a month out, and Betsey couldn't imagine herself being sick for another whole month, even though she found it difficult to ever leave her apartment. Painkillers and fasting were not enough. She resorted to ordering milk and cottage cheese from an online delivery service. She spent much of her time sleeping or wiping down her place with disinfectant.

In the online C. diff support group, Jane from Melbourne posted that she was engaged. She wrote, "Yes, ladies. I found a man who will put up with my shit forever!" Then she posted a picture of her kissing her fiancé in a horse-drawn carriage. She looked wan and frail compared to her beach picture, but she looked happy. Betsey sent her a congratulatory message. "You're an inspiration!" she wrote, and she wondered if she actually felt inspired.

Betsey found articles published by the CDC about the measures hospitals should take with the emergence of antibiotic-resistant strains of her illness. She even found mortality rates.

She had not known death was a possible outcome, but it seemed statistically improbable.

As a temp worker, she had let her insurance go. The vancomycin her doctor prescribed was obscenely expensive. She put everything she could on her credit cards, rotating judiciously between them.

On a particularly bleak day, she called her mother.

"I sure do wish you lived closer," her mother said. "I'd make you some pot roast."

"That's sweet," Betsey said, grimacing at the idea of digesting celery and tough meat. "Mom, I normally do okay. You know I never ask for anything, but it's been real tough lately, being sick and all."

"I think you should just come home. I could help get you fixed up. And Janie quit, so you could take her job." Her mother worked as a stylist at Hair Quest, and Janie had been the receptionist.

"But I'm working on something, Mom. With a real director who's done some big films."

"Why can't you do that here?"

It didn't matter how many times Betsey explained it to her. "Never mind, Mom. I'll figure it out."

"I just want you nearby," her mother said.

"Me too," Betsey said, "but I can't leave."

After they hung up, Betsey called Mannie and asked him if they could practice the pitch by video conference until she got over her flu. He asked if he could come over and bring her soup. She pictured him breathing her spores and told him she'd be over to his place soon, not to worry. Her research suggested that as long as she never used his restroom, and as long as she scrubbed her hands like a surgeon, Mannie would be safe. She could not be so sure about her apartment. Once a week, she washed everything she touched in Lysol and bleach. For a few hours, maybe, she could have company, but who would ever visit besides Mannie?

After finishing her third round of vancomycin, Betsey felt strong and optimistic. She posted an account of her success on the online support group. Several C. diff sufferers emailed her for advice, and she shared the history of her medications, diet, and probiotics, thankful that she would not be like the college dropout girl. Jane sent her a message congratulating her, but then she explained that she had suffered another relapse. She attached a link to another message board featuring a picture of her distended belly. She wrote, "Pretty far cry from my surfer bod, huh? The doctor said a possible danger for me now is toxic megacolon. I'm starting a band just so I can name it that. Also, my husband is gifting me his shit for a fecal implant. Wish me luck!"

Betsey could never consider such a thing. Millions of germs, millions of parasites, someone else's parasites, being injected into her body, into unmentionable places. She asked Jane what that entailed, imagining that there would be a convoluted medical process that would minimize the harsh reality of adopting someone else's feces, but Jane told her that it primarily involved a blender and a turkey baster. She basked in the relief that Jane's journey to recovery would not be her own. That night, she added a quarter cup of Lysol to her bath water. She soaked until her skin stung.

———————

In order to stave off a visit from Mannie, Betsey finally scheduled a pitch planning session at his house. They had only been practicing for an hour when Betsey felt her insides twist like a charley horse wrapped around her lower spine. Sweat slicked her face as she swallowed back the nausea.

"Excuse me," she said.

She walked, one stiff step at a time, to the half bath in the foyer and locked the door behind her. She held her head under the faucet and twisted the cold water to full blast, hoping it would push back the urge to vomit. After a minute, she withdrew and dried her face with the dingy hand towel, but its musty odor invaded her nostrils and she barely made it back over the sink before a mix of tea and stomach acid gushed out of her mouth. She aspirated on her own bile, sending her into a series of deep coughs that caused something to seize then release, deep inside. The pain receded as warm wetness spread into her pants and down her leg. It felt thick and lingered in her panties, molding itself to her. Horrified, Betsey realized that she had just shat herself. She, a thirty-year-old woman, had shat herself in someone else's home.

It seemed a cosmic cruelty that her body would betray her in this way. She cried as she cleaned herself. The C. diff had fundamentally changed her body chemistry so that each bowel movement stunk like rotten eggs. The smell could not be masked.

She rolled her pants into the plastic wrapping of the toilet paper she found under the counter. She stuffed this in her purse and continued crying as she brainstormed options to fix her pantless state with the minimal amount of embarrassment. When she was five, in karate class, she once lingered in the changing room because she couldn't figure out how to tie the knot of her belt, and everyone forgot that she was even there, so she just sat on the dirty floor, ashamed, knowing that each passing minute would make the discovery of her absence an even harsher indictment. This was like that, but a thousand times worse.

She heard Mannie's lumbering footsteps and then the knock at the door. "You okay in there?"

"I had a little accident." She winced at herself in the mirror. "Women's stuff. You wouldn't happen to have any sweatpants or a big tee shirt I could borrow while I do laundry, would you?"

Through the door, she heard Mannie say in a strained tone, "I'll be right back," and then his shuffling gait faded.

After Mannie slipped the shirt through the door and after she donned it like a nightgown, she stepped back into the living room, clutching her purse.

"Where do you keep your washing machine?" she said.

"In the utility room next to the kitchen," he said, gesturing.

He looked at her briefly but then focused on objects adjacent to her, like a tarnished candelabra or the black-and-white photograph of Siamese twins framed on the wall behind her.

After she threw her clothes in the wash, she found some Pine Sol and paper towels. She hid them behind her purse as she walked past Mannie, who was now making tea in the kitchen.

She locked herself in the bathroom yet again and set to work disinfecting each surface like she was wiping away fingerprints at a murder scene. She imagined the spores hibernating on the faucets or the cabinet handles, waiting to hitch a ride with Mannie. She scrubbed until her knuckles burned, raw from the chemicals.

"Are you sure you're okay?" Mannie asked through the door.

"I'm fine!"

After she was sure she had saved Mannie from any possible exposure, she hid the Pine Sol under the sink and returned to the kitchen.

"The tea is a little cold," he said.

"Sorry about that."

"Listen, I don't really know how to say this," Mannie said.

Betsey felt a red flush spread across her face.

"This may not be my place, but I've noticed that you've lost a lot of weight since we've met. And you never eat."

"Oh my god. You think I'm anorexic."

"I've seen a lot of actresses lose work, even go to the hospital—"

"I'm not anorexic. I swear."

He just stared at her.

"You don't believe me," she said.

"I just want you to be healthy."

Betsey began laughing, or at least that was what she had told her body to do, only instead, her eyes welled up and she found herself sobbing. At first, Mannie looked stricken. He edged over to her and patted her on the back. She grabbed hold of him and buried her face in the scratchy wool of his cardigan.

When she pulled away, he handed her a handkerchief embroidered with his initials. And then she told him everything. She used polite euphemisms, but in essence, she told him how her gut had been invaded by a toxic, anaerobic bacteria that nothing could kill. How she felt like a Typhoid Mary full of alien spores that could infect and harm anyone she was close to. How she couldn't eat before she left the house or she might shit ("unexpectedly relieve") herself. How she felt like she was falling apart on the inside.

Finally, she said, "I'm so embarrassed."

"Don't be," he said. "I'm seventy years old. If you knew half the things I contend with on a regular basis, you wouldn't worry one bit about what I thought."

"Thank you."

"Do you need me to push back the pitch?"

Her debt was overwhelming her, and if she didn't make a large paycheck soon, she'd have to move back to Terre Haute and admit that her time in Los Angeles had been a waste.

"No," Betsey said. "I need to do this."

———

Mannie drove them to the pitch meeting in his old Volks-wagen van. At the gate, the guard took their driver's licenses. He looked sixteen.

"You only have walk-ons," he said.

"That can't be right," Mannie said.

"That's what I have you down for," the guard said, rubbing a red zit on his chin.

"Call and check," Mannie said.

The guard sighed. "We are at capacity. It's walk-on or nothing."

Mannie squeezed the steering wheel. His thrombosed veins threatened the surface of the thin skin that covered his hands. Betsey touched his forearm.

"It's not a big deal," she said. "We can walk across the street. Besides, why don't we grab a soda or some tea at Formosa after?"

Mannie nodded and U-turned the car around the guard-house. They parked three blocks away. It was an unseasonable hundred-degree day, and Betsey felt sweaty and dizzy as she walked in her high heels along the gum-dappled sidewalk. When Mannie looked concerned, she assured him that she was just anxious, and she thought, perhaps, that this was true. She had learned to tune out the sharp pain in her abdomen, and she could no longer decipher between the spastic cramps of her disease and the sharp pangs of nerves.

As an added precaution, she had worn an adult diaper, and she could feel it chafing against her inner thighs. She wore a thick wool skirt to hide the bulk, but she could still hear the crinkling of plastic when she walked or sat down. She adjusted her stride, aiming for silence.

The lot was small, but midcentury bungalows lined the edges that had once housed script doctors and starlets.

· "Fitzgerald worked in one of those buildings for a while," Mannie said.

Betsey smiled, and her pain receded a little. This was exactly where she had wanted to be when she first drove across the country with boxes of DVDs in her trunk, ready for film school.

Mannie led her knowingly to a small stucco office building. Next door, golf carts darted in and out of a giant soundstage, and this contributed to Betsey's joy. Once inside, Mannie led her to an office full of composite furniture and unframed posters. A young woman sat behind a desk, reading a script.

"Hi, I'm Mannie." He held out his hand.

"I'm sorry, who?" She looked from him to her computer screen, then back again.

"Mannie Cooper, and this is my partner Betsey," he said. "Rob is expecting us."

The woman typed something into a little machine that looked like a calculator. She stared until it beeped. "He'll be ready for you in just a few. Would you two like any water? A soda, maybe?"

Mannie took a Coke, but Betsey couldn't risk the fluids in her system. She just sat there, glistening in sweat turned sour by dehydration. Betsey watched the woman—her pink cheeks broadcasting health—make notes on the script. *I used to be you*, she thought.

Rob turned out to be a bald, slovenly man. Betsey had expected a power suit and carefully pomaded hair, but instead she found herself seated across from a man in a stained white polo shirt that barely contained his girth. Rust stains marred the ceiling tiles of his office, the gray threadbare carpet revealed patches of concrete, and the paint peeled from the walls, uncovering multiple layers of beige, moss green, and institutional blue. The room smelled like BENGAY.

Rob steepled his fingers over his gut. "How've you been, Mannie?"

"Good, real good," Mannie said. "Betsey here is a real talent."

"You know, I was just at TromaDance and I thought, man, this would be right up Mannie Cooper's alley. What have you been up to?"

"Just prepping this project with Betsey."

Rob glanced at a piece of paper on the corner of his desk. Betsey knew it was coverage. Rob's assistant probably read and synopsized the script so Rob wouldn't have to.

"Our movie is like Gremlins meets Tremors, set in Antarctica," Betsey said, proud of her logline.

Mannie launched into the story, establishing the team of loveable research scientists who discover the herd of killer ice boars and warn the oil tycoons, who of course ignore the research scientists. Mannie and Betsey traded back and forth, weaving their way through the plot, but once they reached the climactic showdown between the evil corporate fixer and the scientists (led by the valiant Bruce Campbell–inspired penguin researcher and his orca specialist girlfriend), she felt a wave of nausea so intense that she blanked. She looked to Mannie, who nodded, bolstering her with wide, hopeful eyes.

"So, uh, a penguin pecks at the fixer's leg, distracting him, just long enough for . . ." Rob stared at her without a hint of smile. Betsey fought back another wave of nausea. Blackness crept in from the periphery, shrinking her vision to a pinhole.

Betsey said, "Just long enough for Bruce to signal a killer whale to leap onto the ice, to leap onto the ice and slide—"

She felt the telltale twist in her gut, then the release, followed by a wet sound down there. Mannie raised an eyebrow. She shook her head. She had the diaper. Just keep going, she thought, shifting in the plastic seat.

"The whale slides across the ice and bites the fixer, drags him back into the ocean." Betsey could smell the rotten eggs wafting up from her seat, but she forced a smile. "And it reminds us of when he saw that whale eat his dad at the zoo all those years ago, but this time, the whale saved him, and his anger is just . . ." Rob sniffed and bunched up his nose. Betsey added, ". . . released. His anger is just released. He finds peace and can finally love Emma, the orca researcher."

"That's how it ends," Mannie said, "with Bruce and Emma together, and the pet penguin beside them."

Rob turned away and pushed open the window behind his desk. When he sat back down, he scooted his chair against the wall, as close to the breeze as possible.

"I lost focus for a minute there," Rob said. "Do you smell that?"

Betsey felt the blood creeping into her face. She hoped the spores weren't airborne, that they stayed put rather than microscopically escaping her clothing and dispersing through the office. Maybe she should tell Rob, if only so that he could protect himself. She gave Mannie a pained look. She twisted around in her chair and stretched her arms to mask her intention of checking the seat. And there it was, a faint trace of brown on the yellow plastic.

Mannie put his hand over his mouth, whether with revulsion or concern, she couldn't decipher. She disgusted herself. She felt less capable than a toddler.

"Where do you want me to pick up again?" Mannie said to Rob. "Where did we leave off?" He shot an encouraging smile at Betsey.

"That whale sliding on the ice," Rob said.

As Mannie retold the ending, Betsey pulled some alcohol towelettes from her purse and slid them under her seat, wiping the smooth plastic as she kept her eyes trained on Mannie and Rob. The effect was that she kept shifting in her chair like a hyper kindergartener, or like a self-pleasuring nympho, depending on one's frame of reference.

Rob held up his hands, cutting Mannie off. "What is going on here?"

"Excuse me?" Mannie said.

"You." Rob pointed at Betsey. "What are you doing?"

Betsey couldn't look at him. "I have a condition."

Mannie shook his head at her. She knew this was his first meeting in years. She wouldn't let the spores take this away from him.

"I have to clean things," she said, "all the time." She held up an unopened wipe.

"Like OCD." Rob smiled. "Me too." He pulled a bottle of Purell out of a drawer and placed it across the desk. "Help yourself."

Betsey squirted some into her hands and rubbed in the gel. "So we end with Bruce and Emma together. With their penguin."

"It's a fun idea," Rob pumped some Purell into his own hands and rubbed his palms together, "but it sounds pricey."

"It could go low-budget too," Mannie said.

"In Antarctica?"

"You don't have to shoot it in Antarctica," Mannie said.

"Yeah, but there's a freaking ice hotel." Rob laughed.

"You can fake that," Mannie said.

"It's meant to be campy," Betsey said, "so if the effects are cheap, it doesn't matter."

Rob leaned back in his polyester chair. "I'm not sure it fits with our slate at this time."

Betsey looked at Mannie. He was already nodding, accepting the news.

"You knew what type of film this would be before we showed up," she said. "Mannie told you." Her head ached and she felt chilled.

Mannie touched her elbow. "It's okay. Let's go."

"It would help to know what isn't working for you," Betsey said, "for other meetings we have."

"Other meetings?" Rob laughed. "Right."

"So we can prepare."

"Mannie and I go way back. If the pitch surprised me, great. But I can't work with what you guys brought."

"If it surprised you?" she said. "You planned on passing before we even walked in the door?"

Rob looked at Mannie. "You had a good run. You should let it go while some people still respect you."

"Come on." Betsey offered her hand to Mannie, but he stood up without it.

"I'm sorry I wasted your time," Mannie said to her.

"You didn't waste my time," she said.

She lingered in the doorway. Mannie stopped in front of the assistant's desk and stared out the window. Several gaffers were tightening bolts on C-stands, securing a large scrim. The warm sunlight passed through the large swath of gauze, emerging bleached and diffused on the set, where a young man, twenty-five years old at best, sat in a director's chair.

Betsey glanced back at Rob, who had already cleared his desk of their script and his assistant's synopsis of their script. She suspected the documents were already lying in a trash can by his feet.

"What?" Rob said, arching an eyebrow.

"I just want you to know," she said, "I shat in your chair."

———

After the pitch, the chills got worse. She stopped in one of the studio's bungalows to use the restroom and clean herself. The smell overwhelmed her, and with the fever, she couldn't hold back the vomit. She was dizzy, and when she sipped a handful of water from the bathroom tap, she couldn't keep it down.

Mannie drove her back to her place. He took her temperature and confirmed her fever. He set her up on the couch with a blanket and brought her Pedialyte popsicles from the grocery down the street. "I get dehydrated from time to time myself," he said, and winked at her.

He turned on the television, and she flipped the channels until she found a movie about voodoo and an elderly woman who hexes a young woman in order to steal her body. She watched the horror spread on the wrinkled face as the woman realized that she was no longer young, that she was in the wrong body.

Mannie sat beside her, and she leaned her head on his woolly shoulder. When the movie ended, she said, "The antibiotics aren't working, you know. I'll have to go back to the doctor."

"You don't know that," he said.

"I know a girl in Australia who has been on nine rounds of antibiotics, and none of them worked. But she just did this experimental procedure and now she's completely cured."

"Is it a risky procedure?" he asked.

"No," she said. "But I'd hate to go through with it."

"Don't borrow worry." He patted her on the shoulder and stood up to go.

"Do you think you could stay a little longer? Maybe watch another movie?"

"Okay," he said.

"How about *Rosemary's Baby*?" she said.

"Good choice."

He found the DVD on her shelves, next to copies of his own films. He set the film to play and then sat beside her, lifting her blanketed feet and placing them in his lap.

LIKE THE LOVE OF SOME DEAD GIRL

t's three in the morning, and the man who lives across the street has brought a woman home for the night. Amanda, unable to sleep, stares at his window—has been staring for hours—when the lights flick on. At three, the bars are closed and Los Angeles is nearest to being at peace. Even from this distance, even through the floor-length windows of her loft and the arched windows of the man's tenth-floor apartment, Amanda can see their bodies merge, a dark silhouette framed by industrial track lights. When they part, he leads her to a drop cloth that encompasses the space in which he paints. Amanda knows from other nights that he often stays up painting until the sun rises and gilds the eastward face of his columned Beaux-Arts building. When she is alone, she will sometimes turn her lights off and pull up a chair. She bought binoculars from the swap meet around the corner, in the block that marks the beginning of Skid Row. She bought them so that she could watch him paint, but she found herself watching on other occasions.

Amanda peels herself off the sweaty sheets and slides Frank's arm from her waist, placing it instead on a pillow. She doesn't know if Frank has ever noticed the painter. She usually watches him when Frank is sleeping at his own place.

When she feels sure that Frank is still in deep sleep, she cracks the window and lights a cigarette. The smokes are a new thing. She has an idea that maybe someday the painter will see her smoking and wave to her, that they will become friends this way. A month ago, soon after he moved in, she noticed that he took frequent smoke breaks, leaning on the ledge of his window. Once he faced her direction, and she dropped out of sight, hoping that he had not seen her binoculars.

The historical district is in flux. Many of the buildings were abandoned until recently, when twenty- and thirty-somethings swarmed the area, renting recently gutted and renovated lofts and failing to budget for curtains big enough to cover the expansive windows. Now it's a dreamland for voyeurs and exhibitionists, but Amanda has never thought of herself as either of those things. The painter is her first case study.

The way he can touch people and the way people choose to expose themselves to him fascinates her. His current paintings are larger-than-life studies of women's bellies. Sometimes a bit of breast or the crease of their sex emerges on the edge of the frame like an afterthought. She watches the women pose for these studies. Many are young and taut, and he paints bluish lines descending to the hollow of their belly buttons, emphasizing their concavity, their firmness. She once saw a squat, fortyish woman with pinned-up hair undress for him. Once naked, the woman crossed her arms to hide her chest. The painter spoke to her, and the woman nodded, relaxing her arms. One by one, he removed the pins from her hair and fanned it out through his fingers so that it flowed over her breasts. Her stomach sagged with the fallen skin of multiple childbirths. A myriad of stretch marks framed her navel. The way he painted it was like geometry or the fractals found in nature, like the repeated fact of the degrees at which a branch will divide from the branch before it. That close, the variances of the tones and textures of her skin became beautiful in their complexity.

He paid her. They thanked each other, and she left. He did not sleep with her, although he does sleep with others. Amanda cannot predict his bedmates. There is too much variance in their traits.

Tonight, the woman is bald. Her eyes clench and her mouth gapes as the painter thrusts into her. Amanda cannot hear her, but she imagines different screams of pleasure she could place on the scene, like different dresses on a paper doll. She prefers the nights when the painter is painting.

She stubs out her cigarette and climbs back into bed. Frank lets out a throaty sound as he rolls over in sleep, his back to her. She presses her lips to the nape of his neck. She can smell the musk of him there. It is a scent that she could not place, or maybe did not notice, until now. She parts her lips, sucking lightly on his skin.

She feels his muscles tense with wakefulness. He rolls to face her. "What are you doing?"

"It's just a kiss," she says.

"What time is it?"

"I don't know," she says.

He props himself up to see the digital display on the alarm clock. "Jesus. I have to teach in four hours. Go to bed."

He lies back down at the edge of the mattress, with space between them.

———

Frank cannot—or will not, depending on the conversation—
have sex. They give each other massages. They run their fingers lightly through each other's hair. They hold hands. They
hold each other. Sometimes they kiss, but it is never deep or
prolonged. Once Amanda thought she felt a lump, so Frank
kneaded her breast. It was methodical, his hands spiraling to
her nipple. After, he pecked her on the lips and said, "I think
you're fine."

Amanda met Frank at an asexual conference five months
ago. She did not always know that there was such a thing as
being asexual. One morning she was sipping her coffee and
watching an interview with Frank on the local news. He was
promoting the conference and called himself a romantic asexual. He described it as someone who wanted companionship,
who wanted an emotionally intimate relationship, but who did
not have sexual urges. Amanda wondered if this definition ap-
plied to her. She had given up companionship five years ago,
figuring that her (nonexistent) sexual wiring precluded finding
a boyfriend, never mind a husband. After Frank's interview, she
hoped she might not have to be alone.

She knew there might be discernable causes for her limited capacity for intimacy, but she'd already been to therapy
and talked about the usual suspects for too long. The therapist probed each trauma and significant relationship and asked
about her childhood memories of her family. She left no stone
unturned and then kept turning stones over until they were
shiny as mirrors, and Amanda was still no closer to wanting

anyone in that way. Before Amanda canceled all her future appointments, she told her therapist it wasn't helping. It wasn't like she was a victim of abuse. She grew up in a healthy family. The man who kidnapped her was a stranger, caught even before the day ended, before he really touched her. A life sentence, and he died in a prison fight—from a rusty knife to the spleen and then an infection—soon after. He was as far in the past as the past could go.

———

Amanda drove to the conference early so that she could sit in the front row for Frank's panel: Considerations of Asexuality in Queer Theory. Frank tossed around a lot of terms she couldn't quite grasp, but his general message reassured her. She didn't have to compromise on what she wanted in life just because she was different. There were others like her, others who might build a life with her.

She asked him to coffee. They found a place around the corner that served lattes with foam shaped like swans. Frank leaned back in his chair and stretched his legs. Amanda liked that each of his movements was slow and deliberate. There was something nonthreatening about the way he sat, close without encroaching on her space. His hand rested on the arm of his chair, several inches from hers. He also happened to be handsome, an aesthetic quality that she could appreciate, if only on a less visceral level than she suspected most other people would.

"How did you know that you were, well, you know?" she asked.

"That I was asexual?" His voice, honed by years of public

speaking, carried across the café. Amanda felt disappointed by the glances of nearby patrons. She had wanted people to think she was with him. He was much more conventionally good-looking than anyone she had ever dated.

"You don't have to worry about outing me," he said. "I made it my job to out myself. I'm outing myself at least two, some-times five times a week. Tomorrow I out myself on national television to a group of bored middle-aged women."

"This is all a bit new to me," she said.

"What is?"

"Using that term," she said, adding in a hushed tone, "asexual."

"Are you?"

"I think so." She stared at the disintegrating swan in her cof-fee, then added, "Yes, I am."

Fifteen years ago, in high school, she'd had a boyfriend. She had known him since she was five and, as a result, she had trusted him. He cheated on her the summer before she left for college, with her best friend. She remembered him touching her in pleasurable ways, but she wondered now, had she ever been more than cerebral in her passion? Maybe she had just loved him as an inexperienced teenage girl. She had assumed with time their physical intimacy would feel transcendent. It never had, and then he transcended with Sarah. If she were honest, a part of her had always expected him to hurt her.

"So the new part is just saying it?" Frank said.

"I'm glad," she said, "that there's a word for it."

She asked Frank out to lunch the next Saturday. They ate

Cuban sandwiches at one of the food stalls in the Grand Central Market. He wiped off the mustard and removed the pickles. It seemed finicky, but he ate the rest, and she mentally noted how easygoing he was. He spoke with enthusiasm about finishing his PhD and someday getting a professorship. He mentioned books she had never heard of. This thrilled her. She shared ownership of a bookstore downtown with an old college buddy. Her friend took on more of the financial burden but relied on Amanda to run it. The Last Booksellers they'd jokingly called it as they drew up plans—how silly to open a bookstore when so many were closing, surrendering to internet sales—but the name stuck. And the neighborhood of artists supported it. They held readings, hosted exhibits during Art Walk, and sold rare editions that bolstered profits. She had lucked into quite a few famous first editions when relatives of the recently deceased at the nearby assisted living facilities donated boxes of literary leftovers, unaware of their value, dusty hard covers with names like Proust and Faulkner embossed on the spines.

He asked to see her store, so they walked across downtown, through Pershing Square where the city was setting up for the weekly movie screening. Tonight, it was *Vertigo*. He insisted they go. She showed him the store, and they browsed together until the movie started. They bought wine at the corner market and reclined next to each other on the grass beneath the palm trees, getting a little drunk and watching the movie as the sky turned from dark indigo to the midnight rust that characterized downtown's light-polluted nights.

She invited him back to her loft, and they stayed up late playing records. She fell asleep on the floor and woke to him cradling her in his arms, carrying her to bed.

"I'm sorry I fell asleep," she said as he lay her down.

"Sweet dreams," he said, then turned to leave.

"Stay with me."

He climbed in beside her. Within minutes, he fell into deep sleep and rolled away so that his back was to hers. They slept together at least a few nights a week after that. Knowing that there was nothing more that he wanted from her made her feel safe. She thought she knew what they were, and by that logic, they couldn't change.

———

In the mornings, the sun shines on the building across the street, reflecting bronze off the windows, obscuring the possibility of spying. She never told Frank about her late-night observations. She knew that those nights satisfied her in some erotic way, but she also knew she compartmentalized such feelings, that they may not translate in real life. She told herself that to touch him would mean nothing, would do nothing for her. But she knew for Frank these feelings would call into question the premise of their relationship.

This morning, she brews coffee and scrambles eggs to ease Frank's mood after disturbing his sleep. He stares at her as he chews, his pale eyes revealing each shift of the pupil, each dilation. It was normally a comfort that she could feel his gaze.

"You smoked last night," he says.

"Just one." She wipes her mouth with the back of her hand, sniffing her fingers for the scent of tobacco.

"You never told me that you smoked. But here you are, a full-fledged smoker all of a sudden?"

"Just on occasion. When my nerves are fried."

"What's wrong?"

She takes a slow sip of her coffee and squints in the morning light. "Business has been slow lately."

He nods. He pats her on the shoulder as a goodbye gesture, pours his coffee into a thermos, and leaves for the campus fifteen minutes south of downtown.

————

When the painter walks into the store, Amanda is cutting open a box of books to shelve in the used fiction section. She hears the bell chime over the door, peers over a row of thick anthologies, and there he is. Dried paint splatters his jeans, but otherwise, he's cleaned himself up, combed his hair, put on a button-down shirt. Instead of perusing the books or the magazine rack, like most customers, he heads straight for the desk and stands there, waiting with a manila envelope.

"May I help you?" She steps into view but maintains distance, worrying that he'll recognize her.

"I'm hosting a sort of informal exhibit at my loft for some of my paintings at the next Art Walk. I was wondering if I could leave some flyers here? Post them on a bulletin board or something?" His voice is softer than she expected. When painting, his posture always seems so self-assured, but now he hunches his shoulders and fumbles the flyers out of the envelope, like he's apologizing for intruding.

She steps closer to see the flyer, which lists his name in bold font: Ryan Bethea. She recognizes one of the two paintings featured. An appendectomy scar glistening against the matte bronze muscles of a young woman's abdomen. It looks fresh, as if the doctor was careless of her beauty. The scar sinks deep, tugging at the surrounding skin, framed by spidery, purple stitch marks.

"Why do you paint scars?" she says.

"I don't always," he says. "She just happened to have one."

"But you focus on it," she says. He gives her a perplexed look, and she says, "At least in this painting, it looks like the scar is the whole point. Why?"

"I've been painting nudes lately. I wanted to avoid objectifying the image, so I focused on women's stomachs rather than the more obvious anatomy." He adds, "I think it's still sexual, just as any aspect of being physical, of having a body, can be."

Up close, she can see that Ryan is older than she previously assessed. A peppering of gray hair marks his temples, and a wrinkle divides his brow, perhaps from hours of concentrating over an easel. She thinks of all the bodies he has known, all those years of nudes, all those years of talking like this.

She says, "Is that something they teach you in art school or do you really believe that?"

"I'm self-taught," he says.

"Really?" She averts her eyes to the flyer. The other painting is of a rib cage emerging like an island from still water, the exposed skin the chilled texture of gooseflesh.

"Why don't you exhibit at any of the galleries?" she says, "You're better than showing paintings out of your own place."

"Thank you." He wraps an arm across his chest, grabbing his own elbow. "I just moved, so I haven't really figured things out yet."

"You could show your work here. It's not a gallery, but we do that sometimes, and we get lots of people who stop by during Art Walk."

"Are you serious?" He smiles and hugs her. "Thank you so much," he says.

She stands stiff and still until he lets go. He apologizes, and she assures him that it's okay.

———

When Amanda visits Ryan's loft to help with the Art Walk selection, she discovers details she could not notice from her former vantage point. The floor is rough concrete. The ceiling is unfinished, a tangle of air ducts and pipes. Just a few shirts and pants hang from a freestanding clothes rack in the corner. There are no closets. No separations or demarcations of space. Across the street, she can see her window. She forgot to turn off the kitchen light. She can see the gray cabinets but not her bed or her chair by the ledge. Maybe some nights he could see her shadow, sitting there, but it's impossible to know.

There are eight large canvases lined up along the wall. She's seen them all before.

"I could paint you," he says, "if you'd like."

She wonders what type of subject he thinks she will be for him. Does he expect perfection? Or rather some unexpected wound, some damaged ideal that he can fixate on?

"Now?" she asks.

"Or whenever you'd like."

"Would I have to be naked?"

"I could work around it, if that makes you too uncomfortable," he says.

He walks toward her. His hands hover down by his sides, poised and careful. *Like he's trying not to scare me off*, she thinks.

"May I show you?" he asks, gesturing at her stomach.

She nods, pulling the hem of her shirt up to reveal a couple inches of smooth skin. He lifts the shirt farther. His rough knuckles skim her belly, and she feels her body tense. Before the fabric slides past her rib cage, she tugs the shirt down.

"I'm sorry," she says.

She recalls other women on other nights looking eager and then sated by him. She liked the idea of them, or she thought she had, when she watched from afar.

"Are you okay?" he asks.

"I have a boyfriend," she says. "I have to go."

She grabs her purse and hurries out the door. He catches her at the elevator.

"I didn't know," he says. "You didn't tell me."

"I'm sorry." She hits the down button repeatedly. "I know."

"Are you okay?"

She won't look at him.

"Are you still going to put my paintings up?"

"Of course," she says, boarding the elevator. When the doors close, the unseen gears shift, and she feels her stomach drop.

————

When Frank comes over, she's a few bourbons in and smoking her third cigarette. She can feel the stiff saltiness of dried tears on her cheek.

"What happened?" he says. He drops his beaten-up brief-case and his jacket on the foot of her bed, then sits beside her on the window ledge.

"Nothing," she says.

"Then why are you upset?"

She grabs an extra glass from the kitchenette and returns to him. "Drink with me," she says, pouring him a few ounces. He leans forward to take the drink, and she notices how the veins skim the surface of his hands, blue threads over delicate bones. If she stares hard enough, she bets she could read his pulse. She places her palm on top of his hand, and although he keeps his hand still, she sees his shoulders stiffen as he braces himself.

"This is hard for you," she says, nodding to their hands. "Even this bothers you, doesn't it?"

"I like being with you," he says. "I thought you understood that."

She slides her hand to his knee. "Does this feel bad?" She moves her hand higher. "Or this?"

He stands up fast, sloshing the drink down his shirt. "Why are you testing me?"

She says, "I thought I didn't care, but maybe I do. Maybe I want you to touch me more than you do. Couldn't you try?"

She takes the glass out of his hand and puts it on the counter. "Maybe it'll be different with us."

In the dark room, his eyes reflect nothing. She grips his hair and guides his face to hers. Her lips glide over his. She lingers there. This is not new territory. He has let their lips meet briefly before. She deepens the kiss.

Normally, when kissing someone, she would taste the sourness of his saliva or feel viscosity on the tongue. She could not separate the act from her distant analysis of the act. It became animal, inferior, and repellant. But now, she tastes some amalgamation of him that she cannot separate into its parts. He tastes familiar. She wants him to grab her, to dig his fingers into her.

He turns away and wipes his mouth.

He says, "I've been nothing but honest with you. I never misled you. I thought you felt the same way."

She returns to the ledge and pours herself another drink. Across the street, the painter's window is dark. She recalls his touch, how her body stiffened. Then a sudden memory of drinking vodka in a dorm room with a friend, the kind of friend you only have your freshman year and then lose track of. She couldn't remember that friend's last name now, but she could still see the concern on her face when she told her about the kidnapping. "No wonder you have issues," she'd said, and they had both laughed. When you're eighteen, maybe it's easier to laugh at the things that derail your life because you think it can't be forever.

She says, "Maybe how we feel isn't natural at all. We're just damaged, and we don't bother fixing ourselves."

"My life's work is legitimizing how I feel and showing that this is natural," he says.

"I'm sure it is for some people."

"But not for you."

"I don't know."

"You need to know," he says, reaching for her and squeezing her hand, despite everything. "I need you to know."

She asks him to stay, but he grabs his coat and briefcase off the bed and leaves. Hours later, when she pulls back the covers, she notices the small gift box he must have meant to give her that night. She unwraps it to find an electronic cigarette with a note: *I hear these are safer*.

————

The night before the exhibit, Ryan shows up at the bookstore to help hang his paintings. All his words are perfunctory. Hold this corner. Place this to the left. Lift it higher. He barely speaks to her. When they finish and Amanda is turning off the lights, he thanks her. "I'm sorry for any weirdness I caused," he says. "I didn't mean anything."

"It wasn't you at all," she says.

That night, she watches as he primes a canvas. He primes it black. Whoever he paints on it will look like a ghost, she thinks, like something half-submerged in dark lake water.

He looks surprised when he opens his door and sees her. "Can you paint me now?" she says.

"What about your boyfriend?"

"I'm not sure I have one anymore," she says, and it's true. Although she and Frank exchanged a couple of brief messages, they were sterile and functional. He asked to meet her for a drink, which seemed like an abnormal step back. She suggested dinner, and he took hours to respond. She told him it would have to be after the exhibit, that she was swamped with preparations. Secretly, she wanted the time and space to map out her confusion.

Ryan widens the door and lets her into his loft.

She strips to her underwear, functional beige cotton. "Is this enough?"

"Whatever you want," he says.

She wants to contradict her body, to expose it, to deny it safekeeping. She takes off her bra, then her panties, conscious of the way her skin doubles on itself as she bends to pull the underwear over her feet.

When she straightens, she knows her stomach is smooth. No lines or birthmarks.

"Paint me with scars," she says.

"You don't have any." He scrutinizes her skin, and she feels less and less inside herself.

"But you can paint them," she says, "here and here." She touches just beneath her breast and right above her navel. The marks of a dead girl. The girl they found after they caught the man who had her—an Amber Alert, they caught him fast, before he got her to his place, before he could touch her the way he intended. The other girl was stabbed after he'd had her a year. When the news sensationalized the case, Amanda saw leaked photos. She saw how he'd dismantled the girl who had the same dark eyes as her. But it didn't happen to her. She knows that.

Now the easel stands between her and a man wielding a palette knife caked in creamy acrylics the color of her flesh. From this angle, she can only see the bare wooden frame and, stapled to it, the tattered edges of the canvas. Light passes through the fabric, faint and diffused, until he paints the first layer of her body, a growing shadow of torso.

"Did you use black or white primer?" she asks.

"I didn't prime it."

"Why not?"

"It'll be good," he says. "Don't worry."

When he mixes a violet red on his palette, his gaze skims over her. He studies her like the scar is real, like he can transfer the wound from her skin to his canvas. Her feet begin to ache against the cold concrete.

At her shifting, he asks, "Need a break?"

"Please."

"Come here."

He waves her to his side where she can see the painting. The contours of her midsection emerge, scratchy and inchoate against the unprimed canvas. Smudginess breaks the lines and blurs the shadows against a backdrop of dry-brushed gray. He has only finished one scar. It distinguishes itself, precise and saturated amidst the gauzy flesh.

"Is this what you pictured?" he asks.

"It's close." She resists the impulse to touch the red, to smear it wider.

"Is it too much?"

She stares at the vivid freshness of the barely healed wound.

He touches her elbow. The gesture is gentle. She can feel the crust of dried paint on his fingertips. She tells him then about the man who took her and about the girl who died. About the scar, she says, "Make it deep, like it was me."

———————

Most people go to Art Walk to let loose. Local galleries are complaining, some branching off to plan an alternate Art Walk that focuses more on art and less on parties. Revelers drink free wine and eat free hors d'oeuvres, and fewer paintings sell than expected for an event with ten thousand attendees.

By nine that evening, Ryan has only sold one painting, the portrait of Amanda. He insisted on bringing it, placing a fan on the acrylic paint throughout the night and carrying it to the store himself in the morning.

The painting will remain on display until closing, at which point a stranger will possess a piece of Amanda. She likes that her image will arrive with prefabricated damage, impervious to any further imperfections. She spends a large part of the evening examining her fictional wounds, the illusory wetness of the paint making them fresher than scars.

"It's perverse."

She turns to find Frank beside her.

He adds, "Like it's glorifying violence against women." His authoritative tone rankles her.

"It's showing a common fact," she says.

He takes a few steps back and surveys the row of female torsos. "It feels like a gimmick. How'd you find this guy?"

"He came to the shop," she says. "He also lives across the street. This one is of me." She points.

Frank steps closer. He zeroes in on the garish splotches of red on the otherwise pristine skin. "Why would you let him do that?"

"I asked him to," she says.

He leans in and whispers so forcefully that spittle hits her cheek. "Why would you want this? After what happened to you—"

"He knows, Frank. Don't make it such a sacred fucking thing." Her voice carries more than she intended. A few patrons stare, entertained by the possibility of a lovers' quarrel. Frank lowers his gaze, spots a stray thread unraveling at his sleeve and plucks at it needlessly.

"This helped me," she says.

He laughs, a quick swallow of air, then reaches for the painting.

He manages to get his hand around the wooden frame and to pull it off the nails before she gets to him. She yanks hard on his elbow and the painting clatters to the concrete floor, then teeters there. Amanda grabs the side, propping it up against the wall.

By now, Ryan sees the commotion and confronts Frank. "Don't touch the art," he says.

"You don't have the right," Frank says.

"That painting doesn't even belong to me. It sold already."

Again, Frank reaches for the painting, but Ryan shoves him aside. Frank punches him, connecting with the jaw, an act of violence unrivaled by any other action he has thus far taken in his life. This much Amanda knows, and through her hor-ror—or, more accurately, from his horror—she feels the shame of excitement.

Ryan clutches his face, and Frank steps away, his fingers splayed.

"I'm sorry." Frank stares at his hands.

"You need to leave," Amanda says.

"I just don't understand why you would want him to do this." He looks to Ryan, who shakes his head.

"Just get out of here, man."

Amanda notices how people have crept away from the art, seeking refuge in the book stacks. "Go outside," she says.

Frank nods, then walks to the exit.

She checks on Ryan's face; there's a sweltering redness but nothing serious. When she follows Frank outside, he's already out of sight.

———

The streets are nearly empty by the time Amanda walks home. A couple of teenage girls scurry past her, barefoot and tugging on their tight skirts, suddenly self-conscious without a crowd to lose themselves in.

She finds Frank at her place, sitting on the ledge and staring out the window.

"Which apartment is it?" he asks.

"You planning on hitting him again?"

"You sit here watching him at night," he says.

"Yes."

"Have you fucked him?"

She hesitates, not wanting to gratify him.

"Have you?" he asks.

"No," she says. "Are you going to fuck me?"

Frank stands, knocking over the small table she keeps by the window.

He pushes her onto the bed and shoves his hand against her breast, then between her legs. "Is this what you want?" he says. She feels her throat burn and she realizes she's crying. She nods and reaches for him beneath his jeans, feels what he won't do. She tries to stroke him, to make him want her, but he shoves her hands away.

He slides off and sits with his back to her at the foot of the bed.

"You lied to me," he says.

"I only want you," she says. "You're the only one I've trusted enough to feel this way."

"You trust me because I'm your fucking eunuch."

She goes to light a cigarette, a real one, and cracks the window to exhale.

After several minutes, she notices the light turn on across the street. She watches Ryan check the dryness of a canvas, then lean it against the wall, primed and blank.

Frank walks up behind her and says, "Go to him."

"You don't mean that," she says.

"You can't even go through with it," he says. "It's just easier for you to blame me."

That he might be right scares her. She leaves without a word, leaves Frank sitting at her window.

She stops at the corner market and buys cheap wine. She

brings it to Ryan, insisting that they celebrate his sold paintings, including her portrait. She drinks most of the bottle herself. When the last drop is gone, she kisses him, unbuttoning
his shirt as soon as he kisses her back.

His touch is practiced. She can recognize his routine, but
it's what she wants, she realizes. To be acted upon as she exca-
vates the nature of her desire. He touches her deliberately, trying to ready her, then presses in, his hips bruising her thighs.
She feels her body tense, resisting him, creating pain, but she
surrenders until there is nothing but numbness. Gravity weighs
on his face, deepening the creases that frame his mouth as he
looks through her with dark, inscrutable eyes. She wants eyes
like pale water, prismatic. She can't see beyond the harsh lights.

Amanda wishes she felt the spurring of reciprocation, but
even as he moves inside her, she thinks, did someone take this
from me? Or is this me? Was this always me, trying to fix an
unbroken thing?

Ryan finishes and she lets him hold her.

After he turns the lights off, after her eyes adjust, she stares
across the street and tries to discern the figure of a man in her
window.

OVERNIGHTS WELCOME

The virus would leave you stock-still for months—years, in the flukish nightmare cases that made the Sunday news specials. One day you could run ten miles, chug a beer in the shower, and endure surprisingly long in bed, leaving your lover spent, slick with summer sweat. But in slips a mosquito, and welcome to paralysis.

It went that way for Zach in Coffeeville. He could still talk, slow and slurred, saliva trickling down his chin, but he struggled to operate his own wheelchair. George would sometimes see Mindy guiding Zach around the square on Sundays, their sulking daughter in tow. Once he saw Mindy spooning ice cream into his mouth. A glob slid out of his limp lips and settled into his lap like a pigeon shit. George felt Zach staring at him then, a tensing of the brows, anger perhaps at becoming George's spectacle—a story he'd share with Jamie later as they perfectly swallowed their mashed potatoes.

George had nightmares that consisted solely of the keening whir of insect wings. Just blackness and that high frequency buzz against the ear, followed by the silence of its landing, its feeding, and the awareness that the virus was being deposited through the skin, buoyed by saliva injected into the bloodstream.

Jamie was pregnant, her maternity tops tenting over her belly

like a fumigation tarp. They never left the house after dark.
The windows were never open. The mosquitoes ruled the
night, which was why the invitation for the Wrights' party was
such a shock.

"Maybe they meant A.M. instead of P.M.?" Jamie said, flip-
ping the invitation back and forth for inspection, then fanning
herself with it.

"Who starts a party at six in the morning?" George said.

It was true; many of the Coffeeville residents had taken to
day drinking, moving their parties to the mornings and calling
them brunches. It was the only way to blow off steam and still
walk safely home in the full light of day. Even still, they had to
avoid the particularly lush backyards. Even then, a stray mosquito could find you in the shade. Zach was playing croquet in
the Wrights' backyard the week before he froze up, following
the ball into the long shadows of the centuries-old oaks. Now
they only played croquet in the harsh glare of the sun, sweat
sprouting beneath the women's broad-brimmed hats. The local bars closed at sundown. There was no point in staying open.
The Lodge was already shuttered forever.

George struggled to see the fine print of the card, despite Jamie's fluttering.

"Can I?" he said, reaching.

The front was a glossy square image of a bright blue door.
The other side listed the times, with an asterisk correspond-
ing to a footnote that read *overnights welcome*. He read that
part aloud.

"My God," Jamie said. "Is it a swingers party?"

"Surely not," George said, but a small unbidden hope unfurled and stood erect in his heart. Mrs. Colleen Dunlap Wright was the great beauty of the town, with a thick rope of hair that gathered softly at her nape, then swung with her stride like the inverted needle of a metronome. She was married to the former mayor, a farmers-market-perusing man and gallery owner who hosted any famous artist or musician who happened to be passing through Mississippi. Colleen was admittedly an exuberant flirt, making both men and women preen, eager to please her.

The last time George had seen Colleen, she was seated at the lunch counter of the Chevron, eating fried chicken with a slice of pie ready on the side. She didn't see him, and although he'd intended to buy a soda from the fridge behind her, there was something intimate about her eating—she was fully engrossed, shoulders hunched protectively over her plate—so he chose to forego his usual Pepsi. He paid for his gas and left, unnoticed.

The last time George spoke to Colleen, he had run into her at the dry cleaner's. She was talking to the owner, jabbing her fingers at a faded yet persistent wine stain that muddied the crotch of a cherry red dress. He was embarrassed to witness her scolding someone, a departure from her usual charm. He grasped at anything to say to fill the awkward void. He told her about a molehill he'd found in his yard that morning.

Colleen smiled then, wide and glossy, and said, "You can tell where they are if you watch closely, especially a couple days out from a good rain, when the ground is still soft, you know? And if you time it just right, you can get them with your shovel."

George pictured a saggy-skinned critter emerging bleary-eyed on a shovel of dirt.

Colleen continued, "The other day I managed to decapitate one. Got it right through the neck."

With that beheading, Colleen became an enigma upon which George projected his own befuddlement with life's great mysteries.

———

The yard had been ravaged by moles. One morning, Colleen went to let the dog in and found her joyfully wagging her tail, a limp mole dangling from her mouth. When she picked it up, she was stunned by how smooth and velvety it was. Her dog had left the skin unbroken. She lightly pinched the mole's foot, a wide paddle with embryonic digits, between her fingers. She could feel its tiny bones shifting, malleable and delicate in her hands, like the links of a necklace chain falling coolly into the palm. The dog meant it as a gift, but a few weeks later she came with another mole, this one long since dead, an already putre-fied corpse. Colleen thought maybe she saw its organs roiling beneath the stretched, translucent skin. Nature's water balloon, she had mused darkly, but a part of her was made serious by the irrefutable decay. She knew then it was an omen. The dog died soon after, and although the vet insisted that the dead mole had nothing to do with it, that it wasn't that type of infection, Colleen felt like entropy was picking up steam, spinning away all comfort, and that somehow all the discontent in her life was connected, originating from a rotten core that she couldn't name.

That was last summer, and now the moles were back. And so were the mosquitoes. No one could sip a bourbon lemonade on the porch swing at sunset, and thanks to the moles, the last lawn party was a disaster. Colleen had broken the heel of her gold pump when her entire foot plunged into a miniature sink-hole, no doubt a result of the extensive tunnels lacing her prop-erty. The croquet balls refused to go in a straight line, unex-pectedly diverted by the undetected molehills. And of course, Zach had been bitten, although no one knew it at the time. It took nine days for the disease to take hold of him, and by the time she found out, it was too late to speak with him. She couldn't call his phone. Who would pick it up besides Mindy? Everything that had passed between them had frozen with him, as if in amber.

Tonight would be the first nighttime party of the year. Col-leen had screened in their expansive back patio. Before the epi-demic, she'd added a gazebo near the wisteria and wrapped twinkling strands of lights around the vines and the iron scroll-work. It had been the perfect spot for a midnight chat, one of those wee-hour conversations that made you feel tethered to the other person. She liked to curate moments of moder-ate intimacy with others. She would seek some nugget of se-cret personality from someone she only knew in a distant, for-mal sense, and she would build worlds around that detail. The next evening, she would tell Kevin what she had learned, and they would speculate, dissect, and hypothesize on how their distant acquaintance, friend, or neighbor lived with this sur-prising trait, past, or secret. They would try to make sense of it, persisting in the premise that people could make sense if you thought about them enough. Usually there was a disagreement about how to interpret some aspect of the persona they had invented based upon this new detail, and this disagreement would fuel tension, and this tension would turn to a shoving, pinning, and biting form of lovemaking. This was their routine, albeit a sporadic one, before the virus, before she told him that she had been bitten, that she carried it and would carry it with her for at least a year, as best as anyone knew.

Now Colleen was patting concealer under her eyes. There was a new crinkly texture there that she couldn't hide. Her skin was getting thinner, she'd noticed. The veins were bluer, closer to the surface. An image of that dead mole flickered in her mind as she smeared layers of thick foundation over her cheeks. After she'd perfected her makeup, she moisturized her hands, lingering over the lines that were forming on her wrists. She had searched the internet. Wrist lines, it turned out, were a neurosis that even women's magazines hadn't yet figured out how to exploit. She'd bought a glycolic acid solution to baste the lassoes of her wrists each evening. It was an act of faith with no evidence of improvement.

In the kitchen, through the art-laden walls, she could hear her daughter, Suzie, opening cabinets and refrigerator bins as she chatted with someone, probably Bella. Bella was gangly and scathing like Zach. After the onset of Zach's symptoms, Colleen had brought a casserole over. Bella had answered the door, and Colleen felt sized up by the girl, who said in an accusing tone, "Why didn't Suzie come?" Maybe she was disappointed in her friend for not showing up that particular night, but Colleen worried that Bella sensed some aspect of the truth: Colleen had ordered Suzie to stay home, to focus on a school project, so that Colleen could focus on her own feelings when she saw him. But she didn't see him then. Mindy told her he was sleeping, that he slept nearly twenty hours a day. Colleen had said something platitudinous and wrong to Mindy, something like, "My condolences," and she was startled when Mindy snapped back at her, saying, "He's not dead," as she shoved the casserole into the fridge.

Now Suzie was describing her crush on an actor in a popular zombie show.

"But he's *old!*" Bella said. "Isn't he like thirty?"

Forty, Colleen thought. She had looked that up and been dismayed that he was younger than she was by a few years.

"It's not like I'd date him," Suzie said. "I just like watching him."

Oh Lord, she thought, *my sweet daughter, lusting after a full-grown man*. She was only twelve. Was that normal? She herself had gone out with an eighteen-year-old when she was just thirteen (and claiming to be fourteen). It had been a secret, sneaking out or pretending to meet friends at the movies. It hadn't lasted long, and when things ended badly, she had spent the summer crying in her room, unable to tell her parents that her heart was broken. As a teen, everything had felt magnified, too intense. It was the most extreme attachment she had ever felt, and she would be mortified if that boy, now a man, had ever known what he meant, because she knew now: it had all been intentional and ill-advised.

She found the girls sitting on the counter, legs dangling, eating huge slices of pecan pie.

"Is that my party pie? I made that for tonight."

"Sorry," Suzie said, mouth full.

"Give me that." Colleen reached out for the plate, stopping an inch from snatching it by force. "You'll ruin dinner. There's going to be barbeque."

"Bella's mom said I could head over there early." Suzie scraped one more bite down before casually relinquishing the pie.

Colleen dumped the plate so hard in the kitchen sink that she had to check it for any cracks.

"What about Calvin? Don't you want to see him before you go?" Calvin had lived next door until a few years ago when he had moved to be closer to the university in Memphis where he taught. He was like an uncle to Suzie. He usually brought some minor surprise, like a trinket for her dresser or a charm for her bracelet. When she was little, Suzie would try on at least five outfits before deciding which one she wanted to show off for any party guests.

"Not really." Suzie shrugged, picking at a scab on her elbow. "It's stressful trying to remember everyone, Mom. You think I can remember all their names and how you know them, but I don't. I hardly ever see most of those people."

"All right, fine. Grab your bag and I'll take you now."

"Bella's mom is picking us up."

"I can take you now," she said, "especially since you're so eager to get going."

"Mom." Suzie cast an exasperated glance Bella's way.

What Colleen didn't want was Mindy on her doorstep, emphasizing her role as the overburdened mother who never had time for parties. She would rather drop the girls off from the curb and wave from her car, watching them run into the house without looking back. She grabbed her cell and texted Mindy.

"I'm taking you," she said, feeling the relief of having handled the situation.

If she were honest with herself, it was probably best for Suzie to get to the house earlier, well before sunset and long before the adults moved on to their second or third beverage, but she found the sudden autonomy of her own progeny to be unsettling. Her daughter couldn't ever know, but if she did, if a couple decades down the road she told Suzie everything, could she understand? She and Kevin had discrete encounters outside their marriage, according to rules that limited the length and intimacy of each engagement, but even having such a meticulous agreement meant that she was compelled to break it. There was nothing intimate anymore about Kevin's permissive calm or the orchestrated order of their relationship. An affair was a way to knock the walls down and figure out where she was left standing.

———

The guests arrived when the sun straddled the hills, the rosy light fading behind the thick drifts of kudzu that would smother the land, strangling the nearby trees until the first frost reclaimed them. They parked their cars and rushed to the blue door as quickly as they could without losing dignity. For most folks, gone were the days of muggy stillness, trading niceties on the front porch, letting the moist air purge your skin, but the Wrights had brought back this piece of summer with their screened-in patio. Calvin asked Colleen for an ash tray and then settled into a plush wicker chair in the corner, puffing on a cigar and sipping from the Scotch he'd brought. Sarah, a willowy girl, actually a woman, but the kind who would always seem girlish, arrived alone and made small chat about the conference she went to for research on procrastination. "It's really liberating," she said, "to realize that I'm not lazy. I'm just too hard on myself. Things need to be perfect and then I get overwhelmed." Calvin gave a grunt and a nod, then swiveled in his seat, scanning the patio for some other conversational thread to grasp.

Small cliques gathered, dragging chairs into pods. Awkward silence was soon lubricated by a growing table of BYOB offerings. When Calvin felt comfortable telling his merkin story—the one where a foreign exchange student brought the piece as a historical artifact, knowing that this was a niche research topic of Cal's, and yet, how does one accept a merkin from a student?—Colleen knew the party was in full swing.

George arrived without Jamie. In the final hour, after she had already fixed her hair and carefully lined her eyes, she lost her grip on her mascara wand and smeared black goo across her lid and cheekbone. "I'll have to start over," she said, scouring her face clean. She had stared at George's reflection in the mirror then and told him to go without her. It wasn't worth the trouble, she said. He knew he should play the dutiful husband. Find a show to watch on TV and cradle her swollen feet in his lap, but he wanted to preserve this piece of separateness. It thrilled him to be alone at a party. It had been so long.

Colleen's lips were a brilliant red, the only noticeable alteration to her natural beauty. George wanted to see the crimson smeared across her face. He wanted to drag his thumbs through the waxy pigment and rub it out. She smiled at him across the room, and he wove his way through the crowd to her side.

"I like your lipstick."

"Thank you," she said. "Kevin says makeup is a form of lying." It was a subtle way of suggesting distance between her and her husband, who was chatting with Holly the has-been actress—now head of a community theater troupe in a neighboring town—and she knew this minor confession of marital dissent increased the likelihood that a man (in this case George, but most men would feel the same way) would want to open up to her, to trade vulnerabilities.

"How's Jamie?"

George avoided her eyes. "She needed a quiet night in."

"When I was pregnant with Suzie, I wanted to hide on a desert island. A desert island with air-conditioning."

"It's hard to imagine you pregnant." He immediately regretted the remark. It was too honest. He could only picture her as perfectly coiffed and immutable. He'd seen the way his wife's body was contorting, the emergence of major arteries bulging beneath her fuzzy skin.

He tried to save himself. "I just meant, you don't look like a mother." He realized too late that he had dug himself deeper.

Colleen laughed, a forced trill. She could hear the tinny fakeness, but she was trying to keep things light. She didn't care what George thought of her—that he objectified her, she knew—as long as she was made to feel put together in other people's eyes.

Of course, George didn't know about the abortion she'd had last year. No one knew, not even Kevin. Not even Zach. It had been an easy decision to make. As best they knew at the time, there was probably a fifty-fifty chance her baby would have suffered severe brain damage, the type of damage that would make any complex thought impossible, but the tests that would determine the damage could only be performed after the point of viability, at which point state law would forbid any termination that wasn't meant to save the mother's life. Even without the complicated issue of paternity, she could never embrace those odds. She made the appointment, and the nurse she spoke with at the clinic was effusive in her support. Colleen felt she was a woman whose choice had been made for her, by the virus, but the reality would creep into her thoughts late at night. She would recognize that she was relieved to have a justification that felt sympathetic, a reason that was in the daily headlines. Some of the more conservative states were easing abortion access now, worried by the burden of so many babies with little more than a brain stem. There was no point in telling anyone, she decided. She was saving Zach the added tragedy, and she was saving Kevin the drama. He was a pragmatic man with his own dalliances, she knew. What did she owe him, really?

"I'll take it as a compliment," she said, grazing George's wrist with her freshly polished nails.

He blushed, and she was gratified. They stood for a moment, eyes shifting to others as they maintained a gentle head nod and polite smiles.

Finally, George spoke, "This is a bit awkward, but the Clarks gave me their permission list for after-school pickup this fall, and you're not on it."

This was the moment at which Colleen knew, rather than mildly suspected, that Mindy had learned about her and Zach. She could feel George scanning her face, and she tried to project placidity. She pulled on her shiny smile and said, "Mindy probably just updated the list and forgot that I'm usually on it."

"Well, it has been a long summer," he said. "Do you want me to ask her about it?"

"Don't trouble yourself. I'll probably see her tomorrow anyway," Colleen said. "She has so much on her plate, bless her heart, I'm sure it's easy to forget the little things. Thanks for letting me know."

"That makes sense," George said, but he knew he had identified a rift between neighbors, and he had his suspicions. The girls were close as could be, and even if they had had a falling out, there would be no need to revoke carpool permissions.

"The girls always ride together," Colleen said. "They're like sisters."

At the end of last semester, when school had let out for the summer, Colleen had dropped Bella off with her bags of locker belongings. She had helped the girls carry the piles of books, projects, and magazine cutouts to the door. Mindy was still at the yoga studio where she worked part-time as a receptionist and instructor. After Bella unlocked the door, Colleen took the liberty of carrying what she could to the living room table, where she found Zach sitting in his motorized chair, watching TV.

There's a surge of constricted emotion that lodges firmly in the back of your throat when you see the object of your love after a long absence. Colleen could not speak at first. She stared, and he raised his eyes to hers. What would she feel in his place? She felt a compartmentalized desire suddenly creeping out of its box to drive to a faraway cabin where they would strategize how to return as a couple. Alone, they would delude themselves into thinking that they could do this thing and still keep the unadulterated love of their children, still keep the intensity of illicit moments. His illness would fade, the affair would fade. If strangers met them on vacation, they would assume all their adult years had been spent together, in wholesome continuity.

But it was different for Zach. His wife loved him. She looked to him like a map to all of her future. Kevin loved Colleen in his own way, she knew, but her absence would never derail him. She was like the parmesan he'd buy to smother his Tuesday pasta: he loved it, but if the cheese were ever left out, the meal went on, by the clock, all the same.

Zach lowered his chin, a shaky head nod. She smiled back, trying to project how much she still cared.

"I'm going to leave your things on this table," she told Bella as the girl gave her dad a quick peck on the top of his head.

"Thanks." Bella snatched the remote and settled into the couch. "You wanna hang out?" she asked Suzie, who promptly plopped down beside her.

Suzie said, "You mind taking my things home with you, Mom?"

"Sure, Sweetie," she said, bristling at the way the girls were unthinkingly ruining everything.

"So good to see you, Zach," she said.

His eyes were as alert as ever, but his face had changed. Although the paralysis was most likely temporary, no one knew for sure how long it would last. It had already been nearly a year—long enough for his muscles to atrophy and for his strong features to turn gaunt. She couldn't say that she'd recognize him on the street if he had suddenly appeared like this, without the gradual metamorphosis. None of it mattered, she had decided. He wouldn't stay like this forever.

He smiled, a pulling of the lips to one side, and said slowly, so that she had to walk right up to his chair to hear him, "So good, Colleen."

That was all he said. It was harmless. She had imbued his words with all the possible subtexts that would validate her feelings.

The girls had looked listless when she told them goodbye, a strange cartoon with long-limbed characters of indecipherable identity—neither animals nor people—blaring from the screen. As she left, she had asked Bella, "Are you sure your father wants to watch this?" The girl had glared back. "He's fine," she said. "Dad, isn't this okay?"

"Okay," Zach said.

And so Colleen left.

Did Bella know even then? How could she have? But the girls weren't just girls anymore. They picked up on things. Did Suzie know? She could feel her mind spiraling down to a pinpoint of obsessive worry when Kevin appeared.

Kevin was the type of man who owned his space, never clutching himself too tightly, never hunching over or shifting diminutively. He strode up to them now, slinging one arm across Colleen's shoulders as he clinked glasses with George.

"How are things at the school?" Kevin kneaded Colleen's skin.

"There's a lot of automation happening, actually," George said. "Some people are happy to have less prep, but a lot of the students and faculty feel a bit isolated, I think. It's just summer school now, but in the fall, I bet a lot of people will have strong opinions."

"Sounds tough." Kevin nodded.

"Is Suzie doing well?" Colleen said.

"She always does. Although Ms. Smith said that she's been glaring at her."

"I'm sure Suzie's just paying attention," Kevin said. "Where should she be looking? The clock?"

"Sure, sure," George said. "I'm keeping an eye on the situation."

"I'm sure you are," he said.

It was at this moment that Calvin bellowed, and then Sarah screamed. She leapt onto her chair and scanned the room wildly, the whites of her eyes flaring. Calvin knocked his wicker chair over and charged for the door. "Mosquito, mosquito!" he cried. The entire party disintegrated as people shuffled and shoved their way indoors with swiftly fading decorum. A deviled egg platter that had been in Colleen's family for generations shattered. An abandoned glass of wine toppled, leaving a ruby stain on the jute rug.

Everyone hurried inside except Colleen. She lingered, curious as to how the tiny interloper had buzzed his way into her patio. She could hear the faint whine of its little wings. George tapped on the sliding glass door and motioned for her to come inside. Instead, she ran her hands along the screen fabric that enclosed the space. Maybe it looked stupid or brave, but she'd already been exposed to the virus. She'd slept with Zach before they'd known a mosquito had infected him. It was after the lawn games had wound down. Holly and Kevin had long since withdrawn into the casita to admire his collection of first editions. Zach had asked her to join him for a walk on the reclaimed railroad, now paved into a cycling trail.

They had found the singular train car that remained in the overgrowth beyond the tracks. Abandoned and rusted, the metal box was covered in graffiti and vines and full of the acrid scent of delinquent urine. She didn't care. He led her into the shadows, wordless. She remembered the pollen sifting through the sun's rays. The feeling of mutual need, visceral and urgent, overwhelmed her, and for those brief moments, she focused on touching him like worship, thinking if she could anoint his skin in kisses, she would feel something pure. They would both feel it, and there would be goodness between them. She had convinced herself that they could have a timeless moment and that would be enough to steady her as she settled into this older phase of life, but she had worshipped beyond reason, stolen too many moments with him over the span of months, and the scent of his scalp lingered, a phantom smell on her pillow even though he'd never laid his head there. A week after that party, she had come down with chills and a three-day headache, but she recovered and Zach fell ill.

She found the hole, a singed circle near the fallen wicker

chair. Calvin probably burnt through it with his cigar. It would be easy to seal, but no one would trust coming outside again.

———

People were losing interest in Colleen's investigation and talking in clusters, but George hesitated to leave. She just stood there, staring at the screen and the dark garden beyond. He liked the way her wavy hair cloaked her face like a hood. George tapped on the glass again.

"She's fine," Kevin said, sipping his whiskey.

Kevin hollered to Calvin then, "Pick a record and put some jazz on, will you?"

Kevin threw back the rest of his drink. "I'm going to grab more booze from the kitchen. Need anything?"

"Shouldn't she come inside first?" George asked.

Kevin leaned down. "She's infected, George."

He said it like he was being kind. George couldn't understand it, this man, this husband, telling this news about his wife to another man.

"Are you sure?"

"They have a test now," Kevin said. "It's not worth the risk."

George felt embarrassment flushing his face. He told himself it was just a crush he'd been nursing. A harmless diversion that would never amount to anything. He still loved Jamie, but all of their conversations had turned to the baby, or the virus and how it could affect the baby, or to the Walmart shopping list. He told himself it was temporary—both his fantasizing and this banal phase of nesting. He certainly didn't mean to be so shamefully obvious. He added, "I'd never."

"Sorry," Kevin laughed, slapping George on the back. "My sick sense of humor." Kevin shook his glass back and forth. "You want some, don't you?"

George had only admired Colleen from afar. He barely spoke to her, never had experiences that belonged to just them as a twosome, alone. George watched her exit the screened-in patio. She drifted into the shadows, toward the twinkling lights of the gazebo. He envied her immunity, wandering in the cooler air of evening. Her ability to walk fearlessly into the night secured her place in his mythology of her—a woman who was both welcoming and untouchable.

Kevin was looking down on him.

"I'm going to be a father soon," George said.

"Yes, I saw Jamie at the Walmart. Any day now, isn't it?" He thumped George on the shoulder, like a brotherly sign of affection at a tailgate with a dash of some unspoken aggression.

Kevin motioned George along and wove his way through the crowd to the corner of the living room that served as a bar, a sleek kitchenette with mirror-backed shelving.

"Are you ready?" Kevin asked, handing George a steep pour of bourbon.

"As much as one can be." He politely took a sip. He usually drank amaretto sours or seasonal Abita in the evenings as he read the newspaper or his backcountry magazine. He used to go camping with his fraternity brothers, the type of camping where you prioritize beer and flame-torched meat, but he'd always wanted to go on one of those multiday hiking trips where you survive on the scantest supply possible and emerge reinvigorated, a self-sufficient animal. It wouldn't happen now.

At least not for years, not until his child had grown beyond helplessness, and definitely not before they'd found a way to eradicate the virus, or mosquitoes, or both. Here he was, neither a survivalist nor a whiskey drinker, about to be a father.

Kevin swallowed his drink and poured another, topping George's off even though he'd barely depleted its contents. "Here's the important thing," Kevin said, leaning heavily on George's shoulder, "you can't expect her to be everything for you. It's going to get messy, and you're going to have to let it fucking implode and still hang on, shrapnel and all. It's a fucking mess."

Kevin raised his glass at George, then downed another shot's worth. George felt the pressure of his stare and suppressed an urge to wince as he took a large swallow of his drink.

"It's already hard enough," George said, aiming for neutral agreement.

"These are hard times," Kevin said. "You just have to figure out what works."

"With all due respect, you don't know what I'm going through. You had Suzie before any of this, and she turned out fine."

The pregnancy was a surprise. George had been terrified that they would end up a statistic, that his child would be born with an impossibly small head with eyes bulging out, mouth fishing for air. He had asked if they should consider their options more, but Jamie was a fierce Baptist. She froze him out for weeks for the mere suggestion. He resented her then, and he still worried that he'd never recover what they once had, which was never the passion he'd witnessed in movies, but it

was faithful and devoted to the needs and desires of each other:
They did their best, and that was love, wasn't it? But a child like
that. He couldn't want it. He tried to imagine holding such a
child and thinking, *She is ours, a part of us forever*, and it made
his skin go cold with a sudden sweat.

When Jamie had the test, months of this dark imagining had
marked him. She hugged him tight with the relief of a woman
who had tethered all her hope and dreams to this one thing,
but he had already built a wall around the outcome, bracing for
the worst so that when the good news came, it felt like a distant
whisper. He could barely feel it.

"Suzie was a preemie," Kevin said. "You get through something like that, you're not just a marriage anymore. You're
something else." He stared George down. "No matter what
happens."

"Good for you," George said, wincing at his bland words.

Then the front door slammed, and Mindy marched into
the center of the party crowd, scanning the room until she saw
Kevin.

"Are they here?" she said.

For a second, Kevin assumed she meant his wife, but who
could *they* mean? Zach was out of commission. He glanced
back at George, who averted his eyes and focused on plucking
an ice cube to chew on. It seemed improbable.

Besides, they had a rule. He had broken it with Holly, but
Holly was discreet. They weren't supposed to sleep with others from Coffeeville. They had a few rules. They were his rec-
ommendations, but Colleen had agreed. No long-lasting affairs. Each experience had to be finite, self-contained, and left

behind. There were the usual safety precautions that they had each tepidly endorsed. They'd only been married a few years when they reconceived their boundaries, but on some level, Kevin always knew he would want something less conventional. "We're the most curious animals on earth," he had said to her. "Isn't it more honest to know that about ourselves?" And she had consented, with a caveat. "Promise me," she had said, "promise me that you'll always love me the most." Kevin had agreed, expecting that it would be true, but also not worrying if life changed his mind someday. Wasn't any promise a commitment contingent on the assessments of that particular day? If the data changed, he would reassess—anyone would if they were honest with themselves—but he still meant his devotion in the act of devotion.

He thought he still loved her the most. He needed her the most. When Suzie came, when they couldn't take her home and her tiny body was contained in a clear box like a medical experiment, he had wanted nothing more than for their lives to remain whole and connected. *This is my family*, he had thought. *We are bound in flesh*.

Now the virus had left him scared to touch Colleen, but it wasn't just that. She barely touched him at all, not even the brief grazing of hands in the kitchen or the passing caresses of a couple readying themselves for sleep. Her attention had shifted away from him, perhaps to become a *they*, to become a *we* defined by the exclusion of others. Perhaps he was one of the others now.

"The girls," Mindy said. "Where are they? I've been trying to call."

Of course, he thought. *They.* "I thought they were with you," he said, registering relief that his imagination had gone so far afield before the parental worry descended.

"We all had dinner and then they went to Bella's room, but they weren't there when I checked in on them. It's not that late. Maybe Suzie forgot something? Are you sure they didn't come back here?"

Colleen surfaced from the back of the room. "I'll check."

Kevin noticed the way Mindy's mouth tightened at the sight of Colleen, the way her eyes followed her.

When Colleen returned, she shook her head and said, "You have no idea where they might have gone?"

"No, I don't," Mindy snipped. "Do you?"

"I wasn't the one watching them."

The party had gone silent. People had encircled Mindy and Colleen, some too drunk to affect the appropriate degree of polite concern, merely seeking a view of the spectacle. Someone hollered out at the women, "Do the girls have boyfriends?"

"Of course not," Mindy said, but then she noticed Colleen's uncertainty and said, accusingly, "Is Suzie dating already?"

"I don't know," she said. "Suzie doesn't tell me anything like that."

The women turned to George.

"You think they'd tell their teacher who they're dating?" he said.

"You at least see who they hang out with, don't you?" Mindy said.

It was true. George had noticed Suzie with a peculiar goth boy at lunch. When he didn't have cafeteria duty, he liked to take his lunch to one of the study carrels in the library. It was against the rules, but the librarian feigned ignorance as long as he was subtle about it, sitting in the far corner away from the book stacks and cleaning up after himself. One day he was peacefully munching on his peanut butter and mayo sandwich when he overheard a boy ecstatically describing the plot of a story by a deceased local author. How refreshing, he had thought, to encounter an adolescent resisting the chains of the internet age. After he had finished licking the peanut butter from his fingers and wiping down his desk, he walked past the budding bibliophile and discovered it was the little goth boy, still regaling Suzie with his literary expertise. George quickly averted his eyes, hoping not to intrude on such an endearing interaction.

George told Mindy about the boy. He couldn't remember his name, so Colleen hollered out to the room, "Does anyone know who the little goth boy is at Coffeeville K through 9?"

Calvin shrugged. "Are you sure there's only one? I saw a whole slew of kids wearing nothing but black on the courthouse lawn the other day."

They were all dismayed.

"Fuck it," Mindy said. "Why don't we just go to the cemetery?"

If you grew up in Coffeeville, the cemetery became a strange vortex for transgressive energy. The teens liked to screw there, and sometimes, to prove their youthful passion, adults would also make the desperate choice of having sex amidst the tombstones. If the cops—there were actually a handful of police officers despite the size of the town—were bored on the weekend, and they often were, they could scan the old cemetery with their flashlight, startling naked flesh. Or sometimes kids snuck out and just told ghost stories. But now the mosquitoes carried the virus, and that fear was much more concrete than the abstract thrills of century-old statues and headstones.

"I'll go," Colleen said. "You should all stay here. It's safer for me to go."

"I'll drive," Kevin offered, his highball in hand.

"Obviously I'm driving," Mindy snapped. "I drove here."

Colleen pulled two cans of bug spray from the cabinet of an entrance table and watched as everyone else doused themselves. Then they all packed into Mindy's van, which she had parked as close to the entrance as possible. George climbed in last, after Kevin, Mindy, and Colleen, and when Kevin looked inquiringly at him, he said, "I know where the popular tombstones are."

They didn't need to drive far. On the way, they passed Mindy and Zach's house with the windows brightly lit, and Colleen pictured him sitting in the living room, waiting for the screen of his phone to glow with news. Moments later, the road dipped and rose again, revealing the edges of the cemetery, made sprawling by centuries and war and yellow fever.

Mindy drove the perimeter of the cemetery as they all peered through the windows, trying to see a hint of flashlight or the silhouettes of the girls.

"I don't see anything," Mindy said, defeated after they had completed a lap. "Where else could they be?"

"The little goth boy likes Larry Piedmont," George said. "You can't see Larry's grave from the road."

"Suzie doesn't even like to read." Colleen was strangely offended that her daughter had taken up such a secret life that she had not only snuck out during a modern plague, but she had also developed an affection for an iconic author after years of refusing to look at any book that her mother had gifted her.

"I'll be right back," Colleen said, hopping out and slamming the door to keep out the bugs.

They all watched her march up the checkered hillside until she disappeared in the shadows of a grove.

"When did she get infected?" Mindy asked.

"Last summer," Kevin said. "No serious issues though. We were lucky. It was like having the summer flu, and then it was gone. Although, it's not really gone, of course . . ." he trailed off.

"It was like that with Zach, right after that party in July, but clearly it just got worse."

Mindy had suspected for a long time. Colleen was a little too eager to visit the house, a little too gracious with the casseroles and offers to help in the initial weeks. And she had seen the way they spoke to each other at school events and parties—that woman, too pretty for fairness, leaning in for each word and Zach, suddenly standing a little taller. When Mindy thought about their disease, she envied it, like it was a sacred bond they'd passed between them.

Zach had confessed. He had sobbed as he told her, his weak tongue mangling each slow word. She resented his broken body then and was ashamed of her resentment—because she wanted to hurt him, but his disease disallowed her that satisfaction. Her care for him became more perfunctory. She scrubbed his body like he was an ailing child, his once taut skin now puffy and loose, hanging away from his atrophied muscles. If she warmed up soup and discovered it was still tepid, she would serve it to him, aware that she had chosen convenience over his optimal satisfaction.

They watched a lot of TV now that his mobility was limited. It was astounding how many shows were about affairs. They would watch the horror unfold on screen, and Mindy would wonder, *Does he feel guilty seeing a reenactment?* One movie embraced the frigid wife stereotype, and the woman—always dressed in pristine shift dresses, hair in a precise bun—apologized to her husband. It was her fault too, she said. She hadn't loved him enough. Mindy felt her face flush watching it. After she had situated Zach in bed and flicked off the lights, she said to the dark room, "That movie was awful."

"Yes," Zach said.

"She didn't deserve that."

"Yes," Zach said. At the peak of his illness, each word took a lot of effort.

"Yes what?"

"Sorry," he said.

He wrote her a letter. They bought him software and equipment that would let him write with eye movements and put his more complex thoughts to paper, where they would be more easily understood. He told her to check the printer, and there it was, three crisp pages, full of apologies and a tenuous explanation. Their life had become routine. He saw each milestone mapped out before them, and he could too clearly see each step as a progression toward death. They never spoke about ideas anymore. They only shared to-do lists, the petty disappointments of their days. Bella was the only thing that kept them going. But, he concluded after so many insults, he wasn't making excuses. He should have confronted this directly. He should have talked to her.

She had ripped the paper into tiny pieces and let it fall like confetti into his lap. She let those pieces stay there for hours. She cried in front of him. She wanted him to see it. "When you get better," she told him, "you'll need to leave." That hurt him. She could see it in his eyes, and against all intention, this reciprocal hurt fostered the tender concern they had lacked for so long.

She began to think of this time as their last year together. *This is our last Fourth of July together*, she thought as they watched Bella light sparklers at the foot of the driveway, the fizzling flames obscured by the low-lying sun. Bella had begged to light more, to push the festivities beyond sunset and draw her name against the dark—a trick they'd done in years past, using Zach's camera set to a slow shutter speed so that each movement branded the image. But Mindy wouldn't allow the risk, and Bella grew bored with the daytime fireworks. Still, Mindy took pictures of Bella in the sunlight, Zach looking on in tired bemusement, to remember that they had been together, that they had at least completed the ritual of celebration. A couple weeks later, Mindy thought, *This is our last time watching Bella open birthday presents as husband and wife*. On the longest day of the year, she watched the morning light stream through the windows and touch Zach's once-dark hair, mussed as always, and thought, *When I see him in the future, when he's well again and only Bella's father, his hair will always be perfectly combed*. How sad, she realized, to never see him in disarray. And then she realized, in counting down the last moment of each category, that she had begun to care again, and to care deeply. The resentment remained, but she also hoped for something real to return.

———

Colleen could hear the mosquitoes swarming her. She had always been susceptible to bug bites with her type O blood. She always thought of herself as unlucky, so it had shocked her that she was resistant to the worst effects of the virus. She hoped she had passed along that luck to her daughter, the budding nihilist.

She found them at the grave, the girls with two boys huddled in front of Larry's tombstone. She had expected some sort of Marilyn Manson getup, black eyeliner and pancake makeup, but the boy next to Suzie wore a simple black tee. He sat cross-legged with a book in his lap, a flashlight trained on the pages. Another boy in flannel sat beside Bella, his arm draped over her shoulders. From a distance, she could hear the boy in black reading. She knew the story. It was about fishermen in a swamp and a mythical catfish. There was nothing goth about it.

When she drew near, Suzie startled first. She screamed, having noticed a shadow, and the boy's flashlight tumbled to the ground. Bella leapt up, ready to bolt.

"Suzie! It's me," Colleen said.

"Mom? What are you doing here?" Suzie clutched her elbows.

"Everyone needs to get to the car, right now." Colleen pointed toward the van, even though she couldn't see it beyond the hill.

Suzie grabbed the boy's hand and gave it a squeeze.

"I'm dead serious. What the hell were you thinking?"

"It's not a big deal, Mom," Suzie said in an all-knowing tone. "Young people don't die from it, unless you're sick already, so it's better to just get it over with. Then I'll be immune like you."

"Where did you get a stupid idea like that?" She turned on the suspected boyfriend. "Did you tell her that?"

"I mean no disrespect, Mrs. Wright. I've done a lot of research—"

Colleen held up her hand to silence him and turned to her daughter. "Are you bit?"

"I hope so." She crossed her arms.

"Get in the car."

The girls and boys looked at each other, deciding.

"Run. Now. Or else."

She swung her arms over her head like she was trying to deter a bear rather than herd teenagers from certain paralysis. The boys ambled after the girls, demonstrating their independence, Colleen thought, by thwarting her with their glacial pace.

As they crested the hill, Bella pointed toward a grove of trees in the middle of the graveyard. "Is that my dad?"

At first Colleen thought it was just the shadow of a tombstone, but then she recognized his hunched silhouette, his chair melting into the lawn. He wasn't moving.

"Don't stop," Colleen said. "I'll take care of him."

Bella hesitated but Colleen shooed her along, physically spun her away from the scene and gave a push. She watched the children, made sure they climbed into the van before she descended the hill. As she got closer, she could see that Zach was asleep, or passed out, his head lolled to the side, accentuating his hollow cheeks. His chair was tilting into the earth. Maybe he was dead. She felt a sharp prickling at the nape of her neck. She had assumed he would recover, that it was just a matter of time.

"Hey," she said, touching his knee, then gripping it to find the warm, living flesh beneath the fabric of his sweatpants.

He startled and jerked his head back before his eyes found her.

"You okay?"

"I'm stuck," he said.

She crouched to discover a cell phone in the grass, next to his wheel, which had sunk into a molehill. She pictured the rodents digging into graves, violating the bodies that still existed like moldering plums below. Only one person in town had died from the virus. He was a great-grandfather, already on dialysis. They said it only killed the very young and the very old. But for most people, would it become a normal rite of passage, to lose control of their body for months or years, relying on family to carry them through to the other side?

"We didn't know you'd be here," she said, placing his phone in the cloth carrier strapped to the arm of his chair. His hand was trembling on his thigh. She wanted to hold it.

"I left right after Mindy," he said. "She didn't want to wait for me, but I couldn't just sit there, doing nothing." He looked up at her, his gaze steadier than she'd expected. "I've spent months looking out the window, watching people come and go. I'd see kids headed this way in the daylight. I didn't think they'd be this stupid, but I thought I could do something. Check to be sure. Do my part." He smacked the back of his hand against the metal arm of his chair. She reached for him, not sure if it was the tremor or some act of angst, until he said, "Stop."

It surprised her, how strong his voice was, not quite steady yet, but getting there.

"You're coming out of it," she said.

"Still can't walk," he said. "I can't even get out of this rut. Look at this. It's a literal rut." He pressed a keypad that triggered the wheels. They spun, kicking up thimbles' worth of red clay, but the chair didn't budge. Zach sighed and added, "Can't even control when I fall asleep. I just nod off. I slept through Bella's violin recital."

Colleen walked over to the base of the nearby trees and gathered up fallen leaves and needles. She packed them into the muddy tracks surrounding Zach's wheels. After three trips of this, when the spongy earth was fully covered, she told him to try again. Even when she helped push, his wheels gripped the leaves and gained purchase only to sputter back into the trap the mole had dug for him.

Colleen saw the van pull up to the curb that was closest to them, a hundred yards away.

"They've come for us," she said.

She sat on her heels next to him, not caring that her knees were soaking in the damp soil. She placed her hand on his knee, on the side the others couldn't see, in the shadow of the trees. The scent of his shampoo drifted to her, along with the unbidden image of Mindy's fingers working their way through his hair.

"I've missed you," she said.

She looked up at him, her chin nearly resting on his knee, so close that she could sense his warmth. His eyes were hooded by the angle of his head against the moonlight. She couldn't see his reaction, but she felt him tense through her hand, a slight shift away from her.

"What we had," he said with the slow rhythm of a man learning to speak again, "it wasn't real."

The rejection came with a flash of shame. She felt like she did as a child when her mother scolded her for eating a bite of her brother's birthday cake before they'd even sung the song. Her lips felt numb.

"It was real to me," she said.

They had rituals, she thought. Who would know their rituals? But even as she thought it, even as she recalled the drives to the blues joint an hour away, the secret Memphis dive bar where they ordered martinis, or the midday meetings at the neighboring town's motel, she realized she could count each ritual on her fingers. Each encounter had been laced with adrenaline, even though Kevin wasn't allowed to be angry, because finally the experience of an affair—beyond the physical and no longer narrowly defined by travel or finite dates, an experience he had taken for granted numerous times—was hers. With a thrill, she had cataloged the differences between the two men—how Zach was quieter, less commanding, less capable of a crafted charm, and therefore seemed like a man incapable of cavalier entitlement—and thought, how wonderful, to know that someone so unlike Kevin could want me and inspire my wanting in turn.

"I love her," he said. "I made a mistake. What you and Kevin have, it's different."

She forced a smile then. It reminded her of something Suzie had learned in school, that the baring of teeth was a sign of aggression. Of course. It was obvious, but she had never thought of it before, not really.

"You're right," she said. "It's different. You couldn't understand, and you've misunderstood me."

She wasn't sure what she meant; she just knew it felt right to flip the script. Maybe he thought she was just like Kevin, but now it was too late. She would rather him think that than know the truth: she'd been swept up by him, or at least by the idea of him. She wanted to tell him that nothing is real in the beginning. You pin your hopes on someone, eventually you disappoint each other, and then you change your hopes. That's when it's real.

"Let's get you out of here." She stood tall and waved at the van, its passengers indiscernible in the night.

————

George and Kevin both sat on the graveyard side of the van with the kids piled on top of each other in the back row. The moon was bright, but the shadows of the trees played tricks, creating movement where there was none.

"What's taking them so long?" Mindy muttered.

Even in the dappled darkness, George could see Colleen kneeling: her shadow lowered, then merged with Zach's.

"She's trying to get the wheel out," he said. Someday he would look back on this and tell himself that he was helping

Mindy, sparing her feelings; really, he just wanted to watch Colleen supplicating herself a bit longer.

When she waved to them, he offered to go to her.

"The bugs must be terrible out there," Mindy said, cautioning him. "What about Jamie?" She turned pointedly to Kevin.

"It's not like Zach can get any sicker," Kevin said. "Colleen's immune. Give her a little more time and she'll figure it out." He stared willfully out the window.

George knew Mindy was right to be concerned, but he had the spray. He wasn't prone to getting bit, and he was sick of the increasingly complicated calculus he was expected to apply to each of his decisions. He could empathize with the girls, choosing to defy the endless rules of self-preservation in order to carve out a moment that was theirs, banned and illogical, sure, but the impulse was true: the way they were supposed to behave didn't make them feel alive, not alive enough anyway.

"I'll be quick," he said, taking care to leap from his seat and shove the door closed.

Colleen met him halfway down the hill. Her eyes were glassy.

"I'm sorry," she said. "You shouldn't be outside like this, but I can't move him by myself."

She tilted her head away from him and ran the back of her hand across her eyes.

He grabbed her arm and couldn't help feeling the thrill of having touched her, skin to skin. "Are you okay?"

"Stop it." She shook him off, but tears ran down her face. "Don't ask me that."

"I was just trying to help."

She stopped crying and glared at him. "I see how you look at me. What do you think is going to happen? Don't you know how pathetic that is?"

"You're imagining things." He felt suddenly sick, thinking that he was so transparent, that maybe even Jamie would know how much his thoughts strayed.

Colleen laughed, one sharp burst. "Oh, yes. I'm imagining everything these days."

He followed her in silence to the top of the hill. He tried to say something to Zach to mask the weirdness of the situation, the weirdness between all of them, but it came out wrong. A terrible joke about being stuck, and Zach gave him a long look of exasperation before saying, "Thank you for risking it." Risking it, risking becoming just like him, George realized.

Colleen lifted one side by the arms of the chair as George held the other. They could move forward only a foot before the wheel would collapse into another stretch of tunnel. In the end, she had to ask Kevin to help as well. They carried Zach away from the compromised earth, back to lower ground, where Mindy was ready to bring him home.

———

When Zach still couldn't speak, he would dream of the easy exchange of words. Even after Mindy forgave him, he would dream of her crying. He would dream that he could suddenly speak again and make her understand, not with the words themselves, but with their urgent tone and his desperate repetition.

Recovery was theoretical. The doctors would say, here are

the numbers, here are the numbers we have so far, because the numbers were new. Each recovery was a statistic in his favor, and the prognosis was nebulous but hopeful. The first case was six years ago in Brazil. They had six years of data for the particular strain that locked him in his body, blocking nerve signals and causing his larynx to swell, rendering him nearly speechless. But now he could speak again.

When she forgave him, when she committed to the process of forgiving him, his dreams shifted to a recurring scene: he finds himself lying in the bed and he feels buried—the quicksand cliché that taps into an ancestral fear at the root of the species, but to put it a new way, he feels like a thousand lead vests have been draped over his body and he could move if only the dentist would peel away the layers.

He is propped up by pillows, and he can see the back of her—the clasp of her bra is missing a hook. The band looks worn and the closure strained so that the fabric is pulling apart, held by a solitary eyelet. He wants to tell her, but his tongue is dry and heavy. She picks up powder. He can see her elbow pivoting as she presses the makeup into her face, but like an eclipse, her body is perfectly positioned between his sight and the mirror. He cannot see her face. She goes through each product on her vanity, applies each cosmetic, but he cannot see her face or say a word.

Each time, when he woke up, he would stare at the ceiling, waiting for her to lean over him, to shift the weight of his head, and when she did, the room would come into focus and he could see her.

Now he could smell the remnants of lavender soap as Mindy

leaned across him to secure his straps in the back of the van. Bella stared at him over the headrest of the last row of seats, her head perched high from sitting in the lap of a boy he'd never met.

"Are you okay?" she asked.

"Daddy's fine," Mindy said.

"I'm okay," he said quietly, but Bella, satisfied, had already turned away.

He could hear Colleen telling Mindy she'd walk home, spare people the room in the packed van. It took a while to get everyone in place, so as they drove by he glimpsed her, walking barefoot along the edge of the road, her dress sandals dangling over her shoulder, held by the hook of her finger. She waved at them and smiled.

———

At her first appointment, laughing, Colleen had said, "I'm long in the tooth," her hand fluttering up to hide her mouth.

Zach had protected her smile, literally. He had measured the gaps between gum and teeth, and when the tissue receded, he made neat little cuts, harvested flesh from the roof of her mouth, and tucked it into the incisions. He made her smile new again.

"No chips, no tough foods, and no kissing for a month," he had told her.

"That's a long time," she had said.

When they first kissed, it was too soon, metallic, but he didn't mind. It was his handiwork, like sipping from your lover's drink. It charmed him that she said "bury" like hurry, and that she would order fried chicken but eat the skin first, flay the cornmeal crust and peel away mouthfuls. A few times, they met in Memphis. There was a bar that was also a Victorian house, each room painted a garish color, plastic chandeliers everywhere, and a suicide note of a former tenant framed and mounted in the stairwell.

"Why did you pick this place?" he had asked her.

"I like all the rooms," she said.

At first, the rooms seemed endless. Acid green, cobalt blue, burgundy and magenta, arsenic gray, deep violet, and dandelion yellow. They visited them all. Each room had a gallery of mirrors and faded photographs. Each room had a worn velvet love seat and an exit marked by an intrusively modern illuminated sign. Someone played piano in the foyer. Tiny speakers mounted beneath the crown molding carried the tune to each cobwebbed corner. The bar offered the facade of difference. At last call, when the lights flickered on, it was just a house with too much paint.

They pretended to be married at the Peabody, or rather, the lady at the front desk assumed and they let her. He had used business as a cover with Mindy. His office was part of a chain of medical offices, so it was easy to claim a regional commitment. When they were lying in bed, letting the cool hotel air evaporate their sweat, he asked Colleen what her story was, and she said, "I told him I was meeting a friend in Memphis."

"That's it?"

"That's all he needs to hear."

"What if he says something? What if Mindy finds out we both were in Memphis tonight?"

"He won't say anything," Colleen had snapped, then placed her hand on his. "Sorry, it's really just not a problem. Trust me."

In the morning, she had begged him to have breakfast with her, to prolong their stay. At first, he had resisted. It would be easier to transition into a smiling lie if he hadn't just been with Colleen. He needed time to transition. But she insisted she was going to eat breakfast with or without him, like it was no big deal when it was obviously a very big deal to her, and he didn't want to be the guy who had the night at the hotel with his mistress and then left her at dawn. Not that Colleen was his mistress. That would be too exceptional and singular for her. The first time they slept together, she had assured him, told him not to worry, that she was discreet. That's when he knew he wasn't her first affair, and it suddenly felt possible that he could try this experience with her because—although the thought wasn't explicit at the time like it was now—he could put what they had back in the box whenever he chose. He realized now that he knew even then, before it started, that he had planned to end it.

At breakfast, she had ordered an egg-white omelet and a mimosa despite it only being Wednesday. She told him a sad high school story about a much older boyfriend who stood her up one day and never talked to her again, then prodded him to share an embarrassing memory of his own.

He had never had his heart broken. His high school relationships were friendships really, and Mindy was his college sweetheart, so he told her about running cross-country, wearing a white uniform and pissing himself during a race. It was a lie, but it made her laugh so hard that he wished it had been the truth.

————

Colleen made Suzie strip down to her underwear and turn in circles as her fingers scanned each inch of flesh. Faint stretch marks peeked out of her bra. She caught herself admiring the glow of her daughter's firm skin even as she searched nervously for signs of a bite. She found a cluster of tiny red bumps on her calf. The quickness of her tears surprised her. She knelt on the bathroom floor, crying.

Suzie touched her shoulder. "It's okay."

All Colleen could do was shake her head.

"I think they're just razor bumps," Suzie said, embarrassed, looking down at her mother.

Suzie let Colleen hug her. There was nothing to be done about it. Colleen sent her to bed like any other night, unsure if their lives had changed.

After the party had ended, after those who were too drunk to drive and too afraid to walk in full darkness with the prowling insects found couches and spare bedrooms and collapsed to wait for the sun, Colleen recalled her words. What did she want Zach to understand that he didn't?

She washed her face before bed, and in the harsh bathroom lighting she could see the blue veins lacing her forehead and cheeks, the sallow shadows of the thinning skin beneath her eyes. She was bound by this skin, held separate by it, but it was pulling away from her, loosening and breaking down.

When Kevin emerged from the shower—he always showered before bed—he kissed her, his thin lips tugging on hers. It had been so long that the taste of him repelled her, strange and alkaline. They had avoided kissing since last summer. They didn't think the risk was high with saliva, but it was still a risk. There could be little cuts from brushing teeth. There could be trace amounts.

She turned away and asked, "What if Suzie was right?"

He kissed her again, on the neck, behind her ear. She watched him in the mirror as he slid his hand over her breast.

"Answer me." She tilted her head away.

"What if she was right about what?"

"About getting bit now. Getting it over with."

"She's not," he said. "They'll find a cure in a year. Even five years. She can take precautions until then."

"But what if they don't?"

"Then they don't."

He clamped his mouth down on hers and pressed her against the wall, pressed himself against her. When he ran his hand up her thigh, she stopped it.

"It's not safe yet," she said.

"I don't care." He kissed her clavicle and slipped her nightgown over her shoulder.

She shrugged her shoulder away from him. "Well, I care."

He blinked at her, wiped his mouth, then lifted his wrist and pointed at a red blemish. "I got bit."

"When?"

"When I was helping your boyfriend in the cemetery."

Colleen knew about his flings. She didn't keep perfect tabs

on him, but she knew. And since the infection, their forced celibacy as a couple had made his liaisons seem ordained, inevitable, and they therefore became bolder, more frequent. Sometimes Kevin would press into her at night and tell her how he couldn't wait to fuck her, and she would murmur something to reciprocate, and she would think how easy it was to perform this desire. As the charade persisted, as they each went through the motions, she felt a polite chasm growing between them. She couldn't believe that he really cared. Their estrangement was set according to a virus-borne timer. She always had thought that it had increased his freedom, but maybe it had granted hers. Freed from the routine of him, she'd begun to feel the anticipation of what might be, like she had as a teenager when she had no clue what the future held, imagining that she could still rupture the barrier that existed between two human minds.

"He's not my boyfriend," she told Kevin then. "He didn't want me."

She could see it in his eyes, the deflating desire. She had deprived him of inflicting his wounds and reclaiming his trophy. There was nothing left to assert; no center remained to resurrect. No love to overthrow, none to return. Not the love she had imagined anyway, an emotion beyond the curiosity of animals.

Now that Kevin might succumb to the virus, she imagined herself in Mindy's shoes. She would perform the role of the dutiful wife and mother. She couldn't ignore how it would look not to. She had never been the person who could start over at the cost of her own security. If reinvention had ever been an option, those years were in the past. No choice could alter the fact: no one else would ever be the father of her child. No one else could ever span the years Kevin had shared with her, remember her young skin glistening on humid nights. In that way, she wanted to be seen—not as a woman crying over a drama she had spun in her mind, an unreciprocated attempt at connection. No, she would bathe him with sponges, feed him vegetables pureed beyond recognition, guide his body into the bed with the help of a neighbor or a state-sponsored caretaker. And when a year or more had passed, if he recovered, would she know him then? Would he know her, really know her, and call her wife in a way that transcended the legal prescription of the term? Would she ever again think, *my husband*, and in turn feel seen in that moment, a lifelong memory in the making, no longer a faded reminder of what used to be?

————

When George got home, he found Jamie asleep on her side. He slid his arms around her belly and tried to stay still, tried to keep his breaths shallow so as not to wake her. The mindful stillness kept him awake. He felt pinpricks along his back and wondered if he was itching, so that then he was itching. He wondered if he had let a mosquito get him in the cemetery. He spent the whole night wondering, eagerly awaiting the sun so Jamie would stir and he could ask her to check the skin he couldn't see. She would groan when the sun filtered through the blinds and struck her face, now round with the pregnancy. He would bring her pomegranate juice. She had been craving it in the mornings. Last month he had complained about the price (each large gulp she took was a dollar), and she had listed the ways he would need to step up to be a good father, like the juice was the red flag tipping her off finally, after all these years together, that he was insufficient.

Maybe he was. He resented how easily his thoughts turned to escape, how often he could imagine with a morbid fixation how the last argument could derail them irreparably.

He would bring her the juice. He wouldn't complain, and after she had finished the last drop, he would ask her to check the skin on his back. Her fingers would graze over him. She would scold him for going outside. Why would you do such a thing? she'd ask. He would swear not to be so reckless. He would do better.

Am I safe? Am I okay? he'd ask. Are you sure?

LANDLINE

Right before the power went out, Eva was Skyping with her boyfriend in Bogotá. He had been unreachable the other night, out late with a new friend, a woman, an artist who made mixed-media collages of pornography—specifically, cutouts of genitalia—layered over ancient Greek and Roman images and Reagan-era political propaganda. She gave him some weed and took him to a concert, then bars until sunrise, and they had really "hit it off, but," he said, "nothing happened." The woman had shellacked his Facebook wall with pictures of them dancing together and cuddly selfies. There was even a kiss emoji on one of them.

"You should maybe just establish some boundaries with her," Eva said.

"You should just trust me," he said. On the pixelated screen, Eva could see his lips pressing into a stubborn slash.

It was the same old fight they always had since the one time he slipped up, only a few months before he left. At the time, they had still lived in Arkansas, where Ben was earning a pittance working an entry-level tech position at a radio station while Eva finished her master's in art history. She had been at a conference. He had been at a local bar. There was a college girl. As he put it when she pressed him, they didn't have sex but they "didn't just make out." He told her he'd freaked himself out about surviving two years apart. He wasn't sure he could do it. She wasn't sure either, but she couldn't tell him that, because then the whole thing would blow up right then and there, and she at least wanted to try. Perhaps she clung too much to memories of the two of them together that burned like lens flares in the photo album of her mind. She often thought about how it touched her that her partner would know her when she was young and girlish and serve as witness to her transition into her present womanly self. That was a form of knowing that could not be replicated. Perhaps it was sunk cost fallacy—she had invested so much in knowing him that the resultant emotional attachment was obscuring a real cost-benefit analysis. She acknowledged this on some level, but she also wondered if emotional attachments were the overriding benefit regardless of any pro–con list she could tally.

"Can you at least maintain the semblance of monogamy on the internet?" she said. "That seems manageable."

"That's not fair," he said. "You're being unreasonable."

At the exact same moment that she clicked on her mouse with the intention of closing out the Skype window and thereby disappearing her boyfriend's unruffled expression, the world went dark. The sudden silence was alarming. The computer's fan ceased its incessant whirring. The air-conditioning rumbled, then released a final gasp. The refrigerator and icemaker stopped buzzing and knocking. Eva's night vision was notoriously ineffective, so at first it seemed the world had descended into a cavernous darkness, but her eyes strained and adjusted until she could make out the cool glimmer of moonlight sifting through the narrow windows. Somewhere, a dog barked. Others soon joined him. Eva thought that maybe the dogs—

conditioned to hear the silence of nature as unnatural—were trying to resurrect the noise of so many machines.

She found her cell phone in the kitchen and checked the time. It was only 1:00. The house, a small duplex, gave the slight tremor it always did when her neighbor slammed the front door. Then the doorbell rang.

Eva smoothed her duckling-print shirt—the one she wore because Ben thought it was cute—and wiped at her eyes. Upon opening the door, she was blinded by an industrial flashlight.

She turned away. "Ralph?"

"Sorry about that." He switched off the light.

After a moment of mottled blindness, she could see Ralph standing in his bright blue TSA shirt, the glint of a badge in the darkness.

"This isn't a normal power outage," he said.

"It's not?"

He leaned into the doorframe. "This is a real event." He looked behind him at the empty cul-de-sac. A few neighbors stood on their patios or wandered in their yards, ghostlike in pale nightwear.

"What do you mean, a real event?"

"Can I come in?"

He strolled past her, guided by the wide beam of his flashlight, and seated himself on the couch.

Ralph often invaded her space. She'd be lounging in her hammock on the patio when he'd appear above the low cinderblock fence separating their property and invite himself over. This usually resulted in an hour of him chain-smoking and lamenting his recent divorce while she served multiple cups of coffee and politely nodded, uttering variations of, "How terrible."

"The power is out as far as I can see," he said.

"How far is that?" She crossed her arms and stared down at him.

"If it's what I think it is, this could be the whole region, the whole coast even," he said. Then, in a fervent tone, "It's a solar storm. Electromagnetic radiation wreaking havoc on all our technology."

Eva had doubts about Ralph. He flirted with her in ways that were just ambiguous enough to make it impossible for her to acknowledge it or shut it down. When he found out she had a boyfriend in the Peace Corps, he made a few derisive jokes about Jimmy Carter and then segued into his experience as a bomb squad guy in the Marines. Then he barely looked at her for a couple months. She would see his head above their patio partition, bobbing over his grill, but for a while he would not even share the briefest hello.

But then her air-conditioning unit broke on a day of record heat, and Ralph insisted that she stay with him. During the day, she had monopolized his saggy black leather couch, working on her laptop and basking in the cool mechanical breeze. In the evening, the heat dissipated a bit. When she packed up her belongings, Ralph asked her why she was leaving. He insisted it was still too hot, but she couldn't imagine sleeping in his space. His house was spare, minimally furnished, impeccably clean, without a television or any books in the living room. Perhaps he was an ascetic or a transient, but the austerity felt unnatural to her.

"Or maybe this is just a normal outage," she said. It had been over a hundred degrees for days.

Ralph turned off his flashlight and leaned back so that his eyes were faint glimmers in the moonlit interior. "Serious flares were spotted days ago, and they've already detected EM radiation."

"Ralph, I've had a rough night." Eva could feel the crust of dried tears and mascara congealing her lashes. The level of abnormalcy was compounding the surreal feeling that her four-year relationship might be over.

"Why are you here?" she asked.

"Check your cell phone," he said. "I bet you don't have service."

She pulled her phone out of her pocket and saw the missing bars.

"Can't a normal outage do that?" She suddenly realized how little she knew about how her cell phone worked. She thought about looking it up on the internet, then quickly realized the futility.

Ralph shook his head. "Unlikely. The FCC requires most towers to have backup power."

She swiped to her favorite contacts screen. She skipped Ben. She didn't want to try him while Ralph was there, at least not after their last conversation. And she scrolled past her mother. That would result in an interrogation about the outage that could lead to the unintentional revealing of personal information. She settled on her college friend Jane. At 1:00 in the morning, Jane was probably at a bar in L.A.

The call failed. She tried a few more times while Ralph

watched her, his posture expansive, hands dangling over the arms of the couch. No call would go through.

"Mark might have a landline," Ralph said. "And we can see the Strip from his sundeck. But you should be the one who asks. He'll say yes to you."

"Say yes in a creepy way?"

"He's annoyed with me." Ralph fiddled with the lens of his flashlight, half unscrewing, then rescrewing the concave plastic.

"Don't you know anyone other than Mark we can ask?" Ralph was the only person in their small, gated community that she saw with any regularity, and that was only because they shared a wall. She knew who Mark was because he had a flat-screen TV installed in his garage with a couple of uphol-stered recliners. He'd blare game shows or conservative news pundits with his garage door open while he threw back beers. Sometimes a neighbor would march over to his driveway and ask him to turn it down. And sometimes, while sipping tea or wine and absorbing the pastel desert sunsets, Eva would watch from her stoop, mildly entertained by the predictable conflict. But there were also times when she returned from walking the loop, the road that skirted the containment wall of their neigh-borhood, that she could feel Mark's eyes on her. She'd glance over, and he'd be sipping a beer, making eye contact without a nod or wave her direction.

Despite this, she wanted to see the lights of the Strip glaring in the distance. Then she'd know Ralph was on one of his cat-astrophizing kicks.

"Only if you go in with me." She surprised herself, placing trust in Ralph. He was weird, but she realized then that she didn't think he'd ever do anything.

Eva found a battery-operated lantern in her garage. Ben had bought it for a camping trip the summer before he left. They had found a wide clearing and peeled back the outermost layer of the tent so that a fine mesh separated them from the outside. They shared a double sleeping bag and curled up to stare at the stars. At twilight, she'd woken with a hint of hangover and had quietly unzipped the tent and tiptoed clumsily to a narrow passage between two nearby rock formations to take a piss. Ben snuck up on her, scandalizing her as she still had her shorts around her ankles. When she was done, she was embarrassed, but he grabbed her and pressed her against the blood-red boulder. She felt animal then. Was it just the unpredictability of him? Of that moment? In a desperate way, she welcomed the power outage. Didn't it produce the same effect?

She switched on the lantern, comforted by its warm glow. She swung it like a purse from a loose strap as she and Ralph walked across the cul-de-sac. On the way, Ralph filled her in on facts about solar storms. Did she know that solar flares had destroyed transformers? Or that it could take months to replace them? Or that in the worst solar storm in history, telegraph machines could spark and set paper on fire without even being connected to an electrical source? Eva imagined her computer igniting, suddenly ablaze.

"Can that happen to computers?" she asked.

"I don't know," Ralph said. He walked the rest of the way in silence. The stars were brighter. She could see more of them than usual. The moon was half-full and waning.

Mark's house looked exactly like Eva's and Ralph's houses—faux stucco and clay tiles—except that it was two stories and had an incongruous wooden deck appended to the roof. It was an eyesore, and every so often there was an HOA vote, but Mark had grandfathered it in as the first resident of the community and refused to take it down. On sunny days, Eva could see him up there, a plump silhouette in a lawn chair with metallic reflectors folded across his stomach to bounce the light onto his face.

Ralph gestured to the door. "He should see you first."

Eva hesitated.

"Don't worry. I have a taser." Ralph patted his hip holster and winked.

It took a couple tries, but after the third set of knocks, Eva could hear footsteps, then violent coughing.

Mark, bald with white, whiskery stubble, opened the door, dragging the yellowed sleeve of his mostly white bathrobe across his mouth. "Goddamn lights aren't working." He finally looked at Eva. "Do you have any idea what time it is?"

Eva gestured to Ralph, behind her. "We need your help."

Mark eyed her. "You're his neighbor. The one with the guy in Mexico?"

"Colombia." She gave Ralph a look of incredulity.

It was odd to think that her neighbors, whom she barely spoke to, talked about her.

"I think we're having a really bad solar storm," Ralph said. "We wanted to see if the power is out on the Strip."

"Oh, Christ," Mark said, "not this shit again."

Eva felt relief. Ralph probably was just paranoid. She wanted to go to bed and wake up to a world of alarm clocks and scrambled eggs and engage in reconciliation messages on social media with Ben. Or maybe she needed to fight with Ben more and see how that shook out. Even if they broke up, she'd rather have the closure of seeing his face as they terminated their relationship than be stuck in unknowing limbo because a solar flare had cast Nevada indefinitely into the dark ages.

"It's probably no big deal," Eva said, "but what's the harm in looking?"

"Go to bed, Ralph. The lights will come back soon."

"You don't know that."

"I'd still like to have a good sleep either way."

Ralph edged closer to Eva and Mark. "If it's anything like Carrington was, this could be a mini-apocalypse."

"Mini?" Eva couldn't resist smiling.

"Like a temporary apocalypse."

Eva laughed.

"You won't be laughing when you can't access your bank or use your cards. No gas. Traffic lights shut down. Car crashes. Hospitals will run out of generator power. Or maybe the generators aren't working right either. It's not just a power outage. The electromagnetic radiation can cause surges, sparks, fires. Machines going on and off at random, like a haunting. Maybe the city burns down with us in it."

"Okay, fine," Mark said. "If it will shut this guy up." He nodded toward Ralph, then swung the door wide.

As they walked past the kitchen, Eva noticed a profound mustiness that was rare in the desert. It reminded her of how her crawl space in Arkansas had smelled—dank and toxic. She could feel the peeled corners of linoleum crunching beneath her shoes.

They felt their way up a narrow carpeted staircase at the

end of the hall. At the top, Mark led them into a room with skylights. In the faint moonlight, Eva could make out a plastic chair and card table covered in piles of papers. Mark unlatched a sliding door and stepped onto a small, dark, wooden balcony. He had constructed a wooden ladder that ascended to the roof and his splintered sundeck, affixed to the house by a few rugged beams.

"You guys go ahead," Eva said, staring up at the shoddy rungs of the ladder. "I'll wait here."

"It's just a few steps," Ralph said.

Eva shook her head. Once, on a hiking trip with Ben in New Mexico, she had climbed a tall ladder embedded in the side of a cliff in order to see a kiva deep in a recessed pocket of the mountainside. Halfway up, she had made the mistake of looking down. A line of people, tiny specks below her, were waiting to ascend. The sudden comprehension of the distance, of the potential severity of a fall, had sent her into a panic attack. She had hyperventilated and hugged the ladder until Ben convinced her to think of the ladder as a vehicle for mindless, mechanical steps, like a treadmill. He counted with her, reminding her to breathe, only moving if she moved, stopping if she stopped. The next day, she couldn't walk without limping. The climb had been easy. What had overstretched her muscles, she thought, were those moments she had gripped the ladder, each limb straining to resist the fall.

Ralph and Mark were on the deck only a minute before Ralph returned to the ladder and extended his hand.

"You should see this," he said. His excitement worried her. She stared at his hand, unsure.

"I'll help you up," he said. "Just eight steps."

She handed up her lantern. "I'll need you to count with me."

Ralph echoed each number and hauled her up as soon as she touched the top.

There was so much darkness. There wasn't the ruddy halo of light pollution that usually embraced the city at night. A hot wind whipped across the deck.

"The Strip is that way." Mark pointed west.

She could see the outline of the mountains, blacker than the abysmal blue of the sky beyond. The valley was a bowl of dark oblivion. Her eyes strained to make sense of it. Normally, the garish lights of the casinos anchored her spatial understanding of the city. She always complained about the wasteful beam that shot out of the top of the Luxor pyramid, but she also came to view it as a guide and center. You could see it from anywhere in the city. You could see it driving in from the surrounding desert, an audacious claim on the uninhabitable land.

But it wasn't all darkness. Now she noticed fires in the distance, perhaps in Summerlin. They seemed small, but she realized she had no sense of scale.

"Holy shit," Eva said.

"I'll be damned," Mark said.

Some headlights crawled along the invisible grid of unlit streets in the foothills. She could hear the siren of an ambulance passing nearby, but from Mark's roof, she couldn't see the roads just beyond the perimeter wall.

"This could be happening in L.A. too. Maybe even as far as San Francisco," Ralph said. "EM radiation is unpredictable."

He gestured at the specks of fires at the base of the faraway mountains.

"It could still just be a normal power outage." Eva sat down on the rough wood and leaned her head against a post.

She wondered how this would affect the completion of her doctoral degree. What if the university shut down, delaying her graduation by a semester, or more? Her entire timeline would be messed up. She was supposed to graduate before Ben got back so that they could both move to wherever he landed a job, something related to journalism, and she would try to find a job there too. At least, that *had* been the plan. Would Ben know what was happening?

"Do you have a landline?" she asked.

Mark shook his head. "Just got rid of it last year. My ex convinced me I didn't need it any longer." He laughed, quick and bitter.

"I need to find a landline."

Ralph turned to Mark. "What about Joe?"

"Nah, he doesn't even have cable."

Ralph nodded. "Best bet is probably going to Thai Town or somewhere in that strip mall."

"They won't be open," Eva said.

"They'll be open soon enough." Mark shrugged and stepped toward the ladder. "Power might be on by then."

"I doubt it. If it's anything like the Carrington Event—"

Mark looked at Eva. "He's been talking about this for months."

"You don't know that's what's going on," Eva said.

"I follow reports on solar activity. There was a large solar blast this morning. The timing makes sense."

This was not that surprising coming from Ralph. In the evenings, when he would invite himself over to her patio, he would often talk about his work as an EOD tech in Afghanistan and Iraq. He would describe a preternatural feeling, like ringing in the ears but more like a tensing in his mind, that he would experience just before finding an explosive. He believed this was true, that humans could have a sense about these things. But Ralph had dedicated himself to an obsessive study of explosives and prior incidents in the region, and Eva suspected this *feeling* of his was nothing more than the processing of his vast knowledge and awareness in the back of his mind. She began to worry that it was the same with this, that maybe he was right.

Mark shook his head and let himself down the ladder, disappearing below the roof.

"Why didn't you warn anyone?" Eva asked.

"Because I still had no idea that the radiation would travel here."

She felt herself crying in that way one does when it's entirely involuntary. Her breathing didn't change. She wasn't gasping or sobbing or making any sound at all. Tears just flowed.

Ralph looked confused. He crouched beside her and gripped her shoulder, giving a reassuring squeeze. "It's going to be okay," he said. "Power will come back on eventually. And we'll figure it out in the meantime."

Eva turned her head, trying not to smile. Laughter rose in her until she couldn't stop shaking. Ralph wrapped his arms around her in a supportive hug. When he started making soft hush sounds and stroking her hair, she pulled away and stood up.

"I'm not crying, I'm laughing."

"Okay," Ralph said, slow and elongated. "You looked upset."

"You seem a little too happy to share all this news. And so what if the power comes back on in a month? That's still pretty fucking terrible."

"I'm not happy," Ralph said. "It's just that I can be calm for this type of thing. I can handle this type of problem."

Ralph pulled out a cigarette and lit up. He inhaled deeply and leaned back, looking up at the sky. "Maybe we'll see an aurora."

Eva started to feel annoyed again but then Ralph winked at her.

"Can I have one?"

"You smoke?"

"I used to, in college, but I quit."

She usually complained to Ben on their video dates about Ralph's smoking. On cool nights, she liked to use her window screen, but she couldn't after Ralph got home from the airport. In the evenings when he was home, he would chain-smoke on his patio for hours, sipping Dr Pepper. Dozens of Dr Pepper cans overflowed his recycling bin each week. When the weather was nice, she would try to read outside, but then she would smell his cheap Pall Malls and Ralph would see her and come over, or just talk over the divider, sometimes for hours. He usually talked about his ex-wife. He missed his stepdaughter and the dog they shared. This kept him tethered to his ex, and he still visited them from time to time, helping around the house. He'd unload everything in these conversations, and although she felt bad for him, she viewed it as weakness, to share so much with someone about whom you knew so little. The more he told her, the less she felt compelled to share her own anxieties, especially regarding her relationship. Ben was just some long-distance boyfriend that Ralph had never met. And for Ben, Ralph was the annoying TSA neighbor who interrupted her reading and made her house stink.

Ralph handed her a cigarette and lit it for her. He cupped one hand around the flame as she inhaled, shielding out the breeze. The gesture struck her as intimate and protective.

They both leaned back, shoulder to shoulder.

"You had a fight," Ralph said.

"Excuse me?"

"Was it your boyfriend? It's not like I'm trying to hear you. But our walls are thin and you sounded upset. I could hear you right before the power went out."

She felt the blood rushing to her face. "What did you hear?"

"He's pissing you off."

"It's hard."

She could feel him staring at her, waiting for more, but she just kept smoking.

"At least I can head over to Katie's to make sure everyone is okay," Ralph said. "If this thing is real, what will you do?"

"Katie isn't your wife anymore."

Ralph looked away. "I know."

"It's not the same thing at all."

"Sure." He took another slow puff on his cigarette. "It's still hard."

Mark emerged on the deck, shoving a small cooler across the floorboards. He wiped the sweat off his face with the sleeve of his frayed bathrobe.

"Help yourselves." He pulled a frosty bottle of beer out and uncapped it.

"Now?" Ralph said.

"Why not now? They'll get warm." Mark nudged the cooler toward Ralph and Eva.

Then Ralph sifted through the contents, digging in the ice and reading the labels.

"No soda?"

"There's Newcastle in there."

"Mark."

"Jesus, Ralph. You think you're an alcoholic but you're not. You're just a goddamn killjoy."

Eva thought about Ralph's soda habit. She couldn't remember when that started.

Ralph stood up and made for the ladder.

"You're leaving?" she asked.

"Oh come on, Ralph. I'm just messing around," Mark said. "I'll get you a water."

"I'm going to find a way to call out and see how far this thing goes."

"I'm coming with you," Eva said.

Mark followed them out of the house and insisted on joining them. "I want to pick up some supplies," he said.

"I thought you wanted to sleep," Ralph said.

"I haven't seen a citywide blackout since the summer of '69 in New York. And you know what really helped pass the time? You know what kept most people on an even keel? A few beers on the stoop."

"Do what you want, Mark."

They walked across the street and climbed into Ralph's truck. Eva slid into the narrow backseat. They only made it as far as the neighborhood exit, where the large gate failed to open. They all piled out of the truck and tried to push it, but the rusted, heavy metal wouldn't budge.

"Shouldn't there be a manual override?"

"Yes," Ralph said. "There should be."

"Can't you just ram it?" Mark asked.

"My truck is government property. If you want to destroy your own car, be my guest."

Mark did not. They had to walk. Eva unlocked the pedestrian exit, and they left the truck parked on the curb, less than a quarter mile from Ralph's driveway.

As they walked along the pocked, seldom-used sidewalk, Eva noticed Mark had a hitch in his gait, like he had a bad hip. He was several inches shorter than Ralph. He was short and kept looking up at Ralph as he interrogated his solar flare theory.

"So let's say this is the real deal. What's your next move?"

"Depends how widespread it is," Ralph said.

"But what if it's the whole coast?" Mark asked, like it was a game, like everything was a distant hypothetical.

"I'll probably get supplies and pack up my truck, check on Katie and Jill, and head out. Get back to wherever there's still power."

"And just leave your place to looters?"

"There's nothing here worth the risk of staying," Ralph said.

Without any lights, the streets looked foreign. The high walls of lackluster gated communities, neighborhoods at the cusp of lower middle class, corralled them into avenues of nothing but road, lampposts, and the occasional bus shed. A car drove by at ten miles per hour, hesitated at the intersection, then crawled away on a dark residential road.

They walked three blocks. When they reached the strip mall parking lot, the first business they saw was a Jeanie's Jackpot, a video poker and "spirits" lounge for aging women who wanted a down-home aesthetic. It scared away the men and made women feel safer about getting their buzz on and gambling alone in the wee hours.

A sixty-year-old woman was sitting on the curb in a purple jumpsuit and gold flats, staring at her cell phone. The glow of the screen cast her face blue and made her makeup look purplish and gothic.

Eva called out to her, "Is Jeanie's open?"

The woman looked up. "Mark?"

"Oh hey, Michelle."

"You two know each other?" Eva said.

"Yeah," she said. "He's a real piece of work, aren't you, Mark?"

"That was months ago."

"You never showed."

"I slept through my alarm. I've told you a dozen times."

"Who needs an alarm at five in the afternoon?" She took a sip from a can of beer and set it back down on the asphalt.

"I'm sorry, okay?" Mark carefully lowered himself beside her. "You have another one of those?"

Michelle swatted his arm. "You stand me up and then you want my beer?" She added, "Power's out."

"Power's out everywhere," Ralph said. He lit a cigarette and offered Michelle one.

Michelle took a puff, then hit a button on her phone. She shook her head. "Damn phone isn't working."

"My cell isn't working either," Eva said. "Do you have a land-line we could use?"

Michelle scoped Eva out as she smoked. "You guys all know each other?"

Eva felt embarrassed. "We're neighbors. Mark and I just met."

Michelle nodded. "Door's unlocked. About an hour ago, the machines started going nuts. Couldn't make sense of it. Power was out but then the John Wayne slots started flashing and spinning numbers. On and off, a few times. My nerves couldn't take it, so I've been out here waiting for the power to come back on."

Eva thanked her and followed Ralph inside. Dozens of video poker and slot machines filled the space in clusters, interspersed among tables covered in checkered cloths. Even in the darkness, with her lantern, Eva could make out the tendrils of fake ivy dangling from ceramic pots on top of the slot machines.

Ralph held the phone to his ear for a moment, but instead of dialing, he handed the receiver to Eva.

"You call first," she said. "I want to know what this is before I call anyway."

Ralph shook his head. "Listen."

Then she heard the silence, the lack of dial tone.

"I'm sorry," he said. "I was wrong. The flare must have fried the copper."

They stared at each other for a moment, as if waiting to see who would have the strongest reaction. The news still didn't feel real. She could gather supplies. Wait for the solar storm to ebb away, using her camping lantern and candles at night, staying in the shade all day, hoping record heat wouldn't smother the valley. If it lasted weeks, she would probably leave the city too. She only had a quarter tank of gas. She couldn't buy more. Credit cards and banks were down. And she would have to drive through hours of desert to get to the next city. She hated to admit it, but she wouldn't feel safe in the house without Ralph on the other side of the wall. Sometimes, when she was trying to fall asleep and thinking too much about Ben—who was probably not doing the same, at least not to the same degree of unwanted distraction—she would feel the tremor of Ralph's door, and then, if she focused, the sounds of late-night foraging in his kitchen and the muted voices of the television. In these moments, she returned to the present and welcome weight of impending sleep and she thought, *I'm not alone in this house, not really*. Maybe loneliness was just the illusion we create when we believe we need one particular person above all possible others.

A light flashed from a nearby machine, and John Wayne's voice drawled, distorted and slow, "What is it now, pilgrim...?"

Eva dropped the phone and leaned into Ralph. They looked over in time to see a blur of icons scrolling through the display. Then the machine went dark and silent.

"Can they catch fire?" she asked.

"I doubt it," he said, placing the phone on its cradle. "But what do I know?"

"Is there no other way for me to reach him?"

"I'm sorry."

"It probably doesn't matter. What could I say anyway? That everything's fine? I'll be okay? Talk in six months, maybe?"

"It *will* be okay. Eventually."

She put her hand over Ralph's and gave it a quick squeeze of acknowledgment. "Where to now?"

"Back home. At least until we figure out the next step."

"I'm not staying here alone," she said. "In the city, I mean."

The lantern barely lit their faces. She wondered if her eyes looked glassy. She could cry, but she wanted to skip that part.

"Of course not," he said. "We just need to go where the lights are still on."

They were startled by Mark knocking on the storefront window. He motioned for them to come outside. Michelle was aiming a disposable camera at the sky.

When Ralph and Eva joined them on the sidewalk, they looked up and saw the aurora. Pink strands and impossible green striations sifted through the atmosphere, traces of solar wind reaching and bending across the sky. The quiet arcs of color hid the stars.

THE WAY THEY SAW HER

In the beginning, the messages seemed harmless to Cleo. Although there was a rash of random first-name Twitter accounts, each followed by a string of numbers—Bob349803592, Cindy39840392, Jake3899—she suspected they belonged to the same person. At first each would simply say hello. When she asked who they were, they would ask how she was doing or what the weather was like or if she'd had a good day. She would ask again, "*Who are you?*" and then they would delete their account.

After a couple weeks of these anonymous greetings, she figured she was being harassed by bots, although she couldn't say why she would be a target. The eleventh time it happened, she asked Brian1991 who he was, and he wrote, "*You should know*," then wiped his account. That was the first time she worried in any serious way. She was forced to wonder, why should she know this anonymous person? What had she done to merit the cryptic attention?

While stuck in traffic on the 10—a time she usually reserved for listening to motivational podcasts to calm her new-job anxiety—she made a list of anyone she'd met or interacted with recently. After two months in L.A., the only people who could connect her name with a face were her boss and coworkers at the studio. Actually, only one coworker could probably connect her full name with her face, but Jill seemed like the type who made a big display of knowing everyone. A performative people person. It was possible, Cleo supposed, that her property manager might recognize her on the street, but he lived in Silver Lake and struck a seriously disinterested vibe when she proudly mentioned where she worked.

Cleo was an only child, a latchkey kid, and as such, she had always desperately courted the approval of her peers, even as she felt like a specimen emerging from experimental isolation. On the rare occasions when a potential friend invited her to hang out at their home, she observed each mundane interaction with fascination. She loved watching it all—the way the parents fought, the battle for the brother's gaming device, the cacophonous sibling debate over dinner. Even when friendships evaded her, she was not one to accumulate nemeses. Once, a neighbor girl had told her it was unfair that she had the limited edition Secretariat from that year's Breyer horse catalog, since that had always been her favorite Triple Crown winner, so Cleo had wrapped the statuette in the tissue paper left over from the shoes her mother had bought her for the first day of school and then deposited the gift on her neighbor's front steps with a card that began, "Dear Friend." The more she remembered, the less she could draw a connection worthy of a vendetta. She even began to wonder if the messenger's insistence that she *should* know them was benign, maybe even well-intentioned. Perhaps this use of *should* was congenial.

———

When Dano30506 messaged Cleo about her favorite dress, the summery one with eyelets, she had just finished assembling her wrought iron bed frame in her new apartment—a studio in an unfinished loft building. There were still tarps on the north-facing windows of the complex. She usually parked her beat-up silver compact car a few blocks away—anything closer was overridden by dumpsters, construction permits, or cars that belonged to people with kinder schedules. At night, when she neared her building, a converted perfume warehouse, the plastic sheeting would flap against the breeze, stiff and milky. They were behind schedule, her property manager said, but don't worry. Utilities would be covered until the common areas were completed. Someday there would be a lounge with billiards, vending machines, and a coworking station. It was hard to picture. Now that space was a cavernous swath of mottled concrete and support beams. A perfect setting for a zombie film.

When she came home from a long day of fielding her boss's calls in the PR department, she hurried past the emptiness and the construction to her tiny studio with its white walls and glossy white concrete floors and exposed ductwork. It was faux fancy with cheap appliances and countertops made from repurposed black floor tiles, but she liked the sterility—a blank slate for her inchoate life—although the floor-to-ceiling windows and the noisy HVAC system disturbed her, provoking her brain to matrix meaning onto passing shadows and white noise. She remembered how she'd always see faces in the floral wallpaper of her childhood bedroom in Ohio. She would sleep steeped in sweat, her face burrowed beneath the flannel sheets because she didn't want to imagine anyone was watching her.

"*I like that picture of you in the yellow dress.*"

If you searched her name in quotation marks, she wore the

dress in the second image result, directly after her LinkedIn profile image. A couple years ago, when her family friend Kayla had gotten married, she'd taken snapshots with various friends and included them on a public blog with their names in the captions. The years she and Kayla had known each other had been spawned by their fathers' work relationship. Those evenings, the parents drank wine and whiskey in the living room and ordered the girls to play, and Cleo had nervously obliged, feeling a deep admiration for the leggy girl who stood three inches taller than her. They pretended to cook with a plastic toy kitchen and played games like Uno and Operation— sometimes Cleo would touch the tweezers to the metal edge of a body cavity and light up the cartoonish man's red nose just to see Kayla gleefully clap her hands. When Cleo's father found a different job with a different company, the playdates ended, even though Kayla lived just down the street. At school, she was polite, but she didn't seek Cleo out at recess, and Cleo didn't have the nerve to ask why. In retrospect, Cleo's father was the intended wedding guest, probably added to the list by Kayla's father, and Cleo was a necessary extension of that invitation. But in the wedding photo, Cleo looked like a close friend of Kayla's, arms encircling each other's waists, even though they now only spoke briefly every other year, usually by Facebook messenger. The image was more flattering than any selfie or snapshot that Cleo had ever taken. It didn't even look like her. Her chin was strong and raised. She looked bold and assertive. After years of tending toward obsequiousness, this photo's persona was the one she still struggled to cultivate in her day-to-day life. Who cares, she finally decided, if the Twit-

ter pest found a perfectly respectable photo of her that any idiot could find in two seconds?

The brain likes to discern patterns when there aren't any.
Evolution had rewarded the quick recognition of allies and
potential threats, faces and approaching footsteps. When the
AC kept clicking and knocking around, she recalled the persistent messages and imagined she heard someone walking in
her room. Her pulse quickened, picturing someone pausing to
leer over her bed. She recalled a Henry Fuseli painting she'd
seen in a textbook in high school where a demonic spirit sits
on the torso of a woman lying supine, her arms flung over her
head and dangling from her chaise. The demon scowls directly
at the viewer as if to say, *you're next*, and, perhaps a greater odd-
ity, a white-eyed black horse observes from the shadows. Now,
in her sterile studio, she imagined the demon on her chest, and
just like her childhood self, she played dead, but this time, she
enacted a digital death. She deactivated her Twitter account.

As she drifted to sleep that night, she thought about
Dan030506 (or whatever name they would use for resurrection) trying to pull up her Twitter profile and instead finding
the words, *This account does not exist*. She reassured herself that
this would be the end of it. She grew smug, lying on top of her
sheets, her fan stirring the air so that she could feel each pulse
of coolness on her exposed skin.

———

The next day she sat at her desk, filing expenses for her boss—
receipts for drinks and dinners with celebrity clients. It gave
her a simultaneous thrill of importance and wave of resent-

ment to see the A-list names and the cost of their outings. No one covered her drinks, professional or otherwise. She'd never attracted that kind of attention. A montage cascaded in her mind's eye—attending each homecoming with friends as friends, being rejected by her calculus partner when she asked him to prom, and numerous flashes of men approaching her at bars and asking her to introduce them to her apparently more attractive acquaintances. She decided Bob/Cindy/Dan must be a bot after all. Or maybe some teenager getting off on pranking strangers without a lived sense of what it meant to be truly alone in a city, left to wonder who would find your body after reading stories where only the stench led neighbors to find the corpse, its face eaten by a starved and ruthless pet. That old cliché was real.

Of course, she didn't have any pets. She didn't even have any neighbors. Not next door anyway. So far, only one other unit was occupied on her floor, three doors down, and she hadn't met the guy; she'd seen him at a distance, collecting mail in the front entryway. Each time she'd spotted him, he'd worn nice blazers with torn jeans, and the scent of weed wafted from his apartment each night. Three doors down, he might never smell the decay.

Once she'd bought a box of frozen coconut-crusted shrimp as a treat. Nearly all her food came frozen from a bag or a box. She heated the shrimp in the oven, poured herself a glass of wine, and sat by the window, alternating bites and sips. On the street below, she noticed an old man with a knife scraping at the sidewalk like he was shucking stale bubblegum, picking up chips of something and inspecting each piece before tossing it

aside or depositing it carefully into a canvas tote bag. She was so
enthralled, so curious, that she ate a shrimp whole and felt it sit
dumbly on the back of her throat, fully blocking her airway. *So
this is what choking is like*, she'd thought. She had recalled that
one couldn't cough when choking, and now she knew it to be
true. Curiosity turned to panic. She considered running down
the hallway and banging on the neighbor's door, but what if
he wasn't even there? She had read that one could perform the
Heimlich maneuver on one's self using the back of a chair, but
she had only tiny, backless bar stools with a two-top to maxi-
mize the space of her tiny studio. She began pounding on her
own diaphragm. She was just about to dial 911, even though she
knew she wouldn't be able to say a word to the operator, when
the coconut breading finally grew soggy enough to deglove the
shrimp and ease the obstruction another inch or two down her
throat, allowing enough air to pass so she could cough. After-
ward, she had finished her wine in three long gulps and then
laughed to herself, thinking of her parents pausing their current network TV show, probably a crime procedural, and re-
ceiving the news that their daughter had died so pathetically.

———

The bosses left for lunch and the office grew quiet. The other
assistants already knew each other and liked to eat at the cafeteria together. She was still new and unknown, so she ate at
her desk, spreading out the contents of a protein pack from the
coffee shop that faced the main gate of the lot. You had to walk
past the security booth to get back in. Normally she hated the
inconvenience of scanning her card to go back inside, but to-

day she liked the protective exclusivity. Surely the studio ran a background check on anyone with a pass. She was nibbling carefully on an overcooked egg when she got the email from Alex1995@gmail.com. Subject line: *Hey Cleo, remember me?*

She pushed her food aside. Her skin tingled with heightened awareness, not unlike the sensation of embarrassment, but she knew logically that any shame was misplaced. Regardless, the effect was the same. She wanted to hide, to remain unseen, even as she found herself clicking on the message, needing to know its contents.

I've been thinking about the way your left lid hangs lower than your right. There's something about it. Makes your smile seem more real. Do you mean it, when you smile?

Nauseated, Cleo stared at the smear of peanut butter and crumbled egg yolk that still sat in her cardboard lunch tray. She heard laughter and hurried to minimize the screen before the first wave of lunch goers rushed back into the open cubicles. Her neighbor Jill scooted in her roller chair toward the shared table that divided their workspace and placed a croissant next to Cleo's keyboard. Cleo was sure that men would ask her for Jill's number. She wore silk blouses with bold prints and knew how to wear fuchsia blush without looking like a clown.

"They gave me an extra pain au chocolat at the pastry cart," Jill said.

Jill was the only coworker who had tried to make small chat with Cleo. She was Miss Congeniality, always retweeting her coworkers' accomplishments with extra emojis or surprisingly perfect GIFs. Whenever Cleo felt jealous about a Twitter post declaring a career milestone or major life achievement—a promotion, a marriage, a dog—she would inevitably see Jill reply with something adulatory soon after. They were in PR. Maybe this was all part of building her brand and network. Maybe Cleo was in the wrong field.

In tenth grade, Mrs. Farmer had found Cleo crying in the back of the theater after the auditions for *A Midsummer Night's Dream*. Mrs. Farmer was always wearing bright, asymmetrical earrings that she made herself out of clay. She sat next to Cleo, a childishly crafted dolphin spinning from her ear. "Better luck next time, my dear," she'd said, clearly not knowing Cleo's name. Cleo told her she'd never even auditioned. She was upset because she couldn't bring herself to. That was when Mrs. Farmer told her words to live by: Pretend. Pretend you are ready for the things you want, or else you never will be. Cleo wanted to know how to please people. She tried drama. She tried debate even though she puked the morning of each tournament. At a career fair, one of the moms—a cheerleader's mom—gave a talk about her PR firm, and that was it. What power, Cleo thought, to make the world see things the way you want it to. But now someone was messaging her, forcing her to see things the way they saw them—the way they saw her.

"I already ate," Cleo said.

Jill's smile grew a bit stiff. "You can just throw it away if you don't want it."

"Sorry, I appreciate it," Cleo registered Jill's displeasure and struggled to course correct. "I just got a weird email," she confided.

"The one from Ted? You'd think he'd know better than to

force his diet on us. I heard he came in late last night to switch all the yogurt and cheese snacks with nonfat versions."

"No, I don't know who it's from."

Jill leaned in expectantly. Then, after an awkward pause, it dawned on her that Cleo was done explaining. "If you're worried about it, you could probably ask IT to see if they can trace the IP. It's a long shot, but you never know."

But Cleo didn't want to share that message with anyone. It felt too intimate. At the end of the day, after she locked her boss's office, she returned to the email. Why, she wondered, would someone seek her out in this way? In college, she had earned As and Bs, but she never drew attention to herself with a prestigious award or a riveting social life. Freshman year she was one of only three girls on her floor who never joined a sorority, and when the dorm emptied on Fridays, they would play Scrabble or Monopoly and eat pizza. It was true that she could not remember their names now, even though it had only been a handful of years, but that wasn't by choice. Those girls had immersed themselves in their other majors, their new friends, and off-campus lives. The closest friends she had were from high school, from debate team and study groups, and they had dispersed to various parts of the country. She had stayed at the local college, living with her parents for the final two years of her degree. Surely if she had offended anyone, she had done so ages ago for reasons she could no longer recall. She had spent her adult years combatting her tendency toward lackluster invisibility. She was never given the chance to seriously offend anyone. That would require knowing a person well enough to disappoint or betray them.

Now she said to Jill, "I don't know why anyone would do this."

"There are some real sickos out there," Jill said, leaning close again. "I've had some weird messages myself. And a couple stalkers."

"But why me? It doesn't make sense."

"And it made sense when it happened to me?" Jill said.

Cleo could see Jill's goodwill melting away, her features closing, hardening.

"I'm sorry," Cleo said. "I just meant, no one knows me. No one pays attention to me."

Jill didn't say anything. She tapped her nails on the desk a couple times and swiveled back to her computer. Cleo let the numbness of rejection seep through her. She had learned to embrace the prickling empty feeling of being embarrassed or discarded. Filing was mindless. She resumed filing.

"Drinks after work tomorrow?" Jill said without looking at her. "I don't usually go out Wednesdays but sounds like you could use a chat."

"That'd be nice," Cleo said, aiming for a casual tone.

She drove home on autopilot. Some lizard-brained part of her was observing traffic signals and picking the usual path without demanding any serious attention on her part. Cleo was oscillating wildly between unease and wild hope. The messages still disturbed her, but now there was Jill to look forward to. Jill laughed easily. It startled Cleo to hear Jill laugh suddenly in a thick bout of silence. She wanted to be jolted. She often felt that she was drifting down a winding creek, reaching for boulders and low-hanging branches but never reaching shore—only the sameness of that soft water carrying her along without any meaningful encounters.

————

That night, she stared at herself in the bathroom mirror, noticing for the first time just how asymmetrical the creases of her upper eyelids were. Her left lid began to look droopy to her. She found herself searching online for images of ptosis and then accounts of corrective surgery. Patients lamenting their progressively weakening levator muscles. She tried lifting her eyebrows and assessing the degree to which each eye reacted. It was subtle, but she could tell: the left side failed to achieve the same degree of wide-eyed shock.

She heated up a frozen egg roll and ate it without any condiments. In the street below, the old man was chipping away at the sidewalk, crouched to nearly crawling on all fours. When he reached the streetlamp beneath her window, he unfurled himself, hands cradling his lower back, his face basking in the harsh fluorescence. She withdrew into the shadows as though he could see her. She crawled into bed without brushing her teeth, not wanting to risk another obsessively self-critical staring session. Sleepless and suffocating beneath the sheets, she listened to the rattle of the AC. Each time it reached the thermostat setting, the unit shut down for a few minutes, ushering in a sudden lapse of sound. She strained to hear. Just when she thought she could make out the knife scraping concrete, the AC would kick back on, industrial blasts of air sluicing through the ductwork.

———

In the morning, before she left for work, she received a notification about the profile she kept on the beta version of a free dating website. She had never gone on a date, through the site or otherwise. She liked browsing through other people's profiles, and sometimes she liked the strange, desperate conversations users would have with her. She hadn't checked it since the move, and her location was still listed as Minneapolis. She hoped to find nothing but the usually banal messages. A mass grave of "Hi, how r u?" The occasional and endearing "I like that book too!" Of course, one always had to deal with guys who had studied the manifestos of self-declared pickup artists, the occasional half insult or "You'd be really hot if . . ." On this day, she would have gladly sifted through a hundred of those messages. Instead she found a message from Dan030506. He'd duplicated his screen name to make sure she'd know. She thought about deleting without reading, but if he had detailed any violent wish, she needed to know.

I'm glad I found you here. But you should change your profile picture. The yellow dress is better. About the questionnaire: I saw that you would rather burn a flag than burn a book. I think you haven't fully thought this through.

Clearly, he'd read through all of her content on the site. When interested, she'd also read through other users' Q&As—comprised of a list of questions generated by users and ranked by popularity. The answers were used to algorithmically generate matches. Had she matched to him? Had he figured out her real identity by hacking the site? Or did she know him from real life and he had used her basic stats and location to find her profile?

She told Jill all about the messages at drinks. Jill picked out the red vinyl booth in the corner, said it was her usual spot. Cleo liked that she had a stake in something so trivial, a territorial love for the corner of a watering hole. She wanted to have spots that were hers, not by right but by assertion of her will.

"You need to accept that people will feel entitled to your attention," Jill said, "but you don't have to give it to them."

"The issue is more a matter of safety," Cleo said.

"Ah," Jill said, sipping thoughtfully on her martini. "Do you think he knows where you live?"

"He, she, they. I don't know who this person is or how much they know."

Jill leaned back in her booth, twirling an olive on a toothpick. "Huh. You really think it could be a woman?"

"One of the names they used was Cindy."

"Seems like a man to me."

"It could be anyone," Cleo said. "Even you."

Jill laughed, but when Cleo did not join her, she grew grim. "What reason would I possibly have?"

"I have no idea. I don't think it is you. I'm just saying, from my perspective, it could technically be anyone."

Jill dug in her purse and placed a twenty-dollar bill on the table. "Well, this has been delightful, but I better run."

Cleo reached for her, managed to graze her fingers before she pulled away and stood from the booth. "I didn't mean it."

Jill nodded. "See you tomorrow."

At the exit, she paused with her hands on the door and glanced back at Cleo. She was inspecting her, deciding how to feel about her. Cleo knew the look.

————

Cleo drove home, parked her car, and walked past the north face of her building. Only one tarp remained, snapping like a flag in the sharp breeze. The rest had become windows, dark eyes reflecting the moon.

As she neared the front entrance, she noticed the sidewalk shucker, his hands dappled in blue and orange paint. He was peeling flyers for a missing corgi off the lamppost, dropping the torn pieces of paper into his frayed and dirty tote.

"You shouldn't do that," she said, surprised to hear the words out loud.

He turned, paint scraper in hand, and eyed her as if scanning for data, then grunted before resuming his scraping.

"What if someone is still looking for him?" she asked.

"Did you even notice this flyer before you saw me tear it down?" His face was tanned to stiff leather so that each word was punctuated by the ripple of the wrinkles in his cheeks.

She shook her head. She hadn't noticed. Now she saw how faded the remnants of the flyer were. The untaped edges had dissolved in the rain. Either the corgi had long since been found, or she was looking at its final picture.

"What do you do with it?" she asked.

"Disassemble and reassemble," he said, flicking another fragment of flyer into his bag. "One man's trash and all that shit." He wiped the sweat off his lip with the back of his forearm. She noticed a faded and blown-out skeleton tattoo. It was dancing. "You don't smoke, do you?"

She shook her head. "Sorry."

"I could really use a smoke. And then I'd take that filter and use it too. Make it art."

His lucidity was unclear. There was something both incisive and scattered about the way he stared at her. Perhaps that was merely the combination of cataracts and a heavy brow.

She retreated to her apartment. By the time she showered and looked out the window, he was gone, but she kept hearing the sound of his knife on the concrete, like the phantom ringing that lingers after tornado sirens.

————

The rest of the week, Jill maintained tersely polite conversation about necessary work tasks, but she never allowed any extemporaneous chitchat. A couple of times, Cleo felt like Jill was looking at her, but when she glanced back, trying to catch her, Jill's eyes were locked on her monitor, her hands typing quickly.

On Saturday, Cleo ran into the neighbor as she was checking her mail. Despite the August heat, he still wore his blazer. The veins on his hands protruded more than she'd expected. He was probably closer to forty than thirty, despite the smooth skin of his face. He caught her staring, and she returned to sorting her envelopes.

"I'm Bryan," he said, extending his veiny hand to her, but she just stared at it.

"Sorry," she said. "My hands are full." She held up the envelopes, awkwardly with both hands even though one could have easily grasped them all.

"And you are?"

"You should know." She meant to test him. To see if he reacted to the phrase with a spark of recognition, but instead he just looked perplexed.

"I'm sorry, have we already met?"

She nodded to her mailbox, which read her full name: Cleo Darby.

"I see," he said, turning to close his own mailbox. He didn't even make eye contact when he left the entranceway. He merely waved a handful of mail in the air in a half-assed gesture of good riddance.

Cleo didn't care. He only mattered if he was the one sending the messages.

————

Like Whac-A-Mole, the messages kept arriving in different accounts. She deleted her dating account only to find a Facebook message from Ed Shepherd. She didn't know Ed Shepherd, and the account only had a few friends, all public restaurant accounts. She looked them up. Restaurants from her hometown and from L.A., but none that she'd ever been to. His profile picture was of Mister Ed, the talking horse, its upper lip curled revealing its big block teeth. He wrote, *What's done is done, but don't forget to smile.*

She reflexively smiled, pressing her hands on her cheeks as if assessing a mold for a sculpture. How stiff and unreal her face felt.

She wrote a response to Mister Ed: Fuck you, you sick fuck. I'm calling the police.

Then she called the police on their nonemergency line and explained the situation, but they couldn't do anything for her. We can't just arrest random people, they said. There was no actual threat. There was no crime. Don't respond to any more messages, they said. Just ignore him, they said, or delete your accounts.

She deleted all of them, even LinkedIn. All that remained was her email, which she needed for work. She wondered about her career. How could she build a network and become a publicist if she had deleted every online iteration of herself? In a civil case, her damages were all hypothetical. She couldn't prove that her life was any worse off postdeletion than it would have been if she had kept all her online personas.

———

Cleo had just finished her first cup of coffee and was rolling calls for her boss, whittling through the phone sheet and the messages they owed clients, when she received the email from Denice Smith. An actual Smith, a real person, who worked on the other side of the office. She invited the office to join her for drinks and maybe even some bowling for her birthday. "RSVP if you want a lane," she wrote, followed by a string of celebratory emojis. Cleo knew better than to RSVP. This message wasn't for her.

Cleo packed her purse so that she could leap up when Jill headed to lunch and walk out with her. She even held the door open.

"Thank you," Jill murmured, avoiding eye contact.

Cleo kept stride with Jill, even though the cafeteria was the opposite direction from the front gate and her usual coffee shop. When Jill quickened her pace, so did Cleo.

Without warning, Jill stopped and turned on Cleo. "Where are you going?"

Cleo forced a smile. "To grab lunch."

"I wasn't planning on company."

"That's okay. I was just going to grab something to go."

Jill nodded, then looked uncertain, like she had overreacted. "Sorry. A client's big interview came out today and it's a disaster. Not at all what we'd discussed."

Cleo felt a surge of relief, the happiness of finding herself a confidante, and tried to affect a sympathetic expression. "Sorry to hear that."

As they neared the cafeteria doors, she added, "Are you going to Action Bowl later?"

"Maybe," Jill shrugged. "Probably not if I'm stuck doing damage control all afternoon."

Jill pushed through the door without holding it for Cleo. The glass swung shut on her shoulder, making her feel klutzy and self-conscious. Still, she murmured after Jill, "Good luck."

Cleo wasn't an idiot. She knew Jill was going to join all the other assistants at the long table in the far corner of the cafeteria. They were already looking this way, smiling at Jill. But Cleo didn't want to wait and see, to confirm Jill's deception. She paid for a turkey and cheese sandwich and a carton of milk and left. She ate at her desk and thought about fixing things with Jill. If they could have another drink together, she could better explain what she'd meant about the stalker, about the feeling of not knowing anything about the person who was accumulating data and connecting the dots of your life.

———

The bowling alley was in a historic building with several floors, and each floor was decorated to represent a different decade. Cleo couldn't recall which decade Denice had chosen. She stood in the tiny art deco lobby checking her email on her phone when she found a new message, now from Jeremy13468@gmail.com.

Don't disappear on me.

Reflexively, she looked up and scanned the room. No one was there except the elderly elevator operator in his gray suit and white gloves. He raised a bushy eyebrow. "You just going to stand there, or you going up?"

Not wanting to be alone, and not wanting a coworker to stumble upon her in the lobby, she joined the operator in the old-fashioned car with its geometric paneling.

"Where to?" He rested his hand on the manual crank that controlled acceleration.

"The '50s," she said. Denice liked knee-length skirts that nipped at the waist. It was worth a shot.

But she didn't recognize anyone there. Families with small children were crowding the lanes or milling near a soda fountain, clutching milkshakes and sundaes. A father helped his daughter toss an unusually small bowling ball down the lane where unusually small pins toppled.

She tried the '60s and the '70s, but she found them in the

'80s. There was a small arcade in the back corner. She drifted to the PAC-MAN machine and pretended to play as she watched Denice and her friends bowl.

Jill wound up and slung her ball so that it skipped the gutter and bounced into her neighbor's lane before scoring for a clearly peeved middle-aged man in acid-washed jeans. Jill doubled over laughing, each of her coworkers high-fiving her on her way to her seat. Cleo had hoped to join them, but now she felt locked out of a ritual that was already halfway enacted.

She tried to focus on the lanes, to find a moment that would allow her entry, but a preteen boy drifted to her side, eyeing the machine. After several minutes, he said, "You didn't even put coins in."

Denice was opening a gift bag from Jill, pulling out bright tissue paper and squealing at whatever she found in there.

Cleo let go of the joystick. "It's yours, kid."

She kept her back to the lanes in case anyone would happen to look in her direction. She had almost made it to the elevator when she saw Jill's boss heading her way. Cleo ducked into the restroom and slid into a stall. She scanned her phone. No new messages.

The door swung open and two women entered, their feet clustering near the mirrors and sinks. Someone popped open a compact and slid open a tube of lipstick. Through the crack in the stall door, Cleo could see a sliver of Jill gently pressing the tip of her lipstick and then dappling it artfully on the apple of her cheek.

"I don't even know why they hired her," someone said. "Who wants someone like that in PR?"

"She was good on paper," Jill said. "And she managed to seem normal in the interview."

"What if she faked the stalker stuff?"

Jill held her face still as she added mascara to the tips of her lashes, barely moving her lips to speak. "I was there when she got one of the messages. She seemed spooked."

"Seemed," the unseen woman scoffed.

"She implied I did it."

"Why would anyone, never mind you, bother?"

"For sport?" Jill shrugged, then blotted away the creases of foundation beneath her eyes.

The woman stepped to the sink, her back obscuring Cleo's view.

"She can't last long. She keeps dropping calls and screwing up the calendar," Jill said. "I know plenty of people who'd be a better fit."

Cleo didn't want to hear anymore, but there was no escaping them, so she let them see her. She opened the door and stood there until they noticed, Jill's eyes first tracking her reflection in the mirror, Cleo's face hovering above her shoulder. Denice turned, eyes wide. There was nothing they could say. Jill breathed her name, like she was going to apologize but realized the futility.

Cleo stood beside Jill then and washed her hands. She smiled at Jill in the mirror. Let the normalcy be uncanny, she thought. The weirdness of politeness in an impolite moment. She wanted them to squirm in their ugly, rented bowling shoes.

———

In the elevator, the operator pretended not to notice the tears that escaped down her cheek.

"The lobby?" he asked, eyes trained straight ahead.

"Yes, please." Her voice held steady.

When he pulled back the grate on the ground floor, he bowed his head and wished her a good night.

She climbed into her car. The parking lot was half-empty by now. Across the aisle, a small car like hers sat beneath the sole lamppost, its silver paint covered in dust. It was hard to tell, but through the slight tint of the windows and the glare of the light, she thought she could discern the silhouette of a driver seated behind the wheel. She knew it could just be a high-backed seat creating the illusion, but she felt that someone was sitting there, watching.

Her phone vibrated against her hip with a notification. She held her phone low to the seat, so that whoever was in the other car (if there was anyone in the other car) would not see her reading their words. But when she scanned her fingerprint to unlock the screen, there were no words. There was only herself staring back at her, a photo taken just moments earlier. In the image on her screen, she sat behind the wheel of her car, gazing right at the camera, which would mean the photographer was behind the wheel of the other silver car, facing her, as if through a mirror.

Prickling unease swept through her, like the cold sweat induced by a virus. Her hands shook as she turned the key, igniting the engine. With the car in park, she idled. Something needed to happen. She flashed her brights and blared the horn. The other car's headlights turned on and echoed her, on and off, again and again, matching her rhythm, mocking her.

She should drive away. She should ignore it all, go home and pull up the covers and play dead. You do not look at the thing.

But she had to know. She pulled out the key to kill the engine and held the cool metal in her palm. If she approached the driver's side, if she peered into that window, who would she find looking back at her?

MODERN RELICS

A human checked them in. Marian wasn't too surprised. She'd read the reports. Automated entities were less effective at coercing people into spending money. The man was a natural pusher, rapidly listing the various services they should consider adding to their hotel stay. Eighty-dollar brunch. Thousand-dollar cabanas on the beach. A couple's massage. After suggesting an excursion in a submarine pod, the pusher looked pointedly at Gerald and said, "This is your honeymoon, yes?"

Gerald smiled stiffly as he fiddled with the loose thread of his denim pocket, unraveling it further. Marian knew Gerald was actively weighing his warring desires: to succumb to opulence and appease the pusher or to decline the offerings of the luxury resort and thereby avoid deepening their crushing credit card debt. He often would acquiesce to unnecessary transactions and add-ons if asked in a public space by a stranger with a moderately imperious tone. Why settle for a synthetic steak if you could get a cut from a cow that had experienced deep-tissue massage each day of its life? Why take the lake view if you could get the ocean view? When Marian had suggested that they'd save money with half pours of champagne for their wedding guests, the venue coordinator had pursed her lips slightly and said, "You only get married once." Gerald had wilted like a double agent under interrogation. Suddenly, he needed a respectable pour of bubbly. He'd insisted.

Now, Marian chimed in before Gerald could fold, "We'll discuss our options and call down from the room."

"Certainly," the pusher said, sliding an activity menu across the counter. "Please be aware that appointments and cabanas often sell out before noon on the preceding day. Sometimes sooner." He nodded toward the large brass clock behind him, which read eleven forty.

Gerald picked up the menu and said, "Oh, look, kayaking!"

The pusher brightened. "Shall I—"

"We'll discuss." Marian shot her husband a stern look.

Gerald's mother had given them a generous portion of her rewards points to book the hotel, a luxury chain that was far beyond the couple's means. Gerald taught high school, and Marian, the librarian for an entire school district, had recently been demoted to part-time hours. Gamified teaching software and algorithms were used to curate books for the students. One of their corporate sponsors would present Marian with a dozen titles that had sentence patterns and vocabularies that allegedly optimized students' verbal scores, and from that scant selection, she would choose her favorites. She no longer taught students how to find books or articles in the library. Instead, it was now her responsibility to fetch the students' selections from the stacks whenever they submitted a request online. Still, she knew this too was a fading purpose. The richer suburbs already had automated retrieval systems with metal bins on miniature train tracks weaving up and down and through the stacks. Occasionally, she would reply to a student's request with a helpful suggestion—a book or an article with more credible research or a more engaging style than the one they had asked for—but the students rarely responded. Fewer and fewer came to collect their books in person. Instead, she placed them on a cart whose inner gears and fans whirred rhythmically as it wheeled the selections to each student's locker. Most students, she suspected, did not realize that she was even a part of the process.

"Mr. and Mrs. Gerald Moore, here are your room keys," the pusher said. "The luggage will be up shortly."

Gerald turned, already slipping the keys into his pocket, but Marian lingered to correct the pusher. "Marian Grace."

"Excuse me?"

"My name is Marian Grace. Do you not have my full name on the reservation?" She turned to Gerald. "Didn't you give my name as well?"

"I did, I did."

The pusher tapped at his keyboard and then smiled at Gerald. "My apologies. I've updated your wife's information in the system."

Marian had deferred to the "Mr. & Mrs." sign that Gerald's mom had picked out for the sweetheart table. After all, Jacky had kindly helped fund their wedding. Marian even let the pastor introduce them as husband and wife, using Gerald's last name alone. After the wedding, Gerald was to let his mother know that they'd decided against the name change. Marian had agreed to entwine the purposes of their lives, but when she said yes, she had not envisioned how "Mrs. Gerald Moore" would feel. When cards arrived from new relatives addressed to his name, but with the Mrs. tacked on, she felt suddenly like a commodity, a potential child bearer, an extension of his hold-ings. Was she perpetuating an unnecessary institution? she had wondered, not for the first time. Had this even been necessary? At the very least, she had decided, she would continue to be "Ms." Grace, the lips pressing for the M and then sliding into that pleasant, husky zee. "Gerald," she had asked several times, often when she was spooning him before sleep, "you'll make sure she understands, right?" And she would say "right" as a plea, over and over, until he murmured back in the affirmative.

In the elevator, on the way to their room, Gerald squeezed her elbow. "I'm sorry," he said. "She must have put our names down when she used the points to book the room."

"It's been five months." They had delayed the honeymoon. Their winter wedding and their school schedules had not al-lowed enough time for the grand exit and immediate depar-ture. They had spent the day after their wedding at Jacky's, watching a sitcom she couldn't remember, packing, and eat-ing leftovers. Then they had driven back to Philly so Gerald could teach and Marian could review her favorites from Read-ing Magic Enterprise's recommended reading list.

In the room, there was a card on the bed—a menu listing voice commands and introducing them to the hotel's AI pro-gram, "Rhonda," with the silhouette of a small-waisted woman in a pencil skirt embossed on the thick cardstock.

"Rhonda, dim the lights," Gerald said. The lights dimmed.

"I don't like it," Marian said.

"Brighten the lights," he said, but the lights remained dim.

"That's not what I meant. Besides, you have to say Rhonda for it to work."

"I do not understand that request," a voice emanated from the walls.

"Is there a way to opt out of this?" Marian whispered. "I don't want the hotel listening."

Gerald shrugged and unwrapped a coffee disk for the sleek steel machine on the desk. "It's not like we're doing anything illegal."

"No, but I don't want some prick, like the guy at the front desk, listening to us having sex later."

"Oh," Gerald said, his finger hovering over the coffeemaker's power button. "Rhonda, stop listening."

"I do not understand that request."

"I don't know what to do." Gerald slumped into the desk chair and watched his coffee brew.

He was defeated so easily, Marian thought, exasperated. Like when they moved across country and only a third of the way into packing their pod he became overwhelmed by trying to make everything fit and had simply slumped into a lawn chair, staring forlornly at the piles of boxes. It had been left to her to orchestrate a plan. She'd quickly listed the furniture they could sell without losing too much value, including the end table she'd bought with her dad from a dusty secondhand shop run by a pastor who'd forced his son to deliver it for free. She'd cried and cried when it sold, like she'd betrayed her still-living father, because a part of her knew she'd eventually regret letting go of any object that could serve as a totem of the ephemeral connection she had felt to another living being. After she'd sold a few more pieces and braced herself against further displays of sentimentality, they'd managed to pack the rest. Gerald had been grateful. She'd felt needed. Sometimes she marveled at the tight-jawed resentment she could feel for something she also deeply desired.

She picked up the phone and called the front desk. A man answered with a snooty tone. The pusher, she thought. She asked to turn off the Rhonda program.

"I'm sorry," he said, "but many of the room's amenities will not function without Rhonda."

Marian hung up on him. Gerald stared expectantly as he blew on his latte.

"Now what?" he said.

"Rhonda, please list room service options for lunch."

The voice began with a lobster roll that cost more than their daily food budget, and the subsequent items were no better: white truffle pizza, caviar, a shockingly expensive seafood bisque.

"Rhonda, stop."

Marian pulled a box of meal bars out of her suitcase and tossed one to Gerald.

"You're a goddess," he said, already tearing into the foil.

She watched him chomp on the granola, pausing only to sip his coffee, and felt that familiar blend of fondness and annoyance: her love for his childlike zeal and her irritation that she usually shouldered the burden of each decision. She had planned nearly all of their wedding, and so she had decided not to plan any of the honeymoon, to leave that responsibility entirely on him. She was already regretting that choice.

"What are we doing for dinner?"

"There are five restaurants in the resort, so I just figured we'd stick around here," he said, allowing a mangled raisin to spill over his lips.

"Did you make a reservation?"

He took forever to swallow. "It's a resort."

"That doesn't mean you don't need a reservation." Marian lay back in the bed, exhausted. "Rhonda, which restaurants on the resort have availability tonight?"

"One moment as I compile results."

Marian listened to Gerald licking the sticky corn syrup off his fingers and then slurping his drink.

Rhonda's voice returned with a quick blip of white noise. "There are two restaurants available tonight. The Blue Lagoon and Casablanca. Would you like me to make a reservation?"

"Rhonda, what is the cheapest entrée at the Blue Lagoon?"

"The Blue Lagoon uses seasonal ingredients that change daily. There are no set prices on the menu."

Marian rolled her eyes at Gerald, then added, "Rhonda, what is the cheapest entrée at Casablanca?"

"I'm sorry. Casablanca does not list prices on their menu."

"Fuck you, Rhonda."

"I do not understand that request."

Gerald asked the ceiling, "Rhonda, which restaurants have availability near the resort?"

"I'm sorry. My services do not extend to external properties."

"Fuck you, Rhonda," they said.

"I do not—"

"Rhonda, stop!" Marian yelled.

Gerald shifted to the bed and reached for Marian's hand. "I'm sorry, love. I'll figure it out."

He always means well, Marian thought. He just had no idea what it took to plan something like this. She gave him a modest smile so as not to overly reassure him. Still, she thought, he should have researched the way she always did, for work, for the move, for their groceries.

They nodded off. When they awoke, Rhonda told them the time was seventeen hundred. Marian felt a heaviness in her chest. Nearly fifteen percent of their honeymoon was already over. She had thought this would feel like an escape, like they'd been freed from their usual worries and obligations and this new chapter of their life was finally beginning, but everything felt the same.

She caught Gerald staring at her, his face still creased by the stitching of the pillowcase.

"What's wrong?" he asked.

"We've already lost a day."

"We still have the entire evening."

"But we didn't see the water when it was bright and turquoise." Suddenly she could smell cheap coconut-scented sunscreen, and she recalled her mother rubbing it into her shoulders. At least, she thought it was her mother. It had been so long ago. Whoever was rubbing her shoulders, she remembered the wholesome absence of worry, and her father, soon after, carrying her into the surf, always keeping her head above the water. She could spend her whole life chasing that feeling.

"We'll see the water tomorrow," Gerald said. "And the next day. And the next."

"I just don't want to waste any more time."

She wanted Gerald to pull her to him, like he sometimes

did when he was feeling tolerant of her melancholy, and to run his fingers across her scalp. Instead, she could see that this was not one of his sympathetic moods. He was tired of her spells of grieving. And she knew he deserved to be. She was her father's daughter, with his somber view on the transience of the world. Before he'd died three years ago, he talked incessantly about the likelihood that he would succumb to a complication from his diabetes. He had turned his will and his plans for his burial into a casual topic of Sunday afternoon phone calls. He had two dogs, and he would carry around a wrist bracelet that had Marian's number on it with the engraved phrase emergency caretaker for dogs. Although he'd been right to worry about his untimely demise—a fulfillment of paranoia that she knew Gerald deeply resented, largely because it confirmed all of Marian's inherited neuroses—the diabetes was not what did him in. It was a coyote attack. Not that the coyotes had harmed her dad personally, but they went after his dogs, as best as anyone could tell, based on the carcass of Doodles and the wounds on Ginger—who'd miraculously escaped and now lived with them, lumpily scarred and pumped full of Prozac, in their tiny apartment in Philly. Marian's father was found in a ravine near a creek bed, his neck broken, not far from what remained of the Goldendoodle. When the emergency responders arrived, tipped off by a startled hiker, they saw the bracelet and called Marian. Thinking that she was just a dog sitter per the engraved label, they broke the news in a brash manner, asking without preamble if she could watch the dogs for their deceased owner. Still, they'd found her immediately. Her father had been right.

Now Marian was wincing at the ceiling fan like it was going to break off and hack her into pieces. She could feel Gerald assessing the situation, assessing her. Suddenly he leapt from the bed and loomed over her with fingers energetically splayed into jazz hands.

"You're succumbing to mawkishness," Gerald said. "Let's go to the pool bar."

"It's too expensive." She was snuggling into her pillow. He yanked it away.

"Hey—"

"Just one," he promised.

With a bit more coaxing, Marian pulled her hair into a bun and they left the room. They took a few wrong turns, but there were always employees eager to intercept and give directions. At one point they passed a robotic crab carrying a tray of dirty dishes to an automated sanitation cart. Its ommatophores swiveled to assess the couple's trajectory, tracking them with green unwavering eyes.

They passed through a wide hallway that had been staged as an art gallery. Marian was no artist, but she found herself embarrassed for the cluster of portraits that used sequins and glitter to depict evening gowns on women with unnaturally configured teeth. Then she gasped at the sight of a brilliantly rendered bird, its wings a jewel-bright rainbow. Its eyes looked sad and stricken to her, full lucid circles peering over a severe black beak. She stepped closer, trying to detect the brush strokes. A curator in a shiny black blazer descended on them.

"It's a Martin Devino original," the curator bragged. "And that is an extremely rare scarlet macaw, a clone he had made before they steepened penalties for the ban. They'll probably go extinct again soon, but we have replicas in the nature preserve. They talk and everything, just like the originals."

"Sounds expensive," Gerald said.

"How awful," Marian said. She hated to think of the bird's resurrection, only to exist as a model for a two-dimensional image that would be sold to a rich tourist at a resort—how it would die, the last of its kind, a second time.

"There's nothing we can do about it." Gerald linked his fingers with hers and squeezed her hand.

They crossed a skywalk. A lazy river wound its way beneath them, carrying along a sunburnt man sipping Corona in his inner tube. On the other side, in the west wing of the building, they found the beachfront portion of the property. The evening sun glittered off the sea, golden flecks masking the blue water.

They found a table at the beach bar, a patio with a crisp white awning. Marian pulled the hem of her skirt down so she could sit on the metal chair without burning her thighs. She watched as Gerald fetched two beers and gestured enthusiastically with the bartender. Both alternated pointing and pantomiming a series of turns.

Gerald returned, heroic. "So Joe, the bartender, told me his favorite restaurant is just a mile or two up the road. An Indian-Caribbean place. Totally affordable. And," his smile grew, "get this! It's next to a mini-mart. We can pick up some things for breakfast to keep in the room."

"Great," Marian said, already picturing the limitations of their minifridge and compiling a list of reasonable food prod-

ucts. String cheese. Apples. Instant oatmeal prepackaged in
cups. Perhaps some kind of beef jerky—although she still
struggled with the synthetic texture of most packaged meat.
A few farms still raised cows the old-fashioned way for elite
restaurants—the resort probably had grass-fed, pasture-raised
beef on their priceless menus—but it was rare to see a field
of cattle along the road. Maybe someday they'd have fields of
replicas fake munching on fake grass—a way to feed nostal-
gia spawned by western films and old dairy ads. We no longer
need the cows, she thought, but we need their ghosts. Then she
thought of the Botanical Preserve and its mechanical beasts.
She didn't want to see the fake macaws. That would mean val-
idating the preserve's decision to buy the cheap spectacle, the
simulacrum of the inefficiently organic creature. Her stomach
lurched, and she turned to find Gerald staring at her.

"What are you thinking about?"

"Food," she said.

He smiled, relieved, like he could solve that problem.

———

Marian changed into a little black dress. She liked to pack light,
and the dress was a way to account for the majority of sartorial
demands that could arise on any vacation. She could feel the
hunger, the acid pooling in her stomach and starting to climb
its way back up her throat. She pinned her hair into a French
twist without looking in the mirror. She caught Gerald ap-
praising her.

"Did you turn off your earrings?"

A couple years ago, she had bought earrings that would covertly track her commute. If she deviated from her preset paths, or if she took too long to reach her destination, it would notify him. The device was programmed to allow for stagnant spells at the library and the school, but if she became immobile outside of her preset safe zones, Gerald would be notified. He could then escalate the warning to the police. If he failed to dismiss the alert within fifteen minutes, the police would come anyway.

"I set them to allow movement within five miles of the resort," she said, checking her lobes for the small synthetic sapphires that hid the necessary hardware. "That makes them a bit worthless, doesn't it? That's over half the island."

"It'll be fine."

"Maybe on our way out we should tell the front desk where we're going. Have them look for us if we don't come back by, I don't know, ten? Eleven?"

"That seems unnecessary."

"Fine. I'll call."

Although Gerald was usually easygoing, talking to strangers rattled him. When they had barely begun dating, he told her about his first office job—how he'd made an elaborate flowchart of all the possible standard responses he would need when discussing business with his boss's clients. For years, he would write a script before placing a call of any importance. Now he avoided phone calls and scripts as much as possible. And now he was sidestepping to block her path to the phone.

"I'd rather you didn't," he said. "I told you I'd plan the dinner. Hurry up and finish getting ready. Let me handle it."

He picked up the phone and explained the restaurant choice

with unusual bravado and ended with his request that someone "notify the authorities" if they hadn't returned by eleven.
When he placed the phone back in its cradle, she'd felt pleased
that he would brave such discomfort for her.

They could have had the valet hail a cab for them, but Gerald was adamant about walking. She watched as he hurried past
the resort's roundabout and knew it was to avoid the valet, to
avoid the awkwardness of refusing a cab when his wife was
clearly dressed for a date.

"It'll be a nice stroll, and then we can maybe take a cab back,"
he said. "I bet it's cheaper to book a cab off property."

They walked to the end of the drive, past a grove of palm
trees, and emerged on a surprisingly narrow street, largely de-
graded to gravel. The sidewalk disappeared suddenly into the
dirt shoulder of the road.

"Maybe we need the cab," Marian said, pausing to look back
at the valet stand, which she could only dimly make out in the
dusky shadows of the portico.

"It'll be fine," Gerald said, already marching ahead.

They had to walk single file. Marian glared at the back of his
head, the glistening wave where he'd failed to comb through
his hair gel. He should have let me go first, she thought, glanc-
ing over her shoulder, listening for signs of traffic. The sky was
deepening, and she worried about her dark dress. It would be
easy to go unnoticed. What if some drunk tourist swiped her?
Her marriage had barely started; there were no children, and
Gerald would die with her, and she'd read fewer books than she
could have ever admitted publicly, given her profession. When
her father died, there were stacks of unused Spanish workbooks

in his office. He always had some sort of self-improvement hobby that never reached its full potential: learning a few chords and songs on guitar when he was forty, then a years-long obsession with making imprecise stained-glass windows, ballroom dancing until his partner-slash-girlfriend dumped him, and so on and so forth. Then he tried to learn Spanish, with the intention of going to Mexico soon after he'd mastered the intermediate-level Rosetta Stone lessons. He never got that far with any of it. Even her mother had a habit of leaving projects unfinished. She'd willingly left Marian when she was only seven to drive to Los Angeles for a career that never took off—Marian knew, she'd Googled her.

An engine rumbled behind her, and she saw headlights approaching from the opposite direction. She anticipated the timing. The cars were going to pass each other, and the road was one-and-a-half cars wide. She pressed against the twenty-foot guardrail that prevented cars from plunging into the swampy channel below. Gerald walked on, unruffled. She yanked the back of his shirt, pulled him beside her.

If they converged on the overpass, the drivers would have to swerve wide, even though the shoulders of the road had shrunk to nothing. She would fling herself over the fence and drag Gerald with her. She pictured themselves doggy paddling in the dank water. She'd once read that Katharine Hepburn had fallen into a canal while filming a scene in Venice. In the interview, decades after her ill-fated submersion, she revealed that she still had ear infections she attributed to that brief exposure.

Marian tensed and leaned her hip against the metal rail, but the cars overtook each other before the bottleneck, before the fatal error might have occurred. Still, her heart. And Gerald, unruffled and oblivious but endearingly in one piece.

"There aren't any streetlights," she said.

"We'll take a cab back," he said without turning, letting the wind throw his words back to her.

"It's too dark already," she said. The sky had turned indigo. Soon, everything would deepen, she would blend into the night, and she wouldn't be able to discern the uneven footing in her slick-soled dress flats.

"It's not that far. Stop worrying." Even in the dusk, she could see his clenched jaw. She had lost his ear. He was growing obstinate.

The canopy of trees was shielding the stars and moon. The night was full of shadow play, deep gray foliage shimmering against blackness. The sound of nature here was novel to her. She had never heard that particular whirring rhythm spawned by insect legs rubbing or innards vibrating, membranes pressed against deeper membranes. She could wonder about the competing instruments that evolved in those chitinous bodies, but she couldn't help but worry about the mosquitoes and the pathogens they carried. The island was not immune, and the pungent repellent she sprayed on her legs and arms had an eighty-percent rate of deterrence. More than that, she worried about the narrow road. She imagined what it would be like to be hit and be thrown or simply to trip and fall into a deep ditch and then realize this was it. Did her father know, when it happened, that it was the end? They told her he wouldn't have felt much pain, not for long anyway, but did he know he was fading forever?

"I'm going to call a cab."

"Oh my god," he said, throwing his head back. "Don't be ridiculous."

This was always a tipping point, when he turned to this script. Nine times out of ten, she knew he was gracious, more patient and tolerant than she could expect in others thanks to her tendency to stew in pessimistic projections and given her resulting need to control, to account for all possibilities. But words like ridiculous, hysterical, emotional—those catchall terms for women when the man was done arguing—those all felt deeply unfair, a lazy insult that had wormed its way into her lover's brain from a half-remembered blockbuster film or prime-time sitcom. An ill-fitting costume for a bit of self-destructive role-playing. She could call him a misogynist, but that wouldn't be true or fair either. Sometimes she did, and instantly felt the wave of guilt for so crudely using a label that didn't do him justice. When there was any sign Gerald would disappoint her—when a fight or a half-baked comment gave her a taste of what the end of their relationship might look like—she would feel a wave of perverse power swelling in her. She could end it all in a moment if she said the right wrong words. It was like when you hike near a cliff and you feel tempted to lean over the edge, to look down as the scree tumbles too far to make a sound. Or the desire to cross the yellow line in the street when the headlights are racing toward you. The call of the void. The death drive. That feeling would surge in her when Gerald acted displeased with her. It begged her to say the thing that they could never come back from and to walk away forever. Because if she walked away, she would never have to worry about what it would feel like to lose him—to have finally lost everyone she'd ever loved. She'd already know.

But she wasn't there yet. She would not say the unforgivable thing.

She pulled out her cell phone, searched for cab companies, and dialed the first result. Gerald shook his head at her, then paced, running his fingers through his hair as he exhaled noisily, an affected huff of displeasure.

On the phone, a singsongy voice with an unnatural rhythm asked for their location. Marian gave the name of the road and described the bridge, to which the voice interrupted, asking for the nearest intersection. She guessed the mileage since the resort. "Pickup will be in approximately five minutes," the voice chirped, then hung up.

"Now we're stuck waiting," Gerald said.

"I wish I'd planned everything." She smacked a gnat on her forehead and examined her palm for guts.

"So you have to swat a few bugs, get a bit sweaty on a tropical island before dinner. It's not the end of the world. Stop being so pessimistic."

She fumed at the smug curl of his lips. Then something icy settled over her. "I'm realistic," she said. "You can't just expect things to fall into place. You can't just ask for a big wedding and then twiddle your thumbs and expect it all to work out. You need a plan, or life will just drift past you."

"You're manifesting negativity."

He'd been reading self-help books. He'd even bought her one for her birthday, which she took as a slight. Clearly, he viewed himself as an advanced guide on some spiritual ladder and she hadn't even found the first rung.

"Not this again," she said. "Not now."

A car crept over the bridge and pulled to the shoulder. The headlights flicked to the brights and back, blinding them.

"Looks like your wife just manifested a car."

Marian tried to peer into the window, but the tint of the glass was opaque in the darkness. She scanned and matched the license plate on her phone, which seemed to trigger the back door opening.

A voice emanated from within. "Marian Grace, welcome."

She climbed into the black interior. Her sweaty thighs stuck to the leather seat as she slid her way across.

Gerald scooted in after her, helped her find the seat belt. She knew this was his way of apologizing, but she said nothing. She just stared out the window, leaving him to stare at her silhouette. She could feel his gaze. Many times, he had told her how he loved the strong curve of her nose. He took her hand and squeezed it, but she kept looking at the passing trees, spidery black spears against the navy sky. They had not been dating long when her father died. Sometimes she wondered if they'd be together at all if she hadn't needed Gerald so desperately in the early stages of their courtship.

She turned to look at him, and he squeezed her hand again.

He pulled her toward him and kissed the top of her head, raised her chin to kiss her mouth. They held one another, locked in their kiss, cocooned by the hum of the engine. Marian was aware of the flakes of dry skin, the way his lips suckled hers, pulling strategically on various parts of her mouth. A part of her wanted this—to finally be held and submerged in their bodies—but she wanted that moment to be later, when they had eaten, returned to their room, and found a way to disable Rhonda. Here, she couldn't help but wonder, what if the car reached its destination in the midst of climax, the doors automated to open for a restaurant host, leaving a stranger scandalized on the sidewalk? Or what if there was an automatic fine or even a police report for this type of transgression in a self-driving vehicle? She had only skimmed the Terms of Agreement. Maybe she'd even lose her job, seeing as how she technically worked with children, although she never actually saw the students anymore.

She pulled away from him. "Later," she said, running her hand along his jawline, trying to project the desire that she knew they both needed.

The car hummed on, then whirred as it slowed for a turn onto an improbably narrow dirt path. The wheels struggled in ruts and dips, overwhelming the car's shocks and jostling Marian and Gerald.

She tapped the map app on her phone, but after a minute of loading the page, the screen fritzed to an error message. She tried again, then tried using a different map. She even rebooted her cellular data, only to discover that they were no longer in range. They could have been driving through a black velvet tunnel. Her eyes strained to see trees or patches of night sky, but there was total darkness. She only saw her own face looking back at her, glowing dimly from the blue light of her phone.

"This isn't right," she said.

"It's probably just a shortcut."

"Why would we be going into the swamp if the restaurant was just down the street? That doesn't make any sense."

"You need to dial back the worry, just a bit." He patted her hand, but she pulled away.

"Someone could have hacked the car. We could be on our way to an ambush, about to get mugged or worse."

"It's probably a simple mistake. Maybe there's more than one place with the same name on the island. Like a local chain."

"You think there are two Curry Curry Coconuts on this tiny island?"

"Or maybe there's just another curry place and the app got confused."

She leaned forward in her seat and yelled, "Stop the car." Undeterred, the car kept moving. She demanded that they pull over, turn around, cut the engine, hit the brakes. Not one of her commands worked.

Gerald was sitting a bit more upright and alert, but he still appeared mostly unperturbed.

"You're going to let this play out," she said. "You're going to assume that everything is fine, until it isn't."

"What do you suggest we do?" he said. "Call the cops?"

She held up her phone. "I already would have if we had service. At least the hotel will know to look for us."

Gerald's gaze flicked away too fast. It was a tell and she knew it.

"What did you do?" she asked.

That was when he told her he never actually placed the call to the front desk. He had merely spoken into the ringtone.

Now, it made sense, the way he had steered her briskly through the lobby, avoiding any dialogue with the concierge.

———

"No normal person does that, you know," he added. "No one assumes they are going to get murdered on their way to dinner down the street. It's embarrassing, to tell this guy that you're so scared of where he lives that you need him to keep tabs on you."

"Oh, I see," she said coldly. "So you were protecting me from embarrassing myself?"

"I mean, yeah?"

She could see his point. She hadn't thought about how that would seem to the pusher, but she also suspected this was a good cover story. In actuality, Gerald didn't want to be judged for avoiding the world-class resort restaurants with menus designed by celebrity chefs so they could eat somewhere cheap and unknown to anyone beyond the island. He didn't want to tell the pusher no. For all his manifestations, he couldn't get past this need to please the wrong people. Sometimes she wondered if she was one of them.

"I still wish you'd made the call. No one knows where we are."

They were in the deep belly of the swamp now. The car continued on its dirt path, the wheels spinning for a second here and there as the uneven, muddy earth caught them.

"We'll be fine," he said. "It's an island. How far can we go?"

Marian leaned forward. "Driver, lower the partition."

The matte black divider lowered, revealing the front cabin of the car and the steering wheel vibrating as it corrected for

each pothole. A touchscreen glowed in front of a digital gear
shift panel.

"Maybe there's an override button, or an emergency services
button," she said.

"Let's wait a few more minutes and see where it takes us."

Marian glared at him and his relaxed shoulders, his deter-
mined peacefulness. She resented it, she realized. How could
he be the one who was supposed to know her best? He oper-
ated in such a fundamentally different way than she did. He
never took the weight of things gone wrong.

She unbuckled her seat belt and climbed over the lowered
partition. Its thin edge dug painfully into her midsection as
she balanced there, reaching for the screen. She could feel Gerald wrap his arm around her thighs, supporting her. "Get back
here," he said, pulling slightly.

But she squirmed forward, gripping headrests and seat edges
to pull herself forward, even as she felt her shins scraping across
the divider. She slumped into the driver's seat and tested the
wheel. It remained impervious to her. She touched the screen
and a grid of options emerged: emergency, map, destination,
and help. She clicked the latter, but the screen revealed the image of pulsing concentric circles, like the ripples from a pebble,
and then displayed an error message before returning to the
home screen. The same was true for any option.

The car continued in darkness. The sound of the rough un-
paved road mimicked white noise, lulling her to near sleep, but
then a stone or pit in the road would jolt her to panic, height-
ening her disorientation. Her stomach ached with hunger, her
throat had grown parched, and her head throbbed as though

she'd been fasting for days. Had hours passed? It seemed so. But the island was too small to explain that much lost time. Perhaps they were driving in circles, deep in the preserve.

The headlights only cast a body's length ahead, revealing dark, glistening earth and nothing more. She remembered a cave her father had taken her to not long after her mother had left. A vacation to distract them from the new configuration of their family. On the longest tour, they squeezed past crevices and walked over fathomless pits covered with flimsy-seeming grates. "You would fall forever," she'd said. But her father explained that there was no such thing as a bottomless pit. There's always an impact, always an end to the fall, he'd said. Deep in the bowels of a subterranean cavern, the guide turned off the lights and revealed total darkness. Marian had squeezed her dad's hand, and he had squeezed back.

But the car was still drifting. Gerald had grown groggy, nodding off for several indeterminate lengths of time.

She turned on the cabin lights to wake him and explained her theory about their circling path.

"I don't know what to do," she said.

He reached forward and gripped her shoulder. "There's nothing to do," he said. "The car will stop eventually."

But she wasn't okay with that. She couldn't quite explain it, but she sensed that her father was wrong. That she had manifested something endless, aimless, and lost forever, so she told Gerald to check his seat belt.

"Is it on?" she insisted as she buckled her own.

He nodded. Even in their predicament, he chuckled.

And she pulled the emergency brake.

The car spun. She felt weightless for a moment, felt her arms drift upward and her hair flying away from her, and then there was impact. They had spun off the road, maybe. Surely there were trees and they had slammed into one. The headlights still cast ahead, cross-eyed, revealing thick leaves and the edge of a trunk tucked into the compressed metal of the hood.

Already, she could feel the weak gelatin sensation in her neck. She turned with her whole body to check on Gerald.

Blood trickled down his forehead and pooled in the hollows beneath his eyes. At first, she thought he had ignored the seat belt, but she could see the metal buckle gleaming in the dome light, the pieces interlocked. Then she saw the dark blot on the interior of the window. Centrifugal force, she realized. His head had spun sideways and met the glass.

"Gerald," she said. She said his name again and again until she finally heard a faint murmur from the back of his throat.

She had manifested this. He believed they were still going to arrive at their destination. He hadn't felt the endlessness of the dark road, like it was swallowing them into a different dimension. She had believed in the danger and pulled the brake and now he was bleeding. In the dim light, it looked as though a web of ink was spreading across his face, pinning him to the black leather seat.

She had to climb back over the partition to get to him. His pulse was strong, and he was breathing. But clearly he'd suffered a concussion, and she couldn't know the extent of the damage.

She sent him an audio text, for later, in case he woke up

alone and was frightened. She made her voice steady, tried to believe the words as she said them.

I'm going for help and will be back soon. Stay put. It's going to be okay.

She found a bottle of water in the side door pocket and left it in his lap. With its branding and cheap plastic, it looked like an insult to his predicament, but she had nothing else to offer, no way to help if she remained with him.

Outside, the air was sweet and boggy, like wet, dying leaves. Somewhere, she could hear a bird cawing, mysterious and rare. Maybe it was a replica, mimicking calls from a previous existence. Even in this moment, as Gerald lay alone, unconscious, Marian wondered, did they give the birds instincts when they remade them? Did they feel a purpose in crying out, or did they simply follow a program to imitate life?

The night was full of echoes, and all directions looked the same. Before she shut the door, she glanced at Gerald, at the vulnerability of his slack jaw and still lashes, and she felt what it might be to lose him.

If she could will him awake, she'd stay. She would. But staying was the same as doing nothing.

So she picked a direction and began walking.

WHAT MAKES YOU THINK
YOU'RE AWAKE RIGHT NOW?

Place alarms on the doors. Not the kind that require a monthly fee to connect to a monitoring service. No, just the cheap battery-powered ones that adhere with double-sided tape. Open the door and hear the insistent squawk of the plastic box. Feel safer. When you prepare to move, forget to take the alarms down. Potential tenants will tour your tiny space and notice, with excitement, the alarm box on the door-frame. Explain that the alarm cannot alert the police or the fire department or the call center of a private security company. The alarm doesn't actually *do* anything except beep and wake you if you try to leave the house while sleeping. Divert their nosy questions about somnambulism. Reassure them and say that the house has never been burglarized.

Install alarms at new place. Fall asleep on couch and wake up in different outfit on top of your bed. Laugh at yourself. It's happened before. Make sure your dog is inside and return to your bed until morning.

Wake up wearing pajamas. Make coffee. Look for your toaster. Begin to realize that last night's episode involved moving the toaster to an illogical location. Check each room, looking where no reasonable person would place a toaster. Check the pantry. Check the laundry bin. Look inside shoe cubbies.

Check the home office and discover a tower of books that you've read this year, books you never consciously placed in a tower. Notice the toaster, perched on your worn copy of *The Magus* like an oversized Christmas star. Pick up the toaster and detect more weight than one should expect from a small appliance. Tilt the toaster and watch water pour out from its dial and two slots. Hope that Sleepwalking You considered, and avoided, the perils of electricity when submerging the device. Hope that Sleepwalking You didn't dunk the toaster in the toilet. Wash hands and order a new toaster.

Tell not-quite-yet boyfriend about the toaster. Be forewarned. He will now sneak up on you as you make a nighttime cheese snack because he assumes you wouldn't consciously choose to eat at three in the morning. He will now recount anything that happened the night before to make sure you remember it. Sometimes you won't remember it.

Research sleepwalking. Learn that alcohol is a trigger but choose to drink anyway. Drink only two glasses of wine and still do things you can't remember because you're a sleepwalker. Do not tell anyone about these episodes. They will just assume you were blitzed.

Go on vacation. Let Sleepwalking You wake your boyfriend and ask him to take a shower with you. Sleepwalking You will start the shower and climb into the stream of water. When the boyfriend climbs into the shower, Sleepwalking You will leave without explanation.

You will wake up as you finish buttoning your flannel nightshirt. Notice that he is staring at you, wrapped in a towel, soaking wet, and the clock reads 3:00 in the morning. Make him explain to you why he is soaking wet. Watch his astonishment as he realizes he's finally witnessed an episode.

Consider seeking professional help. Do more research. Realize that this requires sleep labs and overnights in cities that are hours away. Resolve to not drink wine before bed.

Drink La Croix before bed after grading papers. Decide to reward yourself. Put on your favorite Christmas onesie, the one that makes you look like a giant penguin, and watch a movie on the couch.

Wake up two hours later with the cops at your door. As soon as you hear the persistent knocking, you know it's the police. No one you know would knock like that or holler "Ma'am" through the door. You will notice a distant barking and then realize why the police were called. Sleepwalking You let the dog out. Open the door and apologize to the cops. Watch the cops laugh at your onesie. Replace the batteries on your alarms.

Explain to your boyfriend that the episodes happen in clusters, then disappear for years at a time. When he insists that you need to get help, stop dating him.

Wake up at sunrise fully dressed and on top of a neatly made bed and wonder if you can harness your power for good. When you were little, you once fell asleep in the middle of the day, or at least that was the explanation you settled upon. One minute you were reading in bed and the next—actually three hours later, you could tell by the clock—you were sitting on a couch in the basement as your father spoke with you about what you'd missed on the show he was watching.

You asked him if you'd said any words, if he knew you were asleep. He said that you weren't asleep, that you asked what he was doing. In your cognitive absence, he had explained the entire plot of two episodes of *The X-Files*, including one about a gargoyle. "Remember," your dad kept saying, "remember about the gargoyle?" He reminded you, as though repeating the plot would resurrect your memory: the artist told Mulder that the gargoyle made him kill. More than anything, your father could not believe that his thorough summaries fell on uncomprehending ears.

You later found episode summaries online. You told your dad that you vaguely remembered the conversation you had. You wondered if you actually recalled the episode or if you'd fabricated a memory based on your father's dedicated recap, because as you read the words, you saw the image: the bloody outline of a gargoyle on the concrete wall. The most probable reality is that you lied—to your dad and to yourself—because a part of you worried that something was deeply wrong with your brain. Another part of you, the part that usually wins, would rather not think about cognitive impairments or disease.

But of course you were asleep, or else you would have remembered those three hours. And what happened to the hours before you descended the stairs and spoke to your father? Did you eat any dog food? Isn't it possible that you would walk outside, expose yourself to a stranger, and return to the house, none the wiser? As an adult, you will worry, what if Sleepwalking You commits a crime? As an adult, you will also worry, how could people not know that you weren't really there?

You watch a documentary about a man who sleepwalks out a third-story window and survives. You read articles about people who sleep-kill their lovers. You forgive your ex for insisting that you need help. You ask him to meet you for coffee. The coffee turns to drinks, then dinner, then drinks at your house. Despite the drinks, you remember going to bed after a satisfactory but rather unremarkable act of coitus. After, you remember scrubbing your eyes with a face wipe as you sat on the toilet.

In the morning, you find the mascara-stained tissue on top of the trash, next to two condoms. What you don't remember is climbing on top of him, removing his shirt, and kissing the entire length of his torso. In the morning, he stretches in the slats of sunlight your blinds let in. He smiles, sated, and says, "That was really fun last night." And you will think, how fun was I? And after you answer that question for yourself, you will wonder about Sleepwalking You. You ask him to describe what he means, and he obliges. He details the intensity you cannot remember, a position you rarely use, and how quickly you returned to sleep after. What did my eyes look like? you ask. It was dark, he'll explain, and you will feel resentment blooming: how could he not tell?

You will doubt him. You think of all the rotten men you've known, all the rotten men your friends have known: the men with tequila in the trunk pushing a few shots too many and giving blackout come-ons, the men with insistent dicks and runaway minds, the men who touch you when you least expect it, only to insist that you prompted it. There was a look, or something. And sometimes, flimsiness aside, their words linger.

Sometimes you think, maybe there's something I don't know about myself. You picture yourself rising up in the darkness, eyes shut with dreams. You picture yourself peeling the

sheets off him, coaxing him into wanting you, pulling him up
and taking him in, and even at the thought, you will feel the
soreness between your legs thrumming pleasantly, as if pleased
by the memory that is not a memory.

You will wonder: should I blame him? You will cry, and he
will hold you, and you will decide to make rules. If we follow
the rules, you think, nothing bad will happen. If he follows the
rules, you can trust him again.

Together, you arrive at an agreement. If you have already
fallen asleep during the evening in question—even if only for a
moment—he must ask you the following three questions, and
you must respond in a satisfactory manner before he proceeds
with any intimate gestures. Even if you were to pull him forcefully from the pillow by the lapels of his old-timey nightshirt,
he is to resist your advances unless you can provide a cogent,
nuanced response to the following:

1. What is the last thing you ate?
2. What would you like to do?
3. What makes you think you're awake right now?

The experiment works until it fails. One night, you are
asleep and he is half-asleep. He forgets to ask the questions.
You wake up on top of him. "What's wrong?" he asks when you
stop moving, when you pull away and face the wall. He remembers the questions then, and he holds you, telling your hair over
and over, "I'm sorry." You ninety-nine percent believe him. You
feel ninety-nine percent comforted.

There is nothing that will convince what remains in that one percent of you, so learn to live with it. Perhaps you will get better at compartmentalization. Your relationship will continue on a linear trajectory: the consolidation of living quarters, the procurement of a cat, discussions of procreation, et cetera.

Or perhaps you will listen to that part of you that worries. Perhaps you will think, do I really know him? On particularly troubled evenings, you wonder, who do I know, really?

When he is munching loudly on tortilla chips, when you are staring at him chewing, he swallows thickly and asks, "What are you thinking?"

You should lie. You know you should lie. But you will tell him that you have trust issues, that your mind feels like a betrayal or your body feels betrayed or both or neither. "Maybe I've been raped," you're horrified to hear yourself say.

His hands retreat from the chip bag. "What makes you say that?"

"How many times has someone slept with me without my knowing?" you say. "How would I know?"

"How would they know?" he asks.

This is when you will channel your anger. You accuse him. "How could you not tell I was sleeping?"

"I couldn't tell," he says. "I swear."

"But you should have known," you say. Because you were asleep, each and every time, you cannot know what you looked like to him in the groggy darkness. You blame your body for looking awake. You blame your somnambulant eyes for seeking, finding, and focusing on his in the moonlit room. You imagine your body as a self-driving car; mind, optional.

When he tells you he can't sleep with you until you figure this out, you remind him that the nearest medical facility equipped to study sleep patterns, equipped to wire you like a rat and observe Sleepwalking You, is five hours away. You remind him that you have an individual healthcare plan with a high deductible. That you don't get paid for sick days. You give him all the reasons until he finally leaves.

You expect him to return. For months, when your phone chimes, you will think, this is it. He's finally reaching out to me. You will never reach out to him. That one percent will not allow you. When you miss him terribly, you will think of answers to the questions he never asked. You will imagine that you answered them, that you both laughed, comfortable in the knowing.

1. We sat cross-legged on the kitchen floor and ate vanilla ice cream with fresh basil sprinkled on top. Then I climbed into bed, too tired to keep my eyes open. You kissed my lashes. You held me.
2. I would like to trust you.
3. I don't know. I feel awake. I think I'm awake. Do my eyes seem like my own? And my voice? Please. Give me a puzzle, a riddle, and I'll solve it.

You imagine him sitting in your bed, posing this question:

There are three lovers. One lover always tells the truth. Another always lies. The third lover will only respond with randomness, but you don't know which is which. You may ask three yes-or-no questions. How do you tell who is who?

ACKNOWLEDGMENTS

Earlier versions of some of the stories in this collection have appeared in the following:

"Milking." *Mississippi Review*, Volume 47, Number 1&2, Summer 2019.

"Steering" (appearing in this collection as "The Neighbor's Cat"). *Juked*, Number 15, March 2018.

"Spores." *Pleiades*, Volume 35, Number 2, Summer 2014.

"Like the Love of Some Dead Girl." *Notre Dame Review*, Issue 47, Winter/Spring 2019.

"Overnights Welcome." *Beloit Fiction Journal*, Volume 32, Spring 2019.

"Landline." *Day One*. Amazon Publishing. August 2017.

The title of the story "Like the Love of Some Dead Girl" is a phrase taken from *Ask the Dust* by John Fante.

Deepest gratitude to everyone at Blair, especially Robin Miura and Lynn York, and thank you to Carmen Maria Machado, who judged the contest that gave my book such a wonderful home. Thank you to the editors and journals that gave some of these stories their first homes: Chris Fink at *Beloit Fiction Journal*, Adam Clay and Rachael Fowler at *Mississippi Review*, Ryan Ridge and Ashley Farmer at *Juked*, Phong Nguyen at *Pleiades*, Carmen Johnson at *Day One*, and the editorial team at *Notre Dame Review*. I am forever grateful for the support I received from the Elizabeth George Foundation, the Tin House

Workshop, and Black Mountain Institute while working on these stories.

I'm thankful for the time, support, and community offered by the writing programs I attended at the University of Mississippi and the University of Nevada, Las Vegas. Thank you to the friends who made these places intensely memorable and formative, and to those who eagerly discussed their writing and the stories and poems that inspired them: Brett Finlayson, MaryBeth Finlayson, Olivia Clare, Hanna Andrews, Leia Penina Wilson, Natasha Sushenko, Sean Breckling, Christine Bettis, Becky Robison, Lizzie Tran, Josh-Wade Ferguson, Travis Smith, Jimmy Cajoleas, Marty Cain, Kina Viola, Kaitlyn Wall, Rachel Smith, and Laura Godfrey. To the Stake Out workshoppers who kindly offered feedback on my writing: Tim Buchanan, Brittany Bronson, Timea Balogh, Zach Wilson, Joe Milan, Dan Hernandez. And to Lorinda Toledo, who generously read many drafts of these stories and offered encouragement when I needed it most.

Thank you to the Weird Lady Monsters: Yohanca Delgado, Sarah Gerkensmeyer, Kathryn McMahon, K. C. Mead-Brewer, and Nancy Nguyen. To R. L. Maizes, for sharing wisdom. To my family in Vegas, Jeffrey and Victoria Poland, who welcomed me to a new city and cheered me on. And to Thade Correa, who—when I could not imagine living another year in L.A.—told me about an MFA program in Mississippi and changed my life forever.

To the teachers and mentors who have inspired me through the years—Maile Chapman, Doug Unger, Beth Rosenberg,

Richard Wiley, Jesmyn Ward, Nic Brown, Jack Pendarvis, Tommy Franklin, Chris Offutt, and John Brandon.

Thank you to my parents, Fonda and Vernon. Without your love and encouragement and many childhood trips to libraries and bookstores, this book would never have been.

And to Michael—my great love, my favorite wordsmith. Thank you for being my partner, supporting my dreams, and keeping this conversation going that I never want to end.